# A SILENT TRUTH

## A DETECTIVE MARK TURPIN CRIME THRILLER

### RACHEL AMPHLETT

SAXON
PUBLISHING

# CHAPTER ONE

Julie Tillcott cursed under her breath, her ankle rolling in the strapped high heels while she tried to balance across the gravel path leading away from the gastro pub.

The door slammed shut behind her, then swung open a split second later.

Heavy footsteps hurried to catch up with her, a man's frustrated curse carrying on the light breeze before his rough fingertips grazed her shoulder.

'Jules, wait.'

'Fuck off.'

She shrugged off his touch, hitched up the strap of her handbag across her shoulder and stormed over to the silver V8 sports car that stood alone on the fringes of the car park.

It was far enough away to stand out and be noticed, and far enough away from the likes of the beat-up hatchback she'd seen another couple arrive in, the overweight man wearing a baggy pair of trousers and a crumpled pink polo shirt while his wife slouched along beside him in a pair of knee-high boots and a gaudy dress that resembled a pair of discarded curtains.

Behind her, voices filtered out through the open door of the pub mingled with laughter and the clink of glasses – the sounds mixing with the crunch of the small stones under her feet.

She winced as one bounced into her shoe and she hopped on one foot while shaking the other from side to side to dislodge it.

'Jules, let me explain.'

He was catching up with her, his tone exasperated.

'You had your chance to do that before we got here. Before…'

*Before you made me look like a bloody idiot*, she thought. *Again.*

The stone pinged out from under her heel and she breathed a sigh of relief.

Then she heard the jangle of keys behind her.

Turning, she crossed her arms over her chest and glared at her husband while he dangled the fob from his thumb and grinned.

The steel house key twinkled under electric lanterns hanging from a wire dangling across the car park, taunting her.

'I'll drive,' he said. 'You're drunk.'

'I had two glasses.' Julie pouted. 'Besides, it's my car. Unlock it.'

'And I've had nothing except mineral water.' He aimed the fob at the car as he walked around to the driver's door, then peered over the roof as another couple emerged arm in arm from the pub. 'Get in, before you make a fool of yourself.'

'You...'

'Everything all right over there?' a man's voice called.

She turned to see the couple standing beside a dark green four-by-four, concern etched into the woman's eyes.

'We're fine,' she snapped. 'Enjoy the rest of your evening.'

Simon was barely hiding a smug smile when she climbed in and fastened her seatbelt, and she kept her gaze firmly on the dashboard until they were out of sight of the pub.

'Why do you have to do that?' she asked eventually.

'What?'

'You always do this. Ask me to one of your so-called investment meetings and then make me look stupid in front of everyone.'

'I don't make you look stupid,' he said, his tone conciliatory. 'You hate anything to do with numbers.'

She crossed her arms over her chest, sinking into the seat a little more. 'That makes me feel so much better.'

'I'm just saying. You're good at other things.'

'Then why ask me?'

'Because it makes the people there less wary. A woman's touch and all that.'

'Oh, thanks. So now I'm just your piece of arm candy, is that it?'

'That's not what I meant…'

'Do they even know I'm a joint partner in the business?' she said, twisting in her seat.

His jaw clenched, and then he down-shifted, powering around a tight corner.

'Do they?'

'It didn't come up in the conversation, did it?' He shot her a quick look before turning his attention back to the twisting road. 'But you didn't tell them either.'

'God, I'm sorry. Perhaps that was because you and he were completely ignoring me while I was left to talk to that wife of his about what bloody colour she wants the living room walls painted. As if I care…'

'It distracted her, so that's good,' said Simon. He pressed the accelerator. 'All the time she was wondering about decor and who the neighbours are, she wasn't listening properly to the proposal. She'd been asking too many questions.'

'They were good questions.' Julie bit back the next words, her throat aching and frustrated tears stinging the corners of her eyes. 'I'm tired of playing the sidekick. I'm tired of… of this.'

He laughed. 'Are you kidding me? You love it. How else do you think we can afford a car like this?'

'It's my car, not ours.'

'Whatever. Your cut of the profits every year pays for it.'

'But it's dirty money, isn't it?'

'What?'

The car swerved a little as he gaped at her then quickly corrected his course before a motorbike shot past in the opposite direction. He indicated left, turning into a narrow lane that cut through the Vale towards home.

The back road was one they often used in the evening to get to Charney Bassett.

Less traffic.

Less likely to be caught if they'd had a bit too much to drink.

Julie shrugged away the thought.

They weren't the only ones.

'They don't really want a retirement property in Majorca, Si. She loves living in Wantage. She told me.' Julie flicked her hair over her shoulder and kicked off her shoes, warming to her subject. 'They have a two-year-old granddaughter, did you know that? She has special needs, so if they move to Spain they won't see her unless they travel back here a few times a year. They can't afford to do that, not really.'

His eyes narrowed. 'Did you tell her it was a bad idea?'

She fiddled with the seam of her dress.

'Jules? What did you say before you walked out?'

'I don't want to do this anymore.'

'Then resign.'

'I meant us, not just the business.' She heard it then, the tiredness in her voice. 'I hate what we do.'

A stunned silence filled the car, the only sounds coming from the whoosh of the tyres over the asphalt as Simon kept white-knuckled hands on the steering wheel.

It was why she loved the sports car. She could listen to the road while she drove, drowning out all other thoughts.

'What's brought all this on?' he said finally. 'Is it your time of the month?'

Her jaw dropped. 'You what?'

'Well, it's all a bit out of the blue.'

'No it bloody isn't.' She took a deep breath. 'Can't you see what's happening? What's *been* happening? All we talk about is work, or who's a likely candidate for one of your property deals, or how you can screw such-and-such for another twenty grand, or…'

The car had slowed, and he was frowning, his attention fully on the road in front of him.

'See, you're doing it again. You're not listening to me.'

'Shut up.'

'What—'

She jerked forward as Simon stomped on the brakes, the seatbelt digging into her collarbone while she reached out blindly for something to hold on to.

'Shit…'

Hearing him ratchet the handbrake, Julie raised her gaze and prised her fingernails from the upholstery.

Beyond the front of the car, beyond the pitted surface of the lane and the reach of the headlights, she could see a—

'Is that a deer?' said Simon.

'It looks like someone hit it and it landed in the ditch.'

'There's blood on it.'

'Like I said, it's been hit by a car.'

He said nothing, but flicked the lights to full beam.

'I'm not sure. That doesn't look like a deer, does it?'

Unclipping his seatbelt, he opened the car door.

'Wait – where are you going?' Julie reached across to him, wrapping her fingers around his shirt sleeve.

'To take a closer look.'

'I don't like this.'

'Then stay here.'

The door slammed, and he walked around to the front of the car, his hands by his sides.

Julie watched while he took a tentative step closer, then shoved her feet back into her shoes and climbed out.

'Si, we should keep going.'

'I just want to check it out, all right? I'm not happy about driving on until I know what it is.'

'If it's a deer that's been hit by a car, there's nothing we're going to be able to do for it, is there? What're you going to do? Call a vet?'

'I don't know.'

He shuffled forward, then turned to her. 'Won't be a minute.'

'Wait – I'll come with you.'

Despite their argument, she reached out her hand and slipped her fingers through his.

His grip was cold, clammy.

Swallowing, she realised he was as nervous as she was, and took a shaking breath.

'Come on.'

They walked to the far reaches of the headlight beam, then stopped.

'We should've moved the car closer first,' she said, turning to him.

'Jules, get back.'

He wasn't looking at her but staring into the gloom beyond the light, his face pale.

Wrenching his fingers from hers, he gave her a shove that sent her stumbling a few steps to the right.

Confused, Julie squinted into the darkness, then staggered, a choked scream escaping her lips.

'Jesus Christ,' she managed. 'Those are someone's legs.'

# CHAPTER TWO

Detective Sergeant Mark Turpin leaned back in his chair and emitted an ill-disguised sigh.

Darkness may have fallen over Abingdon but the incident room hummed with nascent activity and an underlying sense of desperation.

The stink of stale coffee and too many anxious officers hoping for a breakthrough filled the air, despite the feeble attempts of the ducted air conditioning.

A light fixed into the suspended ceiling above the photocopier flickered at the fringes of his vision, and he blinked to counteract the niggling headache that was forming.

At the far end of the room, a junior constable sprayed cleaning agent over a whiteboard strewn with jumbled handwriting in different coloured text before scrubbing at the telltale signs of an investigation now closed.

With three arrests made that morning by a small team led by Detective Inspector Ewan Kennedy, a stack of archive boxes next to the whiteboard now waited to be couriered to the Crown Prosecution Service in Oxford the next day.

One down, and plenty more active investigations yet to be solved.

Mark rubbed at his temples and forced himself to reread the witness statement laid out across his computer keyboard, studiously ignoring the stack of files that blocked his view of the screen.

'Still here, Sarge?' PC Alice Fields paused beside his desk, her cap tucked under her arm and the radio fixed to her utility vest turned down low. She eyed the paperwork covering the surface, her lip curling. 'How's it going?'

'Slowly,' he mumbled. 'I figured I'd go through two more of these before heading home just so there's less to do tomorrow.'

'Except they're breeding like rats.' Detective Constable Alex McClellan peered over Mark's computer screen from behind a similar stack of files. 'And I'm going cross-eyed.'

'Call it a night,' Mark said, leaning back in his chair and biting back a yawn. 'I thought you left half an hour ago.'

Alex shrugged. 'I didn't want to leave if you weren't. I'd feel a bit crap doing that.'

Alice's radio squawked, and she stepped away before turning up the volume.

'Seriously, you should go.' Mark gathered up the witness statement and shoved it into an open folder at his elbow. 'These cases are all retrospective, and we've already sorted out which ones we want to talk to next. I thought you and Becky were going out to dinner tonight anyway?'

'Not until eight,' Alex said. He pushed back his chair, groaning as he dug his knuckles into his back. 'God, I've been sitting for too long.'

'That's me out of here,' said Alice. 'There's been a break-in over at Drayton.'

'Stay safe.' Mark watched the young PC hurry from the incident room, then waved Alex away. 'Go on. I'll see you tomorrow.'

'Seven-thirty sharp, Sarge.'

'Right-o.'

Standing, he bit back a curse as his neck twinged in protest, then he began picking up the files he'd stacked on the edge of the desk.

A slight acetone smell carried on the air from the whiteboard and he looked up and nodded at the constable who now started to pack away her desk for the night before turning his attention to the woman striding towards him, a determined look in her eyes.

DC Jan West had been partnered with him when he'd first joined Thames Valley Police after leaving his previous role with Wiltshire Constabulary, and had taken him under her wing as she had done with countless new members of the investigative team.

'Have you eaten yet?' she demanded, dropping her bag on the desk beside him before resting her hand on her hip.

'Not yet. I was going to give Lucy a call and ask her if she wanted me to pick up a takeaway on the way home.'

She nodded, mollified, then cast her gaze over the folders. 'How's it going?'

'We've whittled the crimes into three different categories, and now we're trying to spot trends.' He ran a hand over thick curly hair. 'We've got four potential suspects, but not enough information to tell whether they're linked or working alone.'

'What's your gut feel?'

'My gut says this is going to take forever.'

She grimaced in response, then looked up as DI Kennedy's door opened and he headed towards them.

'Any news from Headquarters yet?' Mark heard the hopefulness in his voice, and bit back a curse.

Kennedy shook his head. 'Not yet. How's it—'

Jan held up her hands. 'Best not ask that, guv.'

'Right. That good, eh? Well, hang in there, Mark. The Professional Standards investigation is only a formality. You won't be stuck doing a desk job for much longer.'

'Understood, guv. It's just that it's been a few months already, and...'

'It's important work you're doing.' Kennedy gestured to the files. 'These people have lost family heirlooms, valuable mementoes, things that are often impossible to replace. And we have a glut of cases all involving vulnerable members of our society being duped into letting fraudsters into their homes. It's on the Chief Superintendent's watchlist this year, and she wants results.'

'Got it.' Mark's shoulders sagged, and he reached out to turn off his computer.

Jan's phone trilled, and she shot him an apologetic glance before turning away.

'I have to get this. I'm on call tonight.'

'I know.'

Since a suspect had died before being arrested on charges of murder and arson earlier that winter, Mark had been relegated to the incident room. Unable to work in major crimes until the representatives from the force's Professional Standards department were satisfied with his statement about his involvement in that accidental death, he was back to working burglaries and fraud cases.

Kennedy hovered at his side while he stuffed his mobile phone in his pocket and slung his backpack over his shoulder, then both men paused to listen to Jan's side of the conversation.

'… dead on scene? Okay, what's the location?' She paused and checked her watch. 'Yes, I can be there in about twenty minutes. Thanks.'

'Suspicious death?' Kennedy asked as she replaced the receiver.

'A young woman's been found dead on a back road between Wantage and Charney Bassett. A couple found her lying in a shallow ditch – only her legs were visible from the road. They thought she was a dead deer to start off with, apparently.'

Kennedy looked around the incident room. 'Is Caroline still here?'

'She should be. I think I saw her heading downstairs to the vending machine.'

Mark saw the DI cast a quick glance his way before turning back to Jan.

'Best take her with you.'

'Guv.'

Mark watched as she collated together her kit and checked her mobile phone and warrant card were in her bag while he battened down a searing envy towards DC Caroline Roberts.

It wasn't her fault he was still relegated to the side benches.

Jan tossed a wave over her shoulder and hurried from the room, car keys jangling in her hand.

'I'm sure this won't be for much longer,' Kennedy said gruffly. 'Hang in there.'

'It's been months.'

'These things take time. Especially when someone dies before he can be arrested. And especially when that person was known to you, and that he was a suspect in another force's investigation, and—'

'—especially when my ex-wife accidentally ran him over.'

'Quite.'

The DI held up a finger as his mobile rang, looked at the number, and then turned back to his office, the phone to his ear.

The door slammed shut behind him.

Alone, Mark forced himself to take a deep breath.

Somewhere within the building a vacuum cleaner roared to life, the contracted cleaners starting their daily sweep through the building to clear away the detritus left by the inhabitants of the busy town police station.

He hoisted his backpack up his shoulder and exhaled while Kennedy's empty assurances went round in his head before the stack of folders caught his eye once more.

'Fuck.'

# CHAPTER THREE

Jan squeezed out from the passenger door and cast a furtive glance at how close Caroline had parked to the hawthorn as branches scraped against the paintwork.

A fine drizzle misted the air around her, clinging to her hair and face and soaking the hedgerow and long grass that feathered her trouser hems.

Up ahead, the rest of the lane had been blocked by Traffic division, a series of wooden sawhorses lined across the road with blue and white tape stretched between them.

In front of those, the approach to the crime scene was cluttered with two patrol vehicles, a dark panel van, and a coroner's vehicle.

Beyond the tape, she could see a silver sports car parked awkwardly across the lane as if it had braked to a sudden standstill.

The flashing lights from the closest patrol vehicle

tore through the pitch-black night and illuminated the bare branches of oak and beech trees that crowded over the narrow lane.

Everywhere she looked, there was a frantic sense of time already slipping away as the first responders paced out the asphalt beyond the tape, heads bowed while they walked side-by-side with their colleagues from the forensics team.

'Sorry,' Caroline said after watching Jan sidle along the car and then pause to pick out leaves from her hair. 'I didn't want to block the rest of the road in case anyone else turned up.'

Jan pulled at an errant tangle of plant life between her fingers, her lips twisting at the soggy mess she'd extracted before flicking it to the ground, unwilling to linger on what it might have contained.

'No problem.'

She fell into step beside the younger detective, noting how Caroline still towered over her despite the heels she wore.

'Any news about Mark's case?' Caroline said, slowing as they reached the first liveried car.

'Not yet.'

'Do you think Kennedy will make me go back to the smaller cases once he's in the clear?'

Jan heard the note of panic in her colleague's voice, and shook her head. 'Both you and Alex have really impressed him these past few months, don't worry.'

Caroline's face brightened a moment under the

strobing lights, then sobered as they took in the small group gathered a few metres ahead, heads bowed while a figure dressed head to toe in protective overalls knelt at the verge.

She cleared her throat. 'Who do we speak to first?'

'Nathan Willis – over there.'

Jan led the way towards the stocky uniformed constable with a clipboard in his hand, his brow creased while he completed all the documentation that Tracy, the team's case manager, and her team would upload into the HOLMES2 database to record the start of the inquiry.

He looked up at the sound of their footsteps. 'I wondered who they'd send out. Any news about...'

'Not yet.' Jan peered at his notes from the beam cast by the police car's headlights, then blinked. 'If you've got a torch handy, can you switch those off? One of us is going to get a headache at this rate.'

'Oh. Sure.' He reached into the car, flicked the switch, then looked up as a set of spotlights burst to life from behind the tape. 'Looks like forensics are all set now anyway.'

'What've you got so far?' Caroline asked, shuffling closer to Jan so she could read over her shoulder.

'A woman in her early twenties, found at seven-fifteen this evening by a Mr and Mrs Tillcott when they were driving home from that new gastro pub outside Wantage.' Nathan grimaced. 'I don't think they're going to be Mr and Mrs for much longer though, given the way they've been carrying on since we got here.'

Jan raised her eyebrows. 'Anything to indicate it might've been a hit and run?'

'Not at first look, no. Forensics plan to take swabs from their car's bodywork just in case though. John Newton's on shift with me tonight, and he's taken a look at the radiator grille and the wheel arches.' He held up a mobile phone. 'We took photos too so I'll upload those to the system as soon as I get a chance.'

'Good. Okay, what else have you got?'

'She's definitely dead.' The constable jerked his chin at the hooded figure at the verge. 'I know the pathologist has to confirm that, but...'

'Injuries?'

'She's had a bloody great whack to the back of the head.' He swallowed. 'Whoever did it, or whatever it was caused by, hit her hard enough that her eye popped out of its socket.'

'Jesus.' Caroline moved a few paces away, then turned back to him. 'Any ID?'

The constable shook his head. 'Once we realised she was dead, we didn't want to touch her clothing until forensics were here and had a look.'

Jan handed back the card, before one of the CSI technicians beckoned to her from within the taped-off cordon. 'Okay, thanks, Nathan. Looks like we're needed.'

# CHAPTER FOUR

Hurrying across to where the hooded figure stood waiting, the spotlight beams sparkling off the asphalt, Jan took in the sight of eight other forensics specialists spread out beyond the cordon.

While Caroline signed in, she watched them work, mindful that everything that would follow over the course of the investigation was dependent on what they found – or didn't find.

The CSI technicians conveyed a sense of busyness, of processes being followed that were second nature, and a patience that kept their heads bowed and voices calm while they tried to make sense of a young woman's death.

Over to her left, one of the technicians cradled a plaster cast, and she realised that despite the wet weather they might have discovered tyre or foot prints in the muddied verge close to the body, or perhaps some other evidence that would help them piece together the victim's final moments.

Further inside the cordon, a group of three similarly hooded figures gathered closer to the overgrown grass, a camera flash illuminating the hawthorn hedgerow every few seconds before notes were compared on a shared tablet computer.

'Have you got gloves?' Jan said, rummaging in her pocket for a pair.

Caroline waggled her fingers in response. 'Ready?'

'As I'll ever be.'

Nodding her thanks as her colleague lifted the cordon tape, Jan ducked underneath and led the way over to where the pathologist stood with Jasper Smith, the CSI lead beside the open door of the panel van.

'Gillian, Jasper.' She nodded to both, then peered around them to see a pair of legs poking out from the long grass. 'What are your initial thoughts?'

Gillian Appleworth lowered the mask from her face and pushed back the hood of the protective suit, sadness in her eyes. 'I can confirm life extinct. I'll be able to tell you more about how and when she died after the post mortem, but there's one hell of a wound to her skull.'

'Was she killed here?' said Caroline. 'We were talking to Nathan Willis about a potential hit and run.'

'Too early to say.' Gillian gave the younger detective a warning glance. 'Especially in these conditions. We'll know more at daylight and once Jasper's team have finished.'

Chastised, Caroline pulled her notebook from her bag and lowered her gaze.

'Could you let me know if your lot find some ID on her, Jasper?' Jan said. 'Nathan didn't want to disturb her clothing until you'd done your preliminary examination.'

'We haven't found anything yet. The fingertip search might turn up something. We'll start that once the preliminaries have been completed.' The CSI lead reached into the panel van's open side door and pulled out a set of protective coveralls encased within a vacuum-sealed plastic bag. 'Pop these on, and I'll take you over there so you can get a sense of what we're dealing with.'

'I'll let you get on,' Gillian said, 'and I'll confirm the details for the post mortem in the morning with you, Jan.'

'Thanks.' Passing the first set of coveralls to Caroline, Jan took another set from Jasper and pulled them over her trousers and jacket. Tugging matching bootees over her shoes, she then swept her hair under the hood and scuffed over the asphalt towards a second cordon.

'I take it your officers explained about the injuries they could see when they found her?' he said, holding up the tape for her and Caroline.

'Enough that I know this isn't going to be pretty.' She could see the victim's legs more clearly now, the pale skin blotchy in places. 'What's that, carpet rash or something?'

'Gillian wondered the same thing, which is why she was being particularly cagey.' Jasper nodded to two of his team who were measuring distances from various natural landmarks and the road to where the victim lay. The figures stood to one side, pausing their work while Jan and Caroline moved closer.

She swallowed.

Whoever their victim was, she was young – early twenties, no more – and underweight. Her right cheekbone protruded from an angled jawline, while the left…

'Jesus, Nathan wasn't kidding about her eye.'

Jasper crouched beside the woman and gently turned her face so that the overhead spotlight shone amongst her hair. 'You can see that there's a considerable indentation here.'

'Got a torch handy?'

One of the technicians handed her one from the kit bag at his feet, and Jan shone it into the undergrowth beside the CSI lead.

'Not much blood around here.'

'That's probably why Gillian didn't want to comment on whether she was killed here or not,' Caroline mused.

'Any other injuries?'

Jasper shook his head, then rose to his feet. 'Again,

Gillian will be able to tell you more after the post mortem.'

'Okay, thanks,' Jan sighed. 'We'll let you get on. Could you call my mobile if you find anything else?'

'Will do.'

She trudged back to the first cordon, peeling away the protective suit and then handing it all to Caroline who wandered off to find a biohazard bin.

Raised voices carried through the buzz of activity around her, and she looked across at the second patrol vehicle to see a man and a woman dressed in evening wear arguing beside it.

She wore his suit jacket over an expensive-looking silk dress, remonstrating with her hands while he shuffled his feet and fiddled with his cuff links.

'What do you want to do next?' said Caroline, then squinted beyond the spotlights towards the couple.

'Let's have a word with Mr and the soon to be ex-Mrs Tillcott to see what they've got to say for themselves.'

Caroline grimaced as the argument increased in volume. 'It might be better if I let you lead this one.'

Jan snorted, then squared her shoulders. 'I thought you might say that.'

# CHAPTER FIVE

Mark heaved himself to his feet as Kennedy called the morning briefing to a start, and tried to shrug away a lethargy that shrouded him in despair.

Even his usual early walk with Hamish that morning had failed to invigorate him while they'd trudged along the muddy towpath back towards the narrowboat he shared with his other half, Lucy O'Brien.

She had tried her best, smiling on his return and handing him a freshly brewed coffee before gently tousling his hair.

'It won't be forever, you know that,' she assured him.

'It bloody feels like it is,' he muttered under his breath now, gathering up his notebook and chucking away a blue biro that had leaked over his fingers too many times. Snatching a fresh one from Jan's top drawer, he made his way over to the semi-circle of chairs gathered around the whiteboard at the far end of the incident room and sank into one at the back beside Alex.

He gave the younger detective a curt nod, biting back his resentment at the man's eagerness as the briefing began, and tried to batten down the feeling that he was a pariah among senior management and therefore destined to investigate burglaries and the like for the rest of his career.

'Right, first update please from Jan about the young female victim found bludgeoned last night over near Charney Bassett,' Kennedy barked.

Mark watched his former partner join the DI at the front of the group, unable to prevent a smile smudging his lips.

Despite everything, he was proud of the way she had taken on more responsibilities the past few months, and missed working with her on a daily basis.

'What did the couple who found her have to say for themselves?' Kennedy began.

Jan shot a rueful smile towards Caroline.

'Oh, plenty. We got the impression that the Tillcotts had been arguing prior to seeing the victim, and they were still at it when we got there.'

'Did they run her over?'

Jan shook her head. 'Doesn't look like it, guv. There were no tyre marks on the road, nothing to indicate that their car had struck something. Although, given the rain that blew in last night, uniform have arranged for a forensic examination of the vehicle later this week just to make sure, and Jasper's team did the same for the road and surrounding area.'

Kennedy nodded, and gestured for her to continue.

'Mr Tillcott was driving, and he says that he was sticking to the speed limit – he's local to the area, and knows the lane well. He told us that it's renowned for deer running out in front of cars at that time of night. That's what he thought she was at first – a deer that had been hit. He slowed down, then says he realised something was wrong so he parked about five metres from the victim, got out and confirmed it was a woman.'

'Did he recognise her?'

'No, guv. Neither he nor his wife have seen her before.' Jan exhaled as she looked up from her notes. 'They were genuinely distressed about the whole situation, that much was clear.'

'Were there any other cars on that stretch of road?'

'They couldn't remember, guv. I think they were too busy arguing to notice.'

'Statements?'

'All being entered into the system this morning.'

'Do we know who the victim is yet?'

'We're still trying to confirm her identity,' Jan said. 'Jasper phoned me earlier this morning to say his team found a handbag several metres away from where her body was discovered by Mr and Mrs Tillcott. He's emailed me photos so I'll pop those into the system when we're done so you can all access them, but I've printed them out.'

She paused while Tracy took the photographs from her and pinned them to the whiteboard beside Kennedy. 'Thanks. It looks to me like a book bag or something you'd carry a lot of items in, rather than an everyday handbag. Of course, it might not have even belonged to her, but until we know otherwise we'll treat it as if it were hers.'

'Anything by way of ID in there?' asked Nathan Willis, his features wan after the late night at the crime scene.

'There's no driving licence for her, or anything else to help us identify who she is.'

'What about fingerprints?'

'She's not in the system, guv. Moving to the other photographs, you'll see they found a mobile phone, and a clasp purse with a bit of change in it.'

'Anything on the phone?' Kennedy said.

'Digital forensics managed to access it earlier this morning but it's hardly been used, guv. There weren't any contacts saved to it.'

'A burner phone then, perhaps. Was there anything else?'

'There was a debit card. Not in her name, though.'

'Eh?'

'The name on it is Mr J S Humphries. The card's been well used – the expiry date's only two months away.'

'J S Humphries?' said Mark, frowning.

'I tracked him down and spoke to him this morning,' explained Caroline, twisting in her seat at the front to face him, then back to Kennedy. 'He was shocked about the woman's death, and said his card had been stolen during a burglary at his house near Stanford in the Vale last month.'

Heart lurching, Mark leaned forward, ignoring the excited squeak from Alex.

'What's his address?'

Caroline flicked through her notes, and then recited it.

'Hang on.' Mark sprang from his seat and jogged back to his desk, another set of footsteps in his wake.

'Which one?' said Alex breathlessly, resting his hand on top of the pile of manila folders next to his computer keyboard.

'You've got the latest cases. Did you sort them into alphabetical order yet?'

'No.' The younger detective's shoulders dropped. 'I was going to make a start this morning.'

'No problem. Split them between us.' Mark launched himself at the pile, whipping away the top half. 'He was one of ours, wasn't he?'

'Can't be two blokes with the exact same name, Sarge. Not in the same area. Too much of a coincidence.'

Ignoring the curious mumbles from the small group of officers at the far end of the room, and conscious of

Kennedy's eyes boring into the back of his head, Mark sifted through the files one at a time, the *swish* of documents being lifted and flicked through the only sound between him and his younger colleague.

They'd been reviewing these cases – thirty-two in total – for four months now with no sign of a breakthrough.

Conflicting witness statements, confused descriptions of potential suspects, vulnerable and frightened victims who'd had their homes broken into and precious mementoes stolen alongside laptops, jewellery…

'Found him.'

Mark's head snapped up at Alex's voice to see the man holding out a folder that had been near the bottom of the pile.

'It wasn't Mr Humphries who reported the burglary,' he explained as Mark took it from him. 'It was his sister, a Mrs Eleanor Rippon.'

'I knew I'd seen it somewhere…'

'Mark, did you have something to share?' Kennedy asked.

Alex led the way back to the whiteboard, leaning against a spare desk rather than taking his seat, and nibbled at a fingernail.

'I think we can link that debit card to one of our burglaries,' Mark said, handing over the file before hovering at Kennedy's shoulder.

The DI raised an eyebrow. 'I know you're keen to get back into the swing of things, Mark, but…'

Laughter broke the tension, and Mark let it subside before continuing.

'I think whoever our victim is, she could be involved somehow.'

Kennedy tapped the photograph of the debit card. 'Does this match the one that was reported as stolen?'

'Yes.' Mark reached out and turned to the next page in the file. 'The burglary took place a week ago.'

He heard Caroline whistle under her breath, and an excited murmur passed amongst the other officers.

Eventually, a quirk formed at the side of the DI's mouth.

'Looks like I'd better have a word with Headquarters and get you reinstated as fast as possible,' he said, handing back the case file. 'I'd imagine your input is going to be required, don't you?'

Mark glanced over his shoulder at a polite cough behind him to see Alex staring at him, desperation in his eyes.

'I'll need help,' he said, turning back to Kennedy. 'There are over thirty cases to review to find out if we can spot a link between those and our victim.'

'Consider it done.' The DI swept his hand towards the whiteboard. 'You'd better bring everyone else up to date with what you've been doing.'

# CHAPTER SIX

Mark tugged his tie away from his collar, balled it up and shoved it into his trouser pocket while Alex and Tracy wheeled a second whiteboard in front of his colleagues.

He took a pen from the younger detective with a nod of thanks.

'You'll be familiar with some of these cases, but bear with me,' he began as officers turned to fresh pages in their notebooks. 'I'll start with the burglary a week ago at Jed Humphries' house.'

Drawing a rough approximation of the area where the woman's body had been discovered, he labelled four small villages as well as Stanford in the Vale.

'Jed is eighty-three years old, and lives in this hamlet two miles from Stanford in the Vale along a dead-end lane.' He sketched a hotchpotch of square buildings. 'His nearest neighbour lives four hundred metres away, and there are only three other properties along here. Jed lives at the far end. While his wife was still alive, he retired from a law practice in Oxford and bought a smallholding. That's since fallen to wrack and ruin, with two overgrown paddocks shielding his house from the lane.' He paused, waiting for his colleagues to catch up and saw that those nearest to him had replicated his crude map in their notebooks. 'Alex, have you got the information about his neighbours to hand?'

'Yes.' Alex straightened his shoulders and crossed to the board. 'His neighbours all work full-time – either from home, or commuting from about seven o'clock in the morning onwards. Jed told the officers who interviewed him that he doesn't have much to do with any of them, apart from waving if he sees them out and about at weekends but given that his is the last house, he's out of the way and forgotten about most of the time.'

'That's why the burglary wasn't reported until six hours after he discovered it,' he added. 'Jed doesn't have a landline, and the thieves took his mobile phone as well as his wallet, which he'd left on a table in his hallway. He had to wait until one of his neighbours came home from work so he could use their phone. Whoever did this left behind his keys, perhaps because he doesn't own a car, and they'd got into the house anyway.'

'How did they get in?' said Caroline.

'That's where things get interesting,' said Mark. 'Jed

says there was a knock on the door that morning, and a woman in a business suit presented herself as a representative from a pension company in Oxford who had taken over several smaller funds. She told him his name had come up along with a few hundred others who were entitled to repayments from a twenty-year-old expired fund. He was intrigued enough to let her in, because she showed him some sort of identification that looked legit. While they were talking in the kitchen, he thinks whoever she was working with came through the front door and made off with his wallet and everything else while he was distracted signing paperwork.'

'So it's a team of fraudsters, not just her?' Kennedy said.

'Probably two, maybe more. We don't know yet, guv.'

'Did Jed get a copy of the paperwork that he signed?' said Jan.

'She said she'd have her boss countersign the documentation and bring it back personally, given that he doesn't have access to email.'

A collective groan flittered among the gathered officers.

'Hang on, you said he used to be a solicitor,' said a voice from the back. 'Didn't he realise he was being conned?'

Mark peered over the heads of his colleagues until he could see PC Alice Fields, her brow furrowed.

'That much was alluded to – gently – when the

patrol first turned up. It soon transpired that Jed's health has deteriorated considerably since his wife died, which is why we've since been speaking to him with his sister in attendance. He's easily confused, although he's still able to look after himself with the basics. Which brings us to the other burglaries in the area,' he said, gesturing to the other villages on the map. 'In each of the cases we've reviewed so far, the victim has been on their own and vulnerable in some way. In some instances, the victim has been elderly, in others recently divorced and living alone – we even have a couple of cases involving single parents.'

'Easily distractible in other words,' Alex blurted, then reddened.

'Exactly,' said Mark, smiling despite the interruption. 'It was Alex here who linked the other cases to the ones targeting older people. We were looking at a very narrow demographic before that, whereas now we can see that each has a similar pattern – a well-dressed man or woman turns up at the door offering information about something specific to that victim's situation that might help them, and they're too professional-looking for their victims to think it might be a scam. Which is why we have so many to review.'

'Who are the local troublemakers?' Jan said.

'Arrests over the past year local to this particular area include two aggravated assault charges, attempted rape, sixteen domestic violence incidents and three thefts relating to farm equipment,' said Alex. 'We interviewed anyone who wasn't still in prison, and all of their alibis check out, so we're at the point where we're looking for someone who's new to the area, or…'

'…travels to the area specifically to conduct these burglaries,' Kennedy mused. 'After all, it wouldn't do to shit on one's own doorstep, would it?'

A murmur of agreement filtered through the group.

'It'd certainly go some way to explain why we haven't managed to get a breakthrough yet,' said Mark. 'If they're fencing the stolen goods somewhere else, then no one's going to recognise the items.'

'What about interviewing pawnbrokers and second-hand dealers in the same area as the burglaries?'

Mark caught Alex's sideways glance, then looked at the DI. 'There's only two of us, guv. We haven't had the time to get to that yet.'

'All right,' said Kennedy, waving them back to their seats. 'Thanks, both of you. Given the potential link between last night's victim and your investigation into those fraud cases, I'm inclined to run the two investigations side-by-side from now on. Mark – I'll still need to clear your involvement with Professional Standards but given that DCI Melrose at Kidlington wants a fast result on finding out who's responsible for the young woman's death and the burglaries, I'll suggest he adds his weight behind that.'

The DI paused for a moment and contemplated the whiteboard. 'Next actions. Mark, Jan – I want you to go and speak to Jed Humphries again. See if you can get a better description of the woman who conned him and let me know if it sounds like our murder victim. Make sure his sister's in attendance, just in case. Alex, I'd like you to get Caroline up to speed on where you've got to with the other fraud cases and draw up a roster to help you with mapping out where every single one of those has taken place. I want to know if there are particular clusters in that area, and I want you both to start phoning around pawnbrokers within a ten mile radius of that area. Get in touch with Wiltshire if there's an overlap with their patch.'

Smiling at Alex as the young DC spoke with Caroline, some of the stress dropped from Mark's shoulders and he felt a lightness in his chest.

He watched as the group of officers disbanded, shoving their chairs back towards desks, the volume increasing while the DI's instructions were disseminated and shared, and then looked up as Jan paused and looked over her shoulder, her eyebrow raised.

'Come on then, Sarge,' she said, and winked. 'We haven't got all day.'

# CHAPTER SEVEN

Jan rested her hand on the steering wheel, willing the traffic lights to turn green, then glanced over at an appreciative groan from the passenger seat.

Turpin sank his teeth into a cheese and pickle sandwich, the thick granary bread crumbling into the creased aluminium foil in his lap.

'I didn't think you'd have brought lunch in with you today,' she laughed. 'Good job I made extra.'

'Mmmph.'

'What?'

He swallowed, wiped his mouth with the back of his hand, and tried again. 'I didn't expect to be going with you. Doing this.'

She watched while he raised his gaze to the windscreen, a wistful look in his eyes.

'I've missed working with you too, Sarge.'

He blinked, then smiled and held up the half-eaten

sandwich. 'What's the pickle? I haven't tried this brand.'

'It's homemade. A new recipe I've been experimenting with.'

'Got any more?'

'Two jars of the stuff on the top shelf of the refrigerator, tucked away at the back and safe from the rummaging hands of ten-year-old twin boys with hollow legs. And a starving DS.'

The traffic lights progressed through their sequence of amber to green, and the traffic inched forward before gathering speed and passing under the A34, Jan shifting through the gears with a deft touch and an air of impatience.

'So, going back to what you were saying about this woman – if it's her – and the way they're ripping off people, Sarge, how come her description didn't flag up within the statements from the burglaries?'

'You mean, how come me and Alex didn't spot it was the same person?'

Heat rose to her cheeks. 'I didn't mean it like that, I—'

'It's okay. It's a fair point.' He scrunched up the foil and opened the glove compartment. 'Got any tissues in here?'

'Spare napkins from the fast food place, just under the service book there.'

'Ta.' He wiped his fingers, then balled up the napkin in his fist and settled in his seat with a sigh. 'The problem is, she changed her appearance on a regular basis.'

'Oh.'

'She had shoulder-length black hair when they found her last night, yes?'

Jan nodded.

'Okay, so in at least nine of the burglaries, she was blonde. In three others, a redhead. She had short hair in four of them…'

'Wigs.'

'And glasses, and theatrical cheek implants.'

Jan slowed to negotiate the bends through Marcham, then floored the accelerator once more. 'You were fighting a losing battle, Sarge.'

'That we were.' Turpin's mobile phone rang, and he switched it to speakerphone. 'Guv?'

'Gillian just called me about another case but she wanted to pass on a message,' said Kennedy. 'The post mortem's scheduled for nine-thirty tomorrow morning. I'd like you both to go so don't make any other arrangements.'

'Copy that.' Turpin ended the call. 'So… hit and run? Falling out with her burglary partner?'

'Could be a random attack, Sarge. Might have just been a case of wrong place, wrong bloody time.'

'True. What was your impression of the couple who found her? I mean, I heard what you said in the briefing, but what did you really think?'

Jan braked at a junction, then aimed the car towards Stanford in the Vale. 'They sell property in Spain.'

'Blimey, that can't be easy these days.'

She chuckled. 'Yeah, well they seem to be doing all right out of it. I took a look at their website when I got home last night. I don't think the properties live up to the photos, put it that way.'

'What were they arguing about?'

'He was a bit cagey, but when I took her to one side while Caroline was finalising his statement, Julie Tillcott said they'd taken a recently retired couple out to dinner at that gastro pub outside Wantage with a view to signing them up for one of the properties. Julie was having a change of heart.'

'She gained a conscience, you mean.'

'Exactly. Walked out, apparently. Which of course scuppered the deal. Mr Tillcott – Simon – wasn't impressed. Says it cost them over a hundred grand.'

'Do you think they killed our victim?'

Jan sighed as she took a left turn into a ridiculously narrow lane with grass growing through the cracked and split asphalt. 'No. No I don't.'

'Me neither.' He waited until they'd travelled another half mile then pointed to a broken five-bar gate on the right. 'This is Jed's place.'

A seven-year-old estate car had been parked next to a privet hedge in need of a trim, one of the vehicle's hub caps was missing and its off-white paintwork was scraped and scratched around the wheel arches.

'That's Eleanor's car,' Turpin said. 'His sister.'

When Jan climbed out she could smell the distinct stench of cow shit, the blue flash of a tractor passing in a nearby field confirming her suspicion as it dragged a dirt-smeared muck spreader behind it.

She couldn't hear the A420 from here.

In fact, she couldn't hear any road traffic.

There were just birds, the tractor, and the sound of the car's engine ticking as it cooled.

'How did they know about him?' she said to Turpin as they made their way to the gate.

'I'm not sure yet.' He opened it – carefully, so it didn't fall off the hinges completely – and let her go ahead. 'Like I said in the briefing, he hasn't got a landline phone or email so we were wondering if they'd scoped the place out before knocking on his door. You can see for yourself, there's nothing else much here. Either that or they might've overheard him and his sister talking somewhere. A pharmacy perhaps, arranging a prescription. Or the local supermarket – there's a small one in the main village. They're clever, these people, Jan. And devious. They didn't get much off of Jed, but some of the burglary victims have lost thousands of pounds' worth of belongings.'

Jan turned her attention to the crumbling stonework covering the front of the double-storey house, taking in the dirt clinging to the windows and then wrinkling her nose at the stench from a drain set off to the right of the gravel path that lacked any stones.

Instead, it resembled a shorter version of the grass on either side of it, evidence that a lawn had once been there but had now been taken over by wildflowers and weeds.

'Is it like this inside?' she hissed while Turpin knocked on the wooden front door.

He shook his head in reply. 'It's just the outside he can't cope with. He doesn't do too bad otherwise. Just don't drink the tea – last time I was here, I think the milk was trying to crawl out of the cup.'

Jan swallowed as the door swung inwards and a woman in her sixties beckoned them inside.

'Detective Turpin, thanks for telling me you were coming over.'

'No problem, Eleanor. This is my colleague, DC Jan West.'

The woman nodded in greeting, then showed them through a door to the left. 'We're in the living room. Jed's not too bad today.'

'Good to hear.'

Jan followed Turpin into a brightly lit room, the front window illuminating a collection of bric-à-brac along the sill despite the grubby panes of glass.

A sofa and two armchairs with embroidered antimacassars took up much of the space, the far wall was lined by two large bookshelves heaving with paperbacks, and she noticed the absence of a television.

'Couldn't afford the sodding licence once I retired, and couldn't be bothered to buy another TV when they started giving out the licensing for free.' A broad man eased himself from the nearest armchair, wheezing as he chuckled, then stuck out a paw of a hand as he towered over her. 'Jed Humphries.'

'I wish we were meeting under different circumstances, Mr Humphries,' she said.

'You and me both. Want tea?'

'No, I'm all good thank you.'

'You said you might have some more information about the burglary, Detective Turpin.' Eleanor gestured to the sofa, taking the other chair for herself. 'Have you found the people who took Jed's wallet?'

'We're following up a number of leads,' Turpin said, 'but I wanted to let Jan have the opportunity to speak with you, Jed, due to your card being found at the scene of another crime last night.'

'A young woman was found dead at the side of the road on the Wantage side of Charney Bassett,' Jan continued. 'She wasn't carrying any identification, but she was carrying a debit card with your name on it, Mr Humphries. Do you recognise this?'

She held out her phone to him, and he peered at the photograph on the screen.

'That's mine,' he said, then frowned. 'Is she the one who conned me?'

'If she isn't, then our thinking is that she might be somehow connected to the people who did.' Jan lowered the phone. 'Would you mind if I showed you a photograph of her? It was taken last night at the scene, but I've done my best to crop the worst of her injuries out of the picture.'

She glanced sideways at Eleanor, who crossed the room to her brother and patted his arm.

'What do you think, Jed? Will you be all right to do that?'

His jaw worked while he ruminated for a while.

'Go on,' he said eventually. 'I saw enough photos when I was practising law. I specialised in car accident claims, did you know that?'

'I didn't, no.' Jan flicked through the photos, careful to avoid the ones she would never show anyone outside of the incident room and reminding herself to delete them before she went home now that they were all on the database. 'This is our dead woman.'

Jed shifted forwards in his seat and took the phone from her between trembling hands.

She saw Turpin leaning closer, tension emanating from him.

They'd had to crop half the woman's face from the original photograph in order to avoid the damage to that side, and Jan's chest tightened while she held her breath.

He squinted at the screen, angling it right and left before mumbling under his breath.

Then he sighed, and handed back the phone.

'It's her. She's got different coloured eyes to when she was here, but it's definitely her.'

## CHAPTER EIGHT

The next morning, Mark pressed his foot to an invisible accelerator while Jan eased out from the police station car park and settled in for the short ride to Oxford.

Despite the busy traffic, despite the faint pungency of old takeaway food and body odour clinging to the upholstery of the pool car, he relished the fact that he had escaped the confines of the incident room once more.

He glanced at the dashboard clock as signposts and Armco barriers flashed past the windows. 'We'll highlight the contact lenses with Gillian – there might be one of them still in the eye that's intact...'

'And if not?'

'Then we'll have to hope that Jasper and his lot can find them among all that undergrowth where she was found.'

'Needle in a haystack,' Jan murmured.

'Yeah, I know. Without an ID though, it's the only chance we've got at the moment.'

Jan braked before turning onto the dual carriageway, tapping her fingers on the steering wheel as the flow of traffic increased. 'Of course, it could be the case that she wasn't wearing them when she was killed. Especially if she only wore them as a disguise.'

'We still need to rule it out.' Mark rested his head against the seat and closed his eyes for a moment. 'This isn't the sort of breakthrough in the burglary cases I was expecting.'

'I took a look at the houses along that lane where she was found. There are only six, and all of them are quite far apart from each other.'

He heard his colleague sigh, and opened his eyes. 'Hopefully one of them's got security cameras or a video doorbell facing the road, or maybe heard something.'

'We'll see.' She turned into the sprawling grounds of the John Radcliffe Hospital and slowed to a crawl. 'Right, keep a lookout for a parking space.'

Minutes later, they walked towards a low-slung building off to one side of the complex, its glass-panelled double doors reflecting a dull light as grey clouds scudded above.

There was a tang of ozone to the air, an oppressive atmosphere that did nothing to counter Mark's bleak mood at the prospect of viewing another autopsy.

He held open one of the doors for Jan, following her

across a tiled reception area to a laminated desk shoe-horned into one corner.

A computer screen took up one third of it, its frame plastered with different coloured sticky notes and remnant reminders while its user peered over the top of it at him, his face forlorn.

'You're five minutes late.'

'Sorry, Clive – traffic was nose-to-tail from the ring road, and we couldn't find a parking space for a while.' Mark signed in and handed back the pen to the mortuary assistant. 'Has she started?'

'No, I haven't.'

He turned at the sound of a brittle voice to see Gillian Appleworth advancing towards them, her feet swooshing across the tiles in protective bootees and a plastic face mask pushed up out of the way, obscuring the blue bonnet that covered her hair.

'Good to see you back in action, Mark.'

'It could be temporary. But, thanks.'

'Get yourselves ready, and I'll see you in there. I've got another four to do before I finish today, so don't hang around.'

Mark traipsed along the corridor behind Jan, peeling off when he reached the men's locker room and instinctively picking up a set of protective coveralls from a pile just inside the door.

After folding up his jacket and storing his wallet, phone and keys in a spare locker, he made his way out again and paused beside the windows overlooking the mortuary car park.

He tried to take a few seconds to prepare himself for what would follow, knowing that despite his stomach flipping at the prospect he needed to learn everything he could over the next two hours in order to help the young woman's family.

She might have been a con artist, a fraud, and a burglar but her death had been violent.

And he wanted to find the person that had murdered her.

'Ready?'

Turning at Jan's voice, he gave her a curt nod and followed her through the stainless steel door to the examination room.

His senses were immediately overwhelmed with the stench of antiseptic and an underlying anticipation about what secrets Gillian could uncover.

The Home Office pathologist reached up and clicked on an overhead microphone, nodded to Clive who was preparing the saws and scalpels she would need, and then glanced over her shoulder to Mark and Jan.

'Before I start, I'll explain what I've found since getting her back here and cleaned up,' she began, beckoning them to join her beside a light box. 'I was right about the whack to the head. It's more towards the base of her skull than I could see last night, but we took these X-rays before you showed up, and she was hit hard enough that there are minuscule fragments of whatever weapon her attacker used embedded in the wound. You can see them here.'

Mark emitted a low whistle as he peered at the images. 'One strike?'

'Yes. I'll confirm once I've finished the post mortem, but I'd submit that death was instantaneous.' Gillian moved across to the examination table, her grey eyes softening as she looked at the young woman laid out. 'She would've fallen to the ground immediately, hence these abrasions on her hands and knees.'

'Did you find any indication that she was killed at the scene?' said Jan.

'Jasper's team confirmed there wasn't a lot of blood once they'd finished clearing the area, and look – these marks on her right thigh are very similar to carpet burns.'

'She was killed, then moved in the back of a car perhaps before being dumped in the lane,' said Mark. 'What about that rash?'

'I'm not sure yet – it could be caused by a plant, or it's an allergic reaction to something else. I've taken swabs and we'll send those to be tested as well. Oh, and this might help with identifying her,' said the pathologist, turning one of the woman's wrists between gloved fingers. 'She has a tattoo of a musical treble clef here.'

Wrinkling his nose, Mark moved closer. 'That's not exactly unusual though. There could be thousands of women with a similar tattoo.'

'Yes, but look – there's a tiny red heart etched into the lower left of the design. That might help to narrow down your search.'

'Good point.' Mark stepped back from the table. 'Thanks, Gillian.'

The pathologist nodded, then pulled down her face mask. 'Okay, let's see what else she can tell us.'

'Before you do, one of the burglary victims we spoke to recognised her from the partial photograph we showed him. He said she had different coloured eyes when she came to his house though.'

'Contact lenses.' Gillian handed back the scalpel she'd taken from Clive and gently prised apart the woman's intact right eyelids. 'There was certainly nothing remaining on the left eye, but... ah...'

Mark swallowed as she used her gloved little finger to move the upper eyelid.

'Clive? Give me back that scalpel will you?' After making a neat incision under the eye, she popped the lids back and tried again. 'There you are, you little bugger.'

'Have you found one?' Unable to keep the excitement from his voice, Mark moved closer, his arm brushing Jan's shoulder.

'Most of one. There's a shard missing but I might find that yet.' Gillian took an evidence pot from Clive and gently placed the remnant contact lens inside. 'I'll go and find one of the specialists over in the ophthalmology department after this. He'll have a focimeter. It'll save you waiting to find a local friendly optician.'

'What does a foci-whatsit do?' said Jan.

'A focimeter. It'll help determine her prescription,' said Clive, logging the evidence before twirling his pen between his fingers. 'That way, you'll be able to give that to any local opticians.'

'It'll help narrow down your search. A bit.' Gillian smiled. 'I'm guessing you still don't know who she is, right?'

'Not yet. Just Jane Doe for now,' said Mark.

'Well, let's get on with the rest of the examination and see what else we can learn.'

# CHAPTER NINE

Mark paused at the threshold to Ewan Kennedy's office, taking in the paperwork strewn across a desk already overwhelmed with sticky notes and files.

Three filing cabinets lined the wall to the left of the door, the top drawer of one open, and Mark risked a sideways glance at the contents.

Budgets, forecasts, performance criteria – all the daily drudgery that an inspector's role entailed.

The back wall was partly covered by a cork board with a hotchpotch display of duty rosters and current directives from the Kidlington headquarters, a pair of framed commendation certificates taking up the remaining space behind Kennedy's chair.

Mark smiled at the child's drawing pinned to the lower right corner of the cork board, a man dressed in a blue top and trousers scrawled across the page in thick crayon and signed "Daisy" along the bottom.

The DI glanced up and beckoned to him, his desk phone to one ear while he pecked at his keyboard and squinted through smeared reading glasses at the screen.

Crossing the threadbare carpet tiles, Mark lowered himself into one of the visitor chairs opposite the DI and tuned out the noise from the incident room while he waited, keeping his gaze on his hands while Kennedy ended the call.

'Sorry to interrupt, guv.'

'You're not. That was DCI Melrose.' The DI removed his reading glasses and rubbed the bridge of his nose. 'Professional Standards are being... difficult. We've explained the current situation to them and that we need your involvement on this murder enquiry, but they want more time to assess the situation.'

'Assess the situation? Guv, how much bloody longer do they need?'

'Something that was pointed out to them. Quite forcefully by Melrose, it has to be said.'

'So where does that leave us?'

'He's just agreed to raise the matter with the Chief Super tomorrow morning. Until then, you're still on the team.'

Mark gritted his teeth before forcing himself to relax.

His dentist had already warned him three weeks ago at a routine checkup that he was wearing down the enamel at an alarming rate.

Instead, he exhaled and slumped a little in his seat. 'Okay.'

'Try not to worry, Mark. I'll do everything I can. So will Melrose.' Kennedy raised his chin and looked through the partition window to the incident room. 'Is Jan here as well?'

'We just got back from the morgue.'

'Of course. What did Gillian have to say?'

'We might have had a couple of small breakthroughs.' Mark explained about the tattoo and the contact lens, and the pathologist's impending visit to the ophthalmology department at the John Radcliffe. 'We're waiting to hear back from the optician there to let us know if she can work out what the prescription is.'

'Good, that's something at least. At the moment, I'll take anything we can get with this one. In the meantime, I'll ask Caroline to work with the media relations team and put something on social media about that tattoo. I'll get Gillian to send over a photograph and ask if anyone recognises it.'

'Sounds good, guv.'

'What did Gillian reckon the cause of death was, Mark?'

'Our victim was definitely hit in the back of the head with something. Gillian said the force was so hard, it left some fibres in the wound. She's having those sent for analysis but after taking measurements, she thinks we should be looking for something like a pole.'

Kennedy frowned. 'Pool cue?'

'Or a garden tool… Let's face it, guv, it could be any number of things. We'll keep an open mind on that until we have more evidence.' Mark straightened, rolling his shoulders until he heard a satisfactory crick. 'Our victim's got a rash on her skin that could be from a plant too, and a mark that looks like carpet burns.'

'Was she put in the back of a car before she was killed perhaps?'

'I wondered that, but Jan mentioned on the way back here that she could've been kept somewhere before being killed and dumped…'

'Any signs of sexual assault?'

'Not that Gillian could tell, no.'

Kennedy's eyes flickered to the incident room beyond the internal window. 'Right, so it sounds like the contact lens is our only hope at the moment. Let's have a word with Alex and Caroline while you're all here.'

He led the way out towards the whiteboard, emitting a loud whistle that carried over the heads of the investigative officers, and pointed at the other detectives.

They gathered up their files and scurried towards him as he uncapped a pen and updated the notes on the board with Gillian's findings.

'You'll get a chance to catch up among yourselves in a moment,' he said, 'but first of all – how are you two getting on with the local pawnbrokers?'

'The legit ones haven't been a problem,' said

Caroline, her top lip curling. 'Some of the others though...'

'We've got two we think you might want to speak to in person,' Alex added. 'Small set-ups, nothing too fancy. I've checked leases on both premises with the landlords and they're on three- to six month rolling renewals.'

'So they can bugger off in a hurry without losing too much money if they want to.' Kennedy lobbed the pen onto a desk and crossed his arms. 'Do we know the owners?'

'They're not in the system, guv.' Alex flipped open one of the files he carried and handed over a sheaf of paperwork. 'That first one, Marcus Targethen, runs a shop on a side street in Wantage just off the marketplace, and the other is a bit farther out from our crime scene, in Botley.'

'Good work. Get the details into the system and we'll do the interviews once we've got more information to hand. I don't want to tip them off just yet, in case they disappear. What about the cases you and Mark had been working through – have you spotted any more trends?'

'We shared out the files among six of us after the briefing, guv.' Alex turned to a map that Tracy had pinned next to the whiteboard that was now covered in a chain of red and green pins. 'The green ones are older cases from last year, the red ones are this year.'

'It's the red ones that we're concentrating on at the

moment,' Caroline said. 'They're favouring more out of the way places, rather than within village centres like they were doing last year.'

'Less chance of getting caught,' said Mark, scratching his chin. 'And less likely that people will warn neighbours if they don't see each other on a regular basis.'

'And because we're understaffed, we haven't made the connection until now.' Jan shook her head. 'It doesn't look great, does it?'

'Nothing we can do about that now. We just have to try to use the information to put a stop to it and find out who killed that young woman,' Kennedy said gruffly. 'Anything else to report?'

'We've identified the four most recent burglary victims within a three mile radius of where the victim's body was found,' said Caroline. 'None of them have a previous record, but I was going to suggest we interview them and find out if they've got any historical security camera footage that might help us.'

The DI checked his watch. 'Split those between you, and make a start on that in the morning. It's too late to be knocking on people's doors today. We'll delay tomorrow's briefing until you're all back here. Alex, can you go and speak to the media team? Ask them to put a statement out across social media by close of business today warning residents in the area about an organised crime group targeting isolated people and asking them to check on family and neighbours.'

The younger DC took back the paperwork and nodded. 'I'll ask them to make sure they include a strongly worded hint for people to share on social media groups as well. Do you want to include the whole area, or just the ones we're seeing targeted here?'

'The whole area,' said Mark. 'There's no point in us chasing them out of one place and sending them to another. Not now that we've got a feel for their movements and where they might be operating from.'

'Agreed.' Kennedy said. 'I realise whoever murdered our victim might see those posts, but given the way this has escalated from fraud and burglaries to murder, people's safety has to be our priority. We can't risk anyone else getting injured or killed.'

# CHAPTER TEN

When Mark pushed through the aluminium gate to the meadow two hours later, he shifted his backpack over weary shoulders and sniffed the air.

There was a distinct tang of woodsmoke wafting across from the riverbank, and as the beam from his torch swung left and right along the path behind a row of terraced cottages, his thoughts turned from the frenetic pace of the incident room to the thought of a glass of Shiraz and a warm stove.

As he turned right, his back to the medieval stone bridge that crossed the River Thames, the wind caught his hair and buffeted against his chest. The grass whispered on either side of him, carrying through the distant murmur of televisions and conversations from the boats he passed.

After a few months on the sidelines of any major

investigation, the past ten hours had been a shock to his system, however grateful he was at being included.

He yawned loudly, stumbled on the uneven ground, and blinked as his tired eyes followed the torchlight past a cabin cruiser moored tight against the riverbank.

His stomach rumbled at the aroma from the paper tote bag in his hand, which had the takeaway's new logo printed across one side and an assortment of food within.

Fish and chips for him and Lucy, and a freshly cooked sausage for Hamish.

On cue, an excited bark resonated on the cold breeze from a long narrowboat at the far end of the path, and then a sooty blur leapt from the gunwale and barrelled towards him.

'Hello, boy.' Mark paused to ruffle the mongrel between his shaggy ears. 'Come on, otherwise this food is going to get cold.'

The dog led a zig-zag route for the last fifty metres, stopping to bury his nose in the long reeds at the water's edge before darting to the worn down grass on the other side of the path as another scent caught his attention.

A figure emerged from the cabin before he reached the narrowboat, tugging a thick wool cardigan around her shoulders and sweeping thick long curls from her face.

'I thought it might be you that Hamish saw.'

'I think he smelled the fish and chips before he realised it was me.'

Lucy O'Brien took the bag of food from Mark with a grin, slipped her hand around his waist and stood on tiptoe to kiss him.

'Beer?'

'There was a queue at the chippy. I only had one next door while I was waiting.'

'Hungry?'

'Starving.'

Hamish gave an agreeable *yip*, and scrambled down the steps into the cabin.

Closing the door behind them, Mark made his way to the far end of the boat, put his backpack on a decorative chair outside the bathroom, shed his jacket and rolled up his shirtsleeves, his shoulders relaxing by the time he slipped off his shoes and padded back towards the galley.

He stretched, thankful that the boat designer had allowed for some additional headroom and girth, and that he wasn't living in the same boat he'd rented when he'd first moved to Abingdon.

A small multi-fuel burning stove hugged the cabin wall opposite a fold-out table, a soft glow emanating through the glass door and giving out a warmth that seeped into his tired muscles.

Crouching to put another small log into the fire, his attention turned to the wash of colour to his right.

A set of six watercolour paintings were propped up on the other sofas that had been built into the main cabin, and an old jar that once contained black olives was now filled with clean paintbrushes propped on the window sill – all evidence that Lucy had been busy at work on commissions all day.

Casting an appreciative eye over the depictions of fishermen, other narrowboats that had travelled from the Midlands or from farther downstream, and people's dogs, he cast aside any guilt about the hours he was keeping.

Lucy was thriving in their new home together, and filling her days with the creative outlet that made her so happy.

He straightened, noticing that she had placed a small vase of flowers in the middle of the table. As he set out cutlery and condiments, he leaned over to smell the subtle scent.

'Can you open the wine while I'm dishing up?'

'Sure.'

He walked over to where she was scooping chips onto two plates, the sausage now cut into small chunks and set on a smaller plate to cool for Hamish. Squeezing behind her, he gathered wine glasses and the bottle of Shiraz from a rack beside the microwave before moving back to the table and pouring generous measures. He set the bottle beside the vase.

Lucy handed him one of the plates and flopped into the seat opposite him. 'I don't know where today went. I was tidying up when Hamish barked.'

'They're looking good.' Mark carved off the end of

his battered fish and cast his eye over the paintings again. 'Is that the last of the commissions?'

'Yes, and one of those isn't a commission, just something that popped into my head. I'll take it up to the gallery in the morning.'

Hamish whined, and she looked down at him.

'It's still too hot, and we're eating. Go and lie on your bed.'

The dog scurried over to a tartan-patterned throw in a corner and reluctantly dropped to a sitting position, his brown eyes keen while they devoured their meal.

'Close enough.' Lucy grinned. 'Anyway, how was your day?'

'Better than yesterday. Remember the woman's body that was found between Stanford in the Vale and Charney Bassett the other night? It turns out she might have had something to do with the burglaries me and Alex were looking into.'

He took a sip of wine, then shared what details he could in between mouthfuls of chips while they finished their meal.

'So you've got a way into the main investigation. That's good.' She leaned back and patted her stomach. 'God, I needed that.'

'Kennedy and Melrose are working on making it official.' He shrugged, picked up their plates and ran hot water into the sink. 'Professional Standards are still dragging their feet.'

Her top lip curled. 'It's politics, isn't it?'

'Probably. Until something else comes along that grabs their attention. It's good to be back in the thick of it though. I mean, I know some poor woman lost her life in horrific circumstances, but…'

'Now you can help find who did that to her, and that makes you happy.'

'Exactly.'

After towelling soap suds from his hands and letting the water drain away to the storage tank they used for the toilet cistern, he picked up Hamish's plate and put it on the floor next to the table.

'Come on then.'

The sausage disappeared in moments, and Mark grinned as the small dog sat licking his lips.

Lucy emitted a huge yawn before screwing the cap back on the wine bottle. 'I'm going to have to have an early night tonight. I might read for a bit.'

'I'll take Hamish for a quick walk.' He drained his wineglass, then slipped a lead off a coat rack near the door and shrugged a padded jacket over his shoulders, shoving his feet into well-worn walking boots. 'See you in a minute.'

The wind had picked up when he stepped out onto the towpath, the sound of an ambulance siren reaching him from the town before it was whipped away.

He exhaled, watching while Hamish scampered ahead with his nose to the ground, and wondered how the interviews would go the next morning.

After all, their victim had been guilty of fraud, and

likely helped steal valuables and treasured mementoes from her victims.

Would any of them feel sorry that she was now dead, perhaps killed by the very people she had been working with?

Cleaning up after the dog, he dropped the bag into a bin nailed to a fence post on the way back to the narrowboat, and followed him into the cabin.

Lucy had broken up the fire, the dull light from dying embers reflecting off the cabin walls, and a lone spotlight left on in the galley.

He yawned while he washed his hands and the wineglasses, then patted Hamish's head and crept into the bedroom.

'So much for reading,' he murmured.

She had fallen asleep with her book still in her hand, her head turned away from him, her hair covering her cheek.

After creeping around the bed and gently removing the book before placing it on a shelf above the bed, he stripped off his clothes and snuggled under the duvet beside her, closing his eyes and listening to her soft breathing.

His last memory before he surrendered to exhaustion was of the soothing motion of the narrowboat rocking on the gentle ebb and flow of the river.

# CHAPTER ELEVEN

Jan looked up from her phone as the back door to the hatchback pool car swung open, Turpin's backpack landing on the seat before he eased into the passenger side with a low groan.

'You all right, Sarge?' she said, raising an eyebrow. She eased out of the public car park that abutted the water meadow and turned left rather than joining the nose-to-tail commuter congestion cluttering the bridge into the town centre. 'You look knackered.'

He ran a hand over a roughly shaven jaw and growled. 'One of the small cruisers upstream from our boat slipped its mooring at four o'clock this morning. Luckily one of our neighbours raised the alarm because he's an insomniac and saw it floating past his galley window.'

Her jaw dropped. 'Where were the owners?'

'Both on the towpath, without a clue in the world what to do. Bloody tourists.'

'What happened?'

'Jeremy – one of our other permanent neighbours – managed to swing his narrowboat around and jump on board the runaway. He reversed the engine before it smashed into the bridge pillars.' Turpin jerked his thumb over his shoulder as they left the town speed limits behind. 'Can you imagine what that lot would say if it'd hit and we had to divert the traffic this morning while a surveyor was called in? It's bad enough when there's a flood.'

Jan gave a low whistle. 'D'you want to stop for coffee before we do the first interview?'

'Do you mind? I've had two but they're not working.'

Twenty minutes later, after following a circuitous route through Culham and Sutton Courtney and doubling back on herself, she braked to a standstill on a service station forecourt outside Drayton and watched through the windscreen while Turpin paid for two takeaway coffees.

Despite his insistence that his tiredness was caused by the misadventures of a pair of tourists from Slough, she couldn't help noticing the dark circles under his eyes and the haphazard way his neck tie hung from his collar.

'Are you sure you're all right?' she said when he

returned and stuck the second coffee in the central console for her.

He remained silent until they were underway once more, blowing across the slot in the plastic cap while caffeine fumes filled the space between them.

'Between you and me, I'm worried about the fallout from the last investigation,' he said eventually. 'It shouldn't be taking this long to come to a decision, and no one's giving me a straight answer, other than to tell me they're still looking into it.'

'Are you sleeping all right?'

'Apart from idiots who shouldn't be in charge of a canoe let alone a cruiser?' He managed a smile. 'Yes, thanks. Just not well enough, apparently. Do I look that bad?'

'A bit fraught, that's all.'

He let out a resigned chuckle. 'Putting it mildly. Okay, to business. Let's speak with Carol and Alan Mildenhall first – they're just past Denchworth, and so nearest to us.'

Jan took the next turning, weaving the car through East then West Hanney before casting a sideways glance at the open notebook in his hand.

'What happened to the Mildenhalls?'

'Our murder victim used a different tactic with Carol – Alan was out playing golf that day, and when she opened the door, she was told that the council had discovered a leaking mains water pipe along the road, and traced its route through the Mildenhalls' back garden. According to our mystery woman, the council were worried it could flood the house at any moment and wondered if she could take a look.'

'Ugh. Let me guess. Carol showed her out to the back garden and while they were out there, the accomplice robbed them.'

'You've got it. The woman took photographs of the supposed pipe route, made quite a show of discussing options and reassuring Carol that the damage could be repaired without digging up the garden, and left after ten minutes saying she'd be in touch.'

'What was taken?'

'Jewellery, cash from Alan's bedside table – he told us he always liked to keep three hundred in there for emergencies – and six miniature limited edition paintings that had been lining the walls of the staircase. Take the next right up ahead. Theirs is the second property on the left.'

Jan parked outside a semi-detached brick home rendered in white plaster and typical of the 1930s style of building popular in the area.

After opening a wooden gate nestled within a neat privet hedge bordering the lane, she eyed the freshly mown turf and its budding flower borders.

New bamboo stakes had been driven into the ground against the boundary fence with the neighbouring property, a paper seed envelope flapping in a gentle breeze.

'I was wondering whether to get the kids growing

some tomatoes and the like over summer,' she said to Turpin, pausing to let him approach the front door and ring the bell. 'Maybe I should buy some runner beans as well. God knows they eat enough.'

'I didn't progress much past potatoes when I was a kid,' he replied. 'And even those were rubbish.'

They both turned to the door as a chain rattled against the other side, and then a man in his late sixties peered out.

'Thought it might be you, Detective Turpin. Come on in.'

'Thanks, Mr Smith. This is my colleague, Detective Constable Jan West.'

She shook hands with the pensioner, his grip firm.

'Carol's in the living room,' he said, waving them through a door to Jan's left. 'Did you want tea, coffee…?'

'We're fine, thanks,' said Turpin. 'Hopefully we won't be taking up too much of your time this morning.'

He introduced Jan to a spritely woman whose golden hair showed little grey and who wore a thick sweatshirt over mud-flecked jeans.

'Sorry, I've just come in from the garden and haven't had time to change,' she said. 'Have a seat.'

Turpin leaned forward in his chair and clasped his hands.

'The reason I asked if we could speak with you today is that the body of a young woman was found late yesterday not too far from here. We spoke to another local victim of a burglary similar in nature to yours, and he's confirmed she was the one who distracted him while her accomplice took cash, jewellery and other items,' he said. 'Rather than assume she's the same person responsible for all the burglaries I've been investigating, we wondered if you'd mind taking a look at a photograph and telling us if she's the same one who came here?'

Carol Mildenhall glanced at her husband, then back to the two detectives. 'All right. It's... it's not too horrible, this photo, is it?'

'I can assure you that while it is of a dead woman, we've cropped out the worst,' said Jan.

'Go on, then.'

She gripped Alan's hand while Jan pulled out a six-by-four-inch photograph that she'd printed out in the incident room earlier that morning and turned it around to face them.

Carol nodded. 'That's her.'

'You're sure?'

'Yes.' The woman sighed as Jan tucked the photo back in her bag. 'The thing is, she showed me identification that looked perfectly legitimate, and was dressed for the part. I was completely taken in by the bluff. While the woman was "assessing" the garden, she was talking about how hard it was to get into the water engineering industry and that this was the first time her manager had let her lead an investigation. I used to run my own accountancy business until I retired, and I told her I understood what she meant and that I'd had to work hard to prove myself.'

Carol sniffed, then held up a hand when Jan proffered a packet of tissues. 'I'm angry with myself, Detective West. They took nothing of sentimental value – we'd even been talking about selling the paintings – but it's… it's the invasion of privacy. The thought that there was someone in here, going through our things…'

'Have you heard from your insurers since we last spoke?' Turpin said gently.

'They paid out,' said Alan. 'Minus the policy excess. Thanks for returning their call so quickly and getting a copy of your report to them as well. We're grateful for that.'

'No problem. I'm just sorry we haven't had the breakthrough I'd hoped for.'

'Yet.' Alan's gaze shifted to his wife, then back. 'So she's definitely dead, is she?'

Jan nodded. 'As Detective Turpin said, her body was found on Tuesday night.'

'Good.'

'Alan!' Carol's shocked gasp mirrored Jan's immediate thought, the woman's eyes wide.

'I'm not going to apologise, love. She lied to you, enabled someone else to steal from us – who could've been carrying a weapon, we don't know – and it sounds like we weren't the only ones.' Alan stuck out his chin. 'Good bloody riddance.'

Turpin glanced down at his hands, giving the other

man a moment to calm down. 'Alan, I'm sorry to have to ask you both this, but it's important. Where were you between six o'clock and ten o'clock on Tuesday night?'

'I beg your pardon?'

Jan watched as both husband and wife turned white, then leaned back as Alan pushed out of his chair and wagged a finger at her colleague.

'Don't you dare come in here, accusing us of murdering her.'

Turpin didn't flinch, and when he spoke his voice was calm, almost soothing. 'It's a routine question.'

'We were at our daughter's house,' said Carol, her hand shaking as she slipped her fingers around Alan's wrist and dragged him back to a sitting position. 'It was her birthday on Monday, but she'd been working so we went around for dinner on Tuesday instead.'

Alan swallowed, colour flushing his cheeks. 'We left around half past ten.'

'Where does she live?' said Jan. 'Nearby?'

'Didcot.'

She shot Turpin a sideways glance, seeing the same confirmation in his stare.

The Mildenhalls had been travelling in the opposite direction to where the woman's body had been found.

'I'm sorry I had to ask,' said the DS as the atmosphere in the room dissipated.

Alan shook his head in response. 'I know. Sorry. It's just…'

'Your home is meant to be a safe place, a refuge.' Turpin grimaced. 'And someone violated that.'

'What do you think happened to her?' said Carol. 'Was it a hit and run?'

'The investigation's ongoing.'

'Was she murdered by whoever you said worked with her?' Alan persisted. 'Did they have a falling out, d'you think?'

'As I said…'

'It's okay.' The man reached out for his wife's hand, squeezing it. 'You can't tell us, can you?'

'Not yet,' said Jan. 'But when we can, we will.'

She received a curt nod in response.

# CHAPTER TWELVE

'Who's next on the list?'

Mark peered at his notes as Jan started the engine and pulled away from the kerb.

Flicking back and forth, he found the details at the second attempt, his heart sinking at the memory of the sadness caused by the loss of personal mementoes, irreplaceable jewellery and an overwhelming sense of fear that now permeated the house he'd first visited four weeks ago.

'Michael and Patricia Phillips,' he replied. 'They're in their forties. Patricia has multiple sclerosis and works part-time from home as a bookkeeper for an engineering company. Michael runs a food manufacturing consultancy based in Didcot. No kids. If you take the next right and go past the riding stables, their house is half a mile outside Goosey.'

'Was Patricia on her own when they were burgled?'

His jaw tightened. 'Yes. And it was one of her bad days health-wise. Most of the time she manages to get around using crutches but if she's in a lot of pain she reverts to a wheelchair.'

'Bastards.'

They fell silent while the sodden countryside passed by the rain-flecked windscreen, Jan flicking on the wipers as a steady downpour ensued.

Mark looked over to a muddy field with four horses standing in a far corner under a sagging oak tree, their backs turned away from the road, and their heads lowered in quiet resolution.

Most of the burglary victims' houses were surrounded by countryside like this.

Isolated, despite the nearby villages.

Quiet, and away from main roads and prying eyes.

Within minutes, Jan turned into a gravel driveway partitioned from the road by a wooden fence.

A matching five-bar gate had been left open in anticipation of their arrival, and as she braked in front of the converted Victorian vicarage, Mark saw smoke puttering out from two of the red brick chimneys at either end of the slate tile roof.

Reaching over to the back seat, Jan extracted a large umbrella and gave him a baleful stare. 'Ready?'

'As I'll ever be. At least there's a porch.'

They made a dash for the ornate stone vestibule that hugged the front door, where Mark brushed the worst of the water from his shoulders while Jan shook out the umbrella and rang the bell.

Michael Phillips opened the door a split second later, beckoning them inside.

'I take it the game's been called off,' said Mark, eyeing the bag of golf clubs propped up against the stairs.

'Again.' Michael rolled his eyes and shook Jan's hand. He'd rolled his shirt sleeves up to his elbows, and his trousers were slightly creased. 'A home visit then, eh? I take it there must've been a significant development to warrant two of you turning up, Mark.'

'Is Patricia here as well?'

'She is – she's just finished a video meeting with her manager. Come through to the living room. We've got the fire lit, so you'll dry out quicker.'

They followed him into a large but cosy space with exposed stonework on the outer walls and the promised roaring fire in a large hearth several centuries old.

'Sit anywhere you like.' Michael crossed to a secondary door and held it open for his wife, who emerged with the aid of sticks, her face resolute.

'Any progress, Detective Turpin?'

'Not yet, Mrs Phillips, but there's been a development we'd like to speak to you about.'

She settled into an armchair beside the fire while her husband perched on the arm of the sofa across from Jan. 'Is that good or bad?'

'Can I start by asking where you both were on

Tuesday between, say, half past two in the afternoon and eleven that night?'

Michael shot a glance at his wife, then turned his attention back to Mark. 'I was at work in Didcot until four, and then I had sales appointments to follow up in person until about half seven. The last one was in Appleford, so I didn't get home until just gone eight, and then we had dinner.'

'I had meetings until six,' Patricia said. 'The engineering firm I work for has projects all over the world so sometimes I'm talking with people on the west coast of the US well into the evenings. After that, I made a start on dinner. Once Michael was home, that was it. We were in bed by half nine. I had an early start the next day with another meeting at seven in the morning.'

'Thank you.' Mark waited while Jan updated her notes, then eyed the couple as he spoke his next words. 'The body of a young woman was found on the roadside outside Charney Bassett on Tuesday evening. I can't give you more details than that, but we are treating her death as suspicious. We received a positive identification yesterday that she matches the description of one of the people responsible for the burglaries in this area.'

He retrieved the photograph and handed it to Patricia. 'Would you mind confirming this is the woman who came to your door?'

She reached out, her top lip curling.

'I blame the painkillers,' she said as her eyes hardened. 'If I'm having a good day, I try not to take them. That wasn't a good day when she turned up on the doorstep.'

'Do you think the medication affected your judgement?'

'Of course. I'd never have fallen for it otherwise, I'm sure. Anyway, yes – that's her.'

'Your dead woman told Patricia that she represented a cleaning company that I'd contacted to get some ad hoc help around the house,' Michael explained as Jan turned a page in her notebook. 'What scares me is the amount of information she had about us, about our lifestyle. They must've watched us for a while.'

Mark crossed to the patio window and looked out over the sprawling lawn that led across to a cluster of trees. Beyond that, farmland stretched as far as he could see.

'I spoke to your neighbours after I saw you the other week,' he said, turning back to them. 'Specifically, I asked them the same question I asked you – whether they'd seen anyone hanging around, acting suspiciously.'

'I take it from the silence that they said they hadn't,' said Patricia, then shook her head as Mark opened his mouth to apologise. 'Whoever did this – whoever that woman was working with – was clever, Detective Turpin. They waited until they saw Michael leave for work, and probably saw me through those windows in my wheelchair. I like to sit in the sun there on the bad mornings. It seems to help with the pain management sometimes.'

'When did you realise you'd been burgled?' asked Jan.

'When Michael got home at about six o'clock. I thanked him for organising the visit from the cleaning company and said that all the prices sounded fair—'

'At which point, I panicked,' Michael added. He got up from his chair and crossed the room to where his wife sat and gently squeezed her shoulder as she dabbed at her cheeks with a tissue. 'Of course, I hadn't spoken to any cleaning companies – we can't really afford it at the moment. I suppose I realised what had happened before I went around the house and checked to see if anything was missing.'

'I felt so stupid,' Patricia mumbled, then sniffed. 'If you saw what I manage on a day-to-day basis here, at work, my health…'

'It's not your fault,' said Mark gently. He retook his seat beside Jan and leaned forward. 'These people are ruthless, cruel and took advantage of you.'

'And now one of them's dead, thank goodness,' Michael spat. 'What about the other one? Any news about her accomplice, whoever he is?'

'We're hopeful that once we have a positive identification for the woman found dead on Tuesday night, then we'll be able to work our way through those who knew her – friends, family…'

'What are the chances of finding out who she was?' said Patricia.

'We're waiting on the outcome of some forensic testing,' Jan explained. 'And we have a team of detectives investigating this now.'

'A bloody shame it took something like this for your lot to sit up and take notice,' said Michael. 'Sorry, Mark, but it had to be said. We know you've been doing your best for us, but it's been obvious that you've been on your own and getting nowhere fast.'

'We've been pursuing a number of leads,' Mark replied, then glanced at his clenched hands, realising how desperate he sounded. 'But this new development – despite how terrible the circumstances – might provide a breakthrough.'

'To hell with her is all I can say,' said Patricia. She stuck out her chin as Mark's head snapped up in surprise at the viciousness in her voice. 'She had it coming, didn't she?'

Five minutes later, Mark trudged down the path towards the car behind Jan, the couple's frustration echoing in his mind.

Everything they had said about his being understaffed and overwhelmed had been correct, although he'd gently rebutted Michael's parting comments with a flimsy explanation about the number of burglaries committed by the mystery woman and her accomplice or accomplices.

The other man had simply shaken his head and

shown them to the door, closing it as Mark's promise to keep them up to date with progress fell on deaf ears.

The *thunk* of the car's locking system disengaging broke his miserable reverie and Jan peered over the top of the roof at him.

'It wasn't your fault, Sarge.'

'I know. How come I feel so bad about it then?'

He eased into the passenger seat, noting the net curtain flicking back into place across the Phillips' living room window while Jan started the engine.

'This is going to be a problem, isn't it?' he muttered as she pulled away. 'No one is going to have any sympathy for our roadside victim, are they?'

Jan pursed her lips. 'I can see it from their point of view, Sarge. She coerced her way into their homes, and stole valuable and treasured belongings. It's hard for them to muster anything but a sense of retribution I'd imagine.'

He exhaled in response, then frowned at a tractor that pulled out in front of them towing a seed drill and set a plodding pace towards Grove.

'I realise she was a criminal,' he said, 'but some people are desperate because they can't get work and don't want to end up on the streets. I'm not excusing what she did by saying that. It's just that she might've got herself into a situation where she was being used by someone, and perhaps didn't have a choice in what she was doing. It's just one more piece of this whole bloody situation we don't yet know about.'

'It's still going to be hard to get anyone to empathise and feel sorry for her,' Jan argued. 'You're right – she might've been in a dreadful situation but she wasn't innocent. She could've told any one of those burglary victims that she was in danger and needed help, but she didn't, did she?'

'No.' Mark cast his mind back through all the statements he and Alex had read through over the past weeks. 'No, she didn't.'

The tractor indicated left before reaching the main road, and his colleague let out a subdued cheer before accelerating towards the next junction.

'Where next, Sarge?'

'Let's get back to the incident room.' Mark sighed. 'Hopefully Alex and Caroline have had better luck than us.'

# CHAPTER THIRTEEN

An overwhelming fug of stagnant coffee and scorched printer toner greeted Mark as he held open the door into the incident room for Jan.

Ringtones blared from mobile phones, clamouring for attention over an accompaniment of desk phones and voices calling from one side of the space to another.

He led the way over to where Kennedy stood with Caroline and Alex outside his office door, pulled out a chair for Jan that faced the small group, and nodded in greeting.

'I hope you had more luck than these two,' said the DI.

Alex shuffled his feet, a blush rising up his neck. 'Both the burglary victims we spoke to were, um, less than dismayed at what happened.'

'Same with ours,' said Jan. 'Shocked, but not upset.'

Caroline shrugged, looked down at her notebook,

and cleared her throat. 'I've taken a look at social media groups local to that area since we've been back, guv. Word's getting around that the dead woman was likely responsible for the burglaries these past six months, and the general consensus there is that – not my words, mind – "she had it coming".'

'Any breakthrough during your conversations today with people regarding her accomplice?' Kennedy asked.

They all shook their heads.

'Guv, I spoke with Nathan when I got back,' said Alex. 'Now that we've got more help from uniform with the burglary side of things, I've had four of them looking for trends in how those people were conned.'

'Go on.'

Alex turned around and waved over the stocky constable walking past with a stack of folders. 'Nate, have you got a minute? Could you give us an update?'

'Sure.' Placing the folders on a nearby desk, Nathan pulled a page from one of them and handed it to the DI. 'We've identified four main themes. Either the dead woman or her accomplice posed as a legal representative in a matter that the homeowner might be interested in, as someone from an insurance company worried about the current valuation of contents, or a utilities company. The least popular con they implemented was pretending to be stranded without a phone and a car on the blink. She'd use the homeowner's phone to make a call for help, and then say her boyfriend was on his way to pick her up.

According to one bloke I spoke to about a theft back in February, the woman accepted a cup of tea from him while she waited. Her accomplice knocked on the door twenty minutes later, saying he'd got the car started and they were never seen again.'

'I remember that one,' said Mark. 'When the victim – Henry Angleton – went upstairs, he found his bedside table drawer slightly open, and then discovered that a valuable watch and his dead wife's wedding ring and engagement ring were missing.'

'It was unusual for her accomplice to make an appearance though, so that's why that last one appears to be the riskiest and least used,' Alex added, as Nathan scooped up his folders and returned to his desk. 'Most of the time, only the woman was seen.'

'I think people viewed her as being more trustworthy, and less threatening than whoever she was working with,' Mark concluded, 'so if he did have something to do with her death, he's going to have to change his methods.'

'Do you think he was responsible for making her rob people?' said Caroline. 'Was she under duress?'

'She had plenty of opportunities to say something to someone,' said Kennedy, echoing Jan's earlier words. 'Any one of the people she helped burgle could've phoned us on her behalf.'

'It depends what sort of hold that man had over her I suppose,' Mark said. 'If he was threatening her or a member of her family, then maybe she felt she had no choice. What I mean is, it might not have been simply physical coercion, but psychological as well.'

Kennedy dipped his chin, conceding the point. 'Jan – any word from Gillian yet about that contact lens prescription?'

'No, guv. She did say she'd be calling in a favour though. I was going to phone her in the morning if she hasn't been in touch by then.'

The DI nodded. 'Fair enough. If that expert at the John Radcliffe can't help her by then, tell her to pass it on to Jasper's team, and quick. We're going to struggle to move this along without an ID to work with.'

'I'm also wondering how many people were conned by her who are too embarrassed or afraid to report it,' said Mark. 'I mean, okay we've got a large number of open cases to work through, but there could be more.'

'Follow that up with the local charities this afternoon. There's at least one based here in Abingdon that's good at posting updates on their website and social media to warn people about the burglaries and offering basic security advice. Tracy can give you the contact details. They're very active about educating vulnerable people about the latest scams so might have more information that people have confided to them.'

'Will do.'

'Okay.' Kennedy checked his watch. 'Do what you need to do for the rest of today. We'll reconvene at midday tomorrow. Caroline, Alex – keep on top of Jasper and his team for anything they manage to glean from the crime scene. We should have his final report later today as well.'

Mark followed Jan back to their desks. 'That charity has its office next to the library. Shall we walk there?'

'You can – I'll have to take the car.' She smiled. 'Football tonight, so I need to get the boys fed early so we can get there on time.'

'No problem. Are you sure you want to come along? I can always go and speak to this lot on my own.'

'I'll be there.' She frowned when she saw the message bank light on her desk phone flashing, picked it up and then groaned. 'If I ever work my way through all of these, that is.'

# CHAPTER FOURTEEN

If it wasn't for the multitude of Easter eggs and fake yellow chicks lining the window of the café, it could have been any Friday afternoon in early spring.

Instead, two weeks before Easter, a weak sunlight struggled to warm the marketplace while a gaggle of men and women hurried to put away gazebos and folding tables, taking apart the farmers' market to begin in earnest somewhere else the next day.

Mark sat at a table set for two outside the café, the legs wobbling on the uneven cobblestones, and cradled a mug of coffee while he waited for the church clock to strike the hour.

He hoped Jan managed to find a parking space this late in the day.

His gaze lazily roamed the headlines of the complimentary newspaper, a wisp of steam wafting his nose and teasing him with an arabica bean aroma.

The newspaper remained on page five, and the coffee stayed three quarters full while it cooled.

Out of the corner of his eye, he watched another busy café across the square, a chill crossing his shoulders when a woman in her thirties emerged from the front door with a smile fixed to her lips while she balanced a tray loaded with cups and a plate of sandwiches.

She served the waiting middle-aged couple – tourists by the look of their clothes, and walkers given the retractable poles placed on the ground by their feet – then turned on her heel, slapping the now empty tray against her leg as she marched back inside.

Clare Baxter hadn't given him a second glance.

He wondered how she was coping these days.

After all, it had been her who had found a teenager in his last dying moments in the alleyway beside the café where she still worked.

Mark took a sip of coffee and fought back the guilt, same as he did every night since October.

Although he tried to avoid the place, he couldn't help but watch and wonder sometimes.

Another ten minutes, and he might have seen the boy.

Another fifteen minutes, and he might have saved him.

'Anything else for you, mate?'

He jumped, his shoe kicking the table with a dull

clang before he looked up at the young waiter staring at him with an apologetic smile.

'Sorry, I was miles away there. I'm good thanks. I'll be on my way in a minute.'

The lad turned away, his attention already taken by two of the market stallholders seeking hot drinks, and Mark's eyes found the café across the cobbles once more as he sipped his coffee.

He could see Clare through the window serving a customer, her features fuzzy from the condensation clinging to the glass.

He should have said something by now, explained his reluctance to spend his money there, but he didn't know where to begin.

Perhaps his presence reminded her too much of that night as well.

He could only hope that she understood.

The owner, Angie, emerged and started wiping down the table recently vacated by a pair of women in business suits, her movements brisk and efficient.

Mark blinked to clear the memories, then stood up and drained the remainder of his coffee.

There was another murder victim who demanded his attention now.

Slipping a couple of pound coins into the saucer, knowing the owner would drop them in the animal shelter charity box on the counter inside, he set off at a brisk pace.

The pedestrianised shopping precinct presented a

tired vista despite the attempts of shop managers to brighten windows with displays and colourful signs alongside the obligatory fake eggs and yellow chicks.

There were too many empty stores, too many instances of boarded-up premises, and too much desperation in the wording of sale signs offering thirty per cent off and more.

A fine drizzle started to soak the interlocking brick pavers, and he hurried along a zig-zag of footpaths towards the library, holding up a hand in greeting to Jan as she emerged from the public car park with a leather bag over one shoulder and her mobile phone in her hand.

She frowned when she saw him.

'Were you watching the café again?' she said as he drew closer.

'How'd you know?'

'I've seen you before. Clare was asking after you as well the other day.'

'Was she? How did you…'

'I went in with Harry to choose a birthday cake for a friend of theirs.' She shoved the phone in her bag, then ushered him towards a three-storey office block beside the library. 'She wanted to know if you were okay.'

He said nothing, stunned.

'You ought to go in there, you know.' Jan nudged his arm as they stepped into a shared reception area. 'Even just once.'

Peering at the list of company names displayed on a

cork board beside the stairs on their left, Mark found the charity on the second floor. He stomped up the carpeted treads, then paused on the landing.

'Maybe I will.'

'Good.' Jan wrenched open a thick door and walked into a small open-plan office with a desk near the entrance, and showed her warrant card to a twenty-something woman who rose from her seat and stared at them with interest.

'We've got a meeting with Andrew Crewford,' said Mark.

'That's me.'

He turned at the sound of the voice to see an earnest-looking man in his forties barrelling towards them, hand outstretched.

'Found us okay, then?' he said, ushering them towards a group of bright orange armchairs in the far corner that surrounded a white Formica table. 'Can I get you a drink – tea, coffee…'

'No, thanks.' Mark sank into one of the chairs and unbuttoned his jacket. 'Hopefully we won't take up too much of your time, but we're hoping you can help us with information regarding current warnings about fraud in the local area. We've had a spate of burglaries these past four months targeting vulnerable people, and now one of the people likely responsible for the fraud has been found dead.'

Crewford's eyebrows shot upwards, and he ran his

tongue across his bottom lip, scooting forward in his seat. 'Dead, eh?'

'That's right.' Mark battened down his disgust at the man's ill-disguised excitement. 'We also wondered if you're providing advice to anyone who may have been conned out of money or valuables recently. Does that sound familiar?'

'Let me have a look. I mean, anything to help the police, right?' Crewford chuckled, then excused himself and walked over to a cluttered desk before returning with a battered lever arch file. 'We have an antiquated computer system, and I don't trust the servers so I always insist on a paper report being printed out by our volunteers. Understand that I can't give you these – people come to us in confidence because they feel that they have nowhere else to go. Often, they're embarrassed at being conned, and don't want to go to the police in case their families find out.'

He flicked through the pages, then turned the folder around to face them. 'This was the first one in the latest spate – we tend to get one or two reports of fraudulent activity each month, but sadly you're right – we have seen a slight spike in complaints and requests for help lately. If you flick through, you'll see we've had six to eight cases each month.'

'What is your charity doing to educate people about the dangers of fraud?' Jan asked, popping her ballpoint pen and readying her notebook.

'We have a lot of information on our website about

what to look out for,' said Crewford. 'We also have a series of flyers containing the same warnings and safety tips that are displayed in the foyer downstairs as well as the Citizens Advice Bureau and the library – places we hope people might see them. The council offices have some in their reception, for example.'

'The cases we're investigating involve door knocking scams, rather than text, email or phone call,' said Mark, flipping through the pages and scanning the text. 'Is that unusual these days?'

'Not really. There are still people who don't have access to the internet or a mobile phone – or who might not want a mobile phone,' Crewford explained. 'And if they do, then despite all the warnings published by charities like ourselves and the police, they still post personal information on social media that can enable someone to target them.'

'What are you doing to help them when they report something like this?' said Jan while Mark handed back the folder.

'First of all, we try to persuade them to report it to the police so you might find some familiar names amongst these reports. If they're reluctant to do that, then we help them with any insurance claims and make sure the gist of the scam – we don't share their names for obvious reasons – are posted to bulletins on our website and social media pages.'

Mark bit back a sigh at the realisation that the charity could do no more, especially if the people they helped were too scared or embarrassed to take a formal approach.

And then the guilt kicked in at the thought of how many cases he and Alex had been swamped with since the New Year, and how little they'd been able to do on their own.

'Have you had much by way of new cases since we released the media statement yesterday?' he said.

'One or two.' Crewford craned his neck and held up the folder to an older colleague. 'Brian – could you make a copy of the reports I've flagged, but remove the names?'

As the other man wandered off towards a clapped-out photocopier, Crewford's attention turned back to Mark. 'Sorry, but like I said – these people come to us in confidence. All I can do is provide the details of the burglaries so you can see if there are similarities with yours.'

'It'll have to do,' Mark replied. He got to his feet. 'Thanks for your time anyway.'

'There is one more thing,' said Crewford as his colleague returned with the copy reports. 'There's a local vigilante-type group on social media who follow a lot of our posts. I think they're trying to work out who's involved with the burglaries as well.'

'In what way?' Jan frowned, shoving the reports into her bag.

'They say they've been collating news stories about the known cases and are trying to put a stop to it.

Keeping an eye on elderly neighbours, checking in on people who live on their own, that sort of thing.' Crewford beamed. 'They're very proactive. It's quite admirable, don't you think?'

Mark's eyes narrowed. 'Why didn't you think to mention this to us before now? You're in touch with our community policing officers on a regular basis here, aren't you?'

'I didn't know if it would be useful.' Crewford squirmed, then reached over to a nearby desk for a pen and tore a page from a block of pale yellow sticky notes. 'Anyway, this is Bill Bereton's number – he runs the group. He lives in Farringdon.'

'How long has this been going on?'

'Oh, at least three months. They're very determined, it seems.'

Mark snatched the note from the man's fingers. 'You should've phoned and told us this before now.'

'I'm sorry.'

'That doesn't help the woman who was murdered, does it?'

# CHAPTER FIFTEEN

'Christ, he's done all right for himself.'

Jan eyed the cathedral-like window at the front of the converted barn, then shot a glance at Turpin. 'What did he used to do?'

'According to Caroline, Bereton used to be the director of a private investment group until four years ago. He's now a non-executive director on the board of trustees for a local hospice charity, and a trustee for one of the local youth groups. Worth a few bob according to the news reports she found online. Makes a few political donations here and there as well.'

'Greasing palms?'

'Probably.' Turpin dropped his phone into his jacket pocket and led the way across to the enormous oak front door set into the middle of the window, and pressed a buzzer on a security panel set into the right of the frame.

Peering through the glass, Jan saw a carved staircase

sweeping up from the hallway to an open landing on the next floor, a minstrels' gallery above that.

An open fireplace had been built into the left-hand wall of the hallway, the grate filled with logs. Beside the stairs, a long oak dresser faced the hearth, a large white ceramic vase filled with tulips adding colour to the wide expanse.

A door beside the fireplace opened, and a man in his early seventies hurried towards them, opening the front door with a flourish.

'William Bereton?' Turpin asked, flipping open his warrant card.

'Call me Bill.' He thrust out his hand, then enveloped Jan's within a tight sweaty grip. 'Andrew phoned to say you needed some help.'

'Something like that,' she said, extracting her fingers and resisting the urge to wipe her hand down her trousers. 'Thanks for seeing us at short notice.'

'Not a problem.' He gave Turpin a cursory glance as he stepped aside to let them in, then slammed the door and spun on his heel. 'Come through to the study, will you? The missus has her sister here, and there's no need to involve the women in this.'

Jan followed a waft of overpowering aftershave past the fireplace and through a doorway under the stairs, noticing that both Bereton and Turpin had to duck under the exposed stone lintel.

'Fifteenth century, I'm told,' said Bereton, spreading his hands. 'Hence why some of the original exposed wattle and daub walls had to be preserved behind glass panels. This whole half of the building is Grade I listed. Apparently, this part was once used for stabling.'

'Impressive,' she admitted, taking in the beams that criss-crossed above her head and the large window that overlooked the rear of the property. 'Nice view from here, too.'

'Isn't it?' Bereton's chest expanded. 'That's why I insisted on my desk facing that way. It aids the thought processes, I find.'

He pointed to a pair of well-worn leather sofas that hugged a smaller unlit hearth, waited until they eased themselves into the thick upholstery, and then walked over to the mantelpiece, resting his arm along the intricate stonework. 'Andrew said this was about the burglaries that have been happening around here.'

'Actually, that's only partially correct,' said Turpin. He unfolded a photograph that Gillian had supplied once she'd cleaned the victim's face prior to the post mortem and thrust it at the other man. 'Do you recognise her?'

Bereton moved to the window and held the image up to the light, squinting a little. 'Can't say I do. What's her name?'

'Could you tell us where you were between half past six and ten o'clock on Tuesday night?'

Returning to the sofas, he gave Turpin a nervous smile and handed back the photograph. 'That sounds ominous.'

'Please, answer the question.'

'I was here, cooking dinner with the wife. It was her sister's birthday yesterday and she's been spending a few days with us.' He gave a slight shake of his head. 'Her husband, Neil, died six months ago and we didn't want her to be on her own.'

'Okay.' Turpin tucked the photo back in his jacket. 'We're still trying to ascertain the woman's identity but she was found on a roadside verge outside of Charney Bassett on Tuesday evening.'

'What happened?'

'Our enquiries are ongoing. Tell me about the group you manage, the one you set up to combat crime in the area.'

Bereton straightened. 'Now, hang on a minute. You can't come in here accusing us of killing her.'

'I don't believe I did.'

Jan watched while the older man chewed his lip, digesting Turpin's words.

Eventually, some of his bluster dissipated and he let out a sigh.

'Look, we're just a bunch of concerned locals, that's all. I mean, several of us have been burgled in the past, and we wanted to do something about it.'

'Have you been burgled recently?' Turpin looked around the study, and Jan noticed his gaze lingering on the window bolts and alarm sensors set into the corners of the ceiling. 'I don't recall seeing your name in our files.'

'No, not me personally. Some others in the group.' Bereton clasped his hands. 'You can appreciate what it's like, living out here in the sticks. Our nearest neighbours are half a mile away, and you saw how sheltered we are from the road. I dread to think what might happen if this place was burgled while Grace was here on her own.'

'What does the group call itself?'

'The White Horse Home Protection Group. You'll find us on social media. I keep saying we ought to get a website but no one listens, and I can't do everything for them.'

Jan glanced up at her notes in time to see Bereton giving a frustrated roll of his eyes.

'What does the group do?' she asked.

'We meet once a month at the village hall in Challow, and discuss any notices that you've put out, anything suspicious that's been noted in the area, and check in on each other,' he said, warming to his subject. 'If someone needs a hand installing new fencing, we'll arrange to meet at that property and lend a hand. That sort of thing.'

'Very neighbourly of you,' Turpin murmured. 'You're aware, then, of the twelve burglaries in this immediate vicinity within the last three months?'

Bereton's jaw dropped. 'Twelve?'

'Within a four mile radius of this house, yes.'

'Well, I…'

'How many people are in your group of "concerned locals"?' said Turpin.

'Six, at present. Myself, an ex-barrister, a chap who used to work for one of the big banks in the City...'

'I take it all of the members are quite... affluent, then?'

'Oh, yes.' Bereton's gaze moved from Turpin to Jan. 'Well, there's no point involving the likes of, shall we say, the less well-off types who live around here, is there? I mean, what on earth could they have that's worth stealing?'

Turpin's eyes narrowed, and Jan took a deep breath.

'It's those less well-off types who are getting burgled while you go around mending fences,' he said through gritted teeth. 'Your immediate neighbours, in other words. And now a woman who might be linked to those burglaries has been found murdered.'

Jan stopped writing as Bereton paled.

He raised his hands to his mouth as if in prayer, then exhaled.

'I'm sorry to hear that,' he said. 'What can I do to help?'

'The security cameras you have here – do you have any facing the road?'

'Yes, there's one on the gatepost. I've recommended all our members install them, just in case.'

'I'm going to need the names and addresses of those members.'

'Of course, no problem. I'll email them to you—'

'I need them now.'

# CHAPTER SIXTEEN

More than twenty uniformed officers and administrative staff were gathered in the incident room when Mark and Jan walked through the door the next morning.

Placing his backpack on his desk, Mark pulled out a fistful of colourful USB sticks and handed them to Tracy as he passed, winking when she gave him a tired smile.

Kennedy broke off from his briefing and wrenched his reading glasses off his nose while they took seats towards the back of the group, and Mark raised a hand in apology.

'I take it you've had a productive afternoon yesterday, you two?' said the DI. 'Care to fill us in?'

'Those files I just gave to Tracy are recordings from six private homes, all of which are situated close to the latest burglaries. We picked up the last of them this morning,' said Mark, loosening his tie. 'We spoke to the unofficial leader of a local group of residents who installed cameras at the end of their driveways in case our victim appears in any of them.'

Kennedy grunted in response. 'Right, Tracy – best get those logged in the system after this. Nathan, can you work with Alice Fields and Sam Owen to review the recordings? Did your so-called leader recognise the victim, Mark?'

'He says he doesn't, and his alibi checked out. Jan spoke to his wife before we left to verify that.'

'We're going to run through the other group members this afternoon, guv, just to make sure their alibis are sound and that they're not already in our system,' Jan added.

'Right, well you turned up just in time to hear some good news.' Kennedy adjusted his reading glasses and peered at the pages in his hand. 'Gillian's expert at the John Radcliffe emailed twenty minutes ago, and he's managed to work out our victim's prescription from the contact lens she found during the post mortem. Pens out, people – you're going to be busy today.'

Mark flipped open his notebook while the DI started to list the tasks.

'Caroline – work with Alex and uniform and start phoning around local opticians. Ask them to pull out records for patients with this prescription. It's going to take time, I know, so I'll have a word with DCI Melrose about approving some overtime for the weekend. We need to move fast on this, because whoever her accomplice is, whoever killed her, is three days ahead of us already.' The DI handed over Gillian's report to her. 'Start with the high street chains. They have centralised databases so if our victim's on one of those it'll save time. Once you've exhausted those, move on to the independent optometrists.'

Caroline nodded, and underscored her note. 'If we have to do that, guv, then I'll start with the ones in Wantage and Farringdon, given that those are closer to where she was found, and work my way out from there.'

Kennedy's gaze fell to Mark. 'I want you and Jan to speak to the two pawnbrokers that Alex identified as potential places where our roadside victim and her accomplice might've fenced their stolen goods, so get that done and report back to me when you're finished.' He paused when a hand shot up from the other side of the group and turned his attention to the young constable. 'Got a question, Sam?'

'Guv, I just wondered, given the amount of information about online scammers and the like, you'd think the victims of these burglaries might've paused to think they were being conned.'

'Speaking to the charity manager we met earlier, they're doing as much as they can to publicise the current scams, but we're dealing with some very shrewd operators,' said Mark. 'And although a lot of people are wary of phone and email scams these days, they seem to let their guard down when someone turns up on their doorstep – especially someone who says they're trying to help them or give them money, rather than selling them something.'

'From the statements we've gone through, in each instance the victim has said how polite and knowledgeable the man or woman was,' Alex added. 'Whoever it is we're up against, he's smart.'

'More worryingly – and, given the turn of events on Tuesday night – he's ruthless, too,' said Kennedy. 'So the sooner we bring him in, the better.'

# CHAPTER SEVENTEEN

Jan cursed as her heel turned on the uneven concrete footpath, then eyed the weary-looking façade of a shop squashed between a laundrette and a butcher's.

A wooden sandwich board was hitched to a chain that trailed from the crumbling brickwork under the front window to one of the sign's feet, and someone had scrawled faded chalk lettering across the blackboard paint promising the best price for gold jewellery and cash for gemstones.

Slowing beside Turpin as they approached, she took in the various electric guitars hanging in the window, their elegant shapes at odds with the dead pig dangling from a hook behind the glass next door.

'Right, this one belongs to Brenda Stephens,' she murmured. 'It's been established for nine years here in Botley – previously she was running the business from a unit off Iffley Road. Looks like she downsized at the same time. Alex said the previous set-up included a lot of furniture and garden reclamation stuff.'

'Okay, let's see what she knows.'

Turpin pushed the door and held it open for Jan, who immediately placed her finger under her nose to stop a sneeze erupting.

A dusty, damp smell assaulted her senses, and she blinked for a moment while looking around at the different china knick-knacks and gaudy paintings that leaned against one wall.

More guitars cluttered a corner, acoustics propped next to electrics and a couple of battered amplifiers that appeared in need of new switches.

She spotted a crate of comic books in another corner, then turned at the sound of a cigarette-induced hacking cough.

'Help you?' a woman rasped.

Pencilled-in eyebrows were raised above heavily made-up eyes that glared at them, deep wrinkles creasing her cheeks and forehead. Wrapped in a bright blue cardigan, she rose from a wooden bar stool beside a glass-topped counter and put down a paperback book, its pages splaying over an assortment of necklaces that had seen better times.

'Are you Brenda Stephens?' Jan opened her warrant card.

'That's me. What d'you want?' The woman squinted through the gloom to where Turpin flicked through a row of vinyl records. 'Unless you're buying, sonny, don't touch.'

He backed away, and Jan saw his mouth quirk before she turned back to the shop owner.

'Ms Stephens, we're investigating the death of a woman in her early twenties earlier this week. Do you recognise her?'

'Lemme see.' Snatching the photo from her, Brenda pulled pink plastic-framed glasses from amongst her nicotine-stained hair and peered at the woman's face.

'No. Don't know this one. What happened to her?' She thrust the photo back at Jan and collected her cardigan around her waist, hugging herself. 'She been stealing?'

'What makes you say that?'

'Well, you wouldn't be here otherwise, would you? What did you think? She came in here trying to flog stolen goods, is that it?'

'Did she?'

'No. I just told you. I've never seen her.'

'What sort of customers do you get in here?' Turpin said, moving to the counter and crouching to look at the jewellery on display.

'Mostly students.'

'Just students?' Turpin shot her a sly grin. 'Are you sure? We could always get uniform in here and bring the sniffer dogs along.'

Brenda rolled her eyes, one of her false eyelashes

dangerously close to falling off under the weight of the layers of mascara plastered to it.

'All right, no need to do that,' she grumbled. 'A few users, no dealers. I don't get involved with them, dirty bastards that they are.'

'Have you had anyone come in here acting suspiciously?' said Jan.

A barking laugh preceded a vicious coughing fit, and Brenda slapped her hand against her chest, oblivious to the step backwards Jan took to avoid the explosion of spittle.

'Oh my fucking God, woman. Of course I have,' the shop owner cackled, wheezing while she made her way around the counter. She pushed the book aside and rested her hands on the glass, a large diamond ring sparkling on her wedding finger. 'Everyone who comes in 'ere looks suspicious, don't they? Nobody *wants* to walk into a place like this. It's not like they're here by choice, is it? They come in here when they're desperate.'

'And you're sure you've never seen this woman?' said Jan.

'No, can't say I have. What'd she do?'

'We're more interested in finding out how she ended up dead in a ditch outside Charney Bassett,' said Turpin. 'It's a straight run down the A417 from here.'

'Like I said, I never met her.' Brenda glared at him. 'And if that's all, I've got a business to run here.'

Jan looked over her shoulder, taking in the empty

shop and then the brief flicker of pedestrians passing the front window. 'Doesn't look very busy at the moment.'

'I got house calls to make, and I'm already late. So, if you don't have any more questions, you can bugger off.'

# CHAPTER EIGHTEEN

Forty minutes later, Mark looked up at the chipped and peeling gold lettering etched onto what was once a glossy black signboard, then lowered his gaze to the bay window jutting out into the narrow cobbled alleyway.

A sorry collection of cheap furniture, tasteless china ornaments and dirty jewellery lined the display, framed by a series of faded notices listing everything from opening hours to warnings about a lack of cash on the premises.

'I want to put on protective gloves just looking at this place,' Jan said, frowning at the layer of dirt ingrained within the rotting window frame.

'How long did Alex say this bloke had been here?'

'Three years. There's nothing on the database to suggest that there's been any trouble. I checked with local uniform and they say they've never had cause for concern either – Mr Targethen drinks in one of the pubs in the Market Square on a regular basis, and tends to keep to himself, according to the bloke who owns this building. Targethen does a bit of house clearance work in between running this place, and fancies himself as an antiques dealer on the side.'

'Don't they all.'

Mark took one look at the smears on the door handle, then used his elbow to push his way inside.

He ducked as something brushed against his hair, a chill running across his neck before he turned to see a wisp of loose brown tape from a broken electrical junction box above the open door. It fluttered in the breeze until Jan pushed it aside.

To his left and right, shelves lined the walls, disappearing into a dusty gloom and stacked haphazardly with old china cups and saucers, copper pots and dirty silverware.

He could hear a radio station playing in the background, a tinny collection of jumbled voices with too much treble and little resonance before he spotted an ancient smartphone propped up against a stack of leather-clad books on the counter, a miniature speaker beside it.

A thin man in his fifties eyed him from behind a glass-topped counter that was as cluttered as the shelves. He leaned an arm on a till, his mouth in a zip of a line and a harshness in his gaze.

'Well, if it isn't the police,' he sneered. 'What brings you here?'

'Are you Marcus Targethen?' asked Mark, moving closer.

'I am.'

Mark held out his warrant card, then the photograph, now creased in several places. 'Do you know this woman?'

The pawnbroker leaned forward, but didn't take the photograph and instead swivelled a desk lamp around to illuminate it.

'Nope.' He rocked back on his heels. 'Why? Has she been trying to fence stolen goods or something?'

'That's what we're trying to find out. Do you get much trouble like that in here?'

'What did you say your name was?'

'DS Mark Turpin.'

Targethen grinned, exposing uneven teeth blackened with rot. 'I don't get any trouble in here, detective. I don't hang around with those sort of people. I run a perfectly legitimate business here.'

'Are you busy?' Jan asked, her tone incredulous.

'It's a quiet time of the day, that's all. Gives me time to do the paperwork.' Targethen swept his arm in the direction of a chipped mahogany sideboard behind the till, where a stack of receipts and bills wobbled beside an ancient laptop computer. 'You interrupted me.'

'Then we'll keep this short,' said Mark. 'Where were you between half past six and ten-thirty on Tuesday night?'

Targethen poked his finger towards the door. 'Over

at the pub in the square. Watching the footy. Ask the landlord, he'll tell you. I got there at six, and walked out at five to eleven. Then I went home.'

Mark waited while Jan took down the details, and looked past the shop owner to the spreadsheet display on the laptop. 'Do you keep a record of everything that you buy and sell?'

'Of course.'

'Any cash jobs?'

'Look, only now and again, and only if it's a particularly crappy piece. No jewellery, mind – I'm careful with that stuff, just in case your lot do turn up. Only the odd chair or ornament here and there. But I still put it in that inventory list,' he hastened to add. 'The accountant sorts it all out at the end of the year and tells me what I owe the tax man.'

Mark raised an eyebrow in response.

'Where do you find most of your stock?' asked Jan.

'Most times, people walk in here with bits and pieces. Stuff they've inherited that they don't want to keep, or unwanted presents.' The blackened teeth grinned again. 'Plenty of engagement rings and unwanted reminders. They figure at least I'll give them some money for it rather than taking it down the charity shop or handing it back to an ex.'

'Do you have CCTV cameras?' Mark said.

'I've never had any trouble, so I don't bother. Expensive things to run, them.'

'I'm surprised your insurance premiums haven't gone up if you haven't got cameras.'

'I've got good locks on the doors and windows. That helps.' Targethen's eyes narrowed. 'What's this about, anyway? That woman – what's she done?'

'She was found on the side of the road a few miles away from here. We're treating her death as suspicious.'

The pawnbroker's face paled. 'She's dead?'

'I thought you didn't know her.'

'I-I don't. It's just shocking, isn't it?' Targethen swallowed. 'I've got two nieces, and I keep telling my sister she ought to pay for them to have some self-defence classes. It's just not safe out there anymore, is it?'

Mark took one last look at the contents of the counter and shelves behind the till. 'Thanks for your time, Mr Targethen. We'll be in touch if we have any more questions.'

He slid a business card across the counter, then followed Jan outside, blinking in the grey light from an overcast sky.

He didn't look back, feeling Targethen's stare boring into him through the smeared window panes, and instead set a brisk pace back to the market square.

As Jan unlocked the car, he finally eyed the entrance to the alleyway and growled under his breath.

'When we get back to the incident room, I want to take another look at the background checks Alex pulled out of the system.'

'I'll give you a hand,' she said, dropping behind the wheel and putting her bag behind her seat.

'We'll check out his social media for the nieces as well,' he said, reaching forward to turn up the heater.

'Okay. You didn't believe him about the self-defence classes?'

'I do, but you saw his reaction when I told him about our mystery dead woman.'

'He's lying,' said Jan, starting the engine. 'He looked frightened when you said that. So you think he did know her?'

'Yes. And I want to know why he's scared.'

# CHAPTER NINETEEN

Mark rolled his shoulders and took a swig from a takeout coffee cup before turning his attention back to his computer screen, pecking his fingers at the keyboard while recalling the day's interviews.

It was already half past five, but with the investigation team working over the weekend, all of his reports needed to be completed straight away to keep the rest of them up to date.

Especially Kennedy.

The DI had looked up from his computer as Mark and Jan walked past his office window twenty minutes ago, a frown etched across his forehead and his phone to his ear. He'd nodded in greeting before returning his attention to the caller, his voice inaudible through the closed door.

'Do you think that's Headquarters on the phone?' Jan said, nudging her shoe against his under the desk.

'No idea. Looks official though, doesn't it?' Mark didn't turn around to look, and instead kept his eyes focused on the keyboard. 'Why can I never find the bloody K when I need it?'

Jan grinned. 'You should get some touch-typing lessons, Sarge. Alex did while he was at university. Seen how fast he is?'

'Like I have time to do that.' He stabbed the keyboard, pressed another button and watched with satisfaction as a message appeared to confirm his report was now recorded in HOLMES2. 'Okay, that's Targethen's interview in the system. How're you getting on with the Brenda Stephens one?'

'All done, minus the swearing.'

Mark chuckled. 'I liked her.'

'So you don't think she's involved?'

'Not with our dead woman, no. I've asked for a uniform patrol to keep an eye on the place though, just in case we do need to pass it over to the drugs team. Somehow, I think Ms Stephens treads a fine line but never crosses it. She wouldn't have lasted this long in that business if she had. Not these days.'

'Sarge, got a minute?'

He looked over his shoulder to see Caroline walking towards him, then leaned across and pulled a spare chair over from the desk beside him. 'Have a seat.'

'Ta.'

'What's up?'

'I was going through Jasper's report from the search

at the crime scene, and the statements we got from the Tillcotts on Tuesday night. There's something bothering me about all her missing ID.'

'In what way?' Jan walked around to Mark's desk. 'If she was on the take, then it makes sense that either her accomplice took it, or she didn't have anything on her in case she was caught and identified.'

'I agree, but none of that explains why he – or they – didn't pick up her handbag or take her mobile phone out of it when they dumped her on the side of the road,' Caroline said. 'I mean, why go to all that bother removing her ID, but leave the bag?'

Mark wagged a finger. 'Bearing in mind the evidence at the moment suggests she was killed elsewhere then dumped there, he had to move her from the car to the ditch on the roadside. Perhaps the bag was over her shoulder but slipped off while he was doing that—'

'—and he would've been planning to look for it,' Jan added.

'That's what I'm thinking,' said Caroline. 'He was going to take the bag, but he was interrupted. By the Tillcotts' car approaching.'

Reaching out for his notebook, Mark scrawled down her theory then raised his head at the sound of footsteps.

'Got a minute?' Kennedy said. 'That is, if I'm not interrupting something here.'

'Caroline's got an idea about the woman's handbag,'

said Mark, and explained. 'In which case, we need to speak to the Tillcotts again.'

'They didn't mention any other cars passing them when we interviewed them on Tuesday night, did they?' said Caroline, glancing at Jan, who shook her head.

'No, I specifically asked them that when we were still thinking it might've been a hit and run,' she said. 'But at the time, they said they couldn't remember. If someone had dumped a body on the side of the road though, they wouldn't be hanging around would they? They'd have passed the Tillcotts at speed, so I'm sure they would've noticed that.'

'Fair enough, but what if the killer drove off in the other direction?' Mark swung his chair back and forth. 'They might've spotted tail lights or movement ahead of them but not put two and two together at the time. Their recollection might be better now.'

'Or worse,' said Kennedy. 'I agree it's worth speaking to them again, so add that to your list tomorrow. In the meantime, while you're here, I've got some good news for you. Professional Standards called Melrose an hour ago and told him they're not pursuing their investigation anymore. You're back on the team full-time.'

Mark slumped in his seat, his heart thumping. 'Really?'

'How come it took them so long?' said Jan.

Kennedy raised an eyebrow in response, and she blushed.

'Sorry, guv. It's just that this has been going on since last year.'

'Politics,' he replied. 'As always.'

'Thanks anyway,' said Mark. He rose and shook Kennedy's hand. 'I appreciate you being in my corner, guv.'

'No doubt we'll both pay for that somewhere down the line. In the meantime, I suggest you all go and find Alex, then knock off early and go and have a drink to celebrate.'

'What about you?' Jan asked. 'Care to join us?'

'Unfortunately, I've still got the paperwork to process. Have fun.'

The DI stalked back into his office and slammed the door.

'Come on,' Mark said, looping his arm through hers and Caroline's. 'You heard him. Let's go and find a pub.'

# CHAPTER TWENTY

Bright sunshine reflected off the windscreen of Jan's car the next morning when Mark crossed the gravel parking area beside the water meadow.

Fresh puddles sparkled amongst the small stones, potholes brimming with water from the late night rainstorm that lashed the roof of the narrowboat and lent an ozone-heavy richness to the air.

'Morning,' he said, closing the door. 'Scott not playing football this morning, then?'

'Later,' Jan responded. 'He's taking the twins swimming first – his match isn't until four o'clock.'

He watched a rag-tag procession of pedestrians while she steered the car over the bridge and through the town centre before passing the police station.

'Thanks for the drinks last night,' she added. 'It was good to catch up with Lucy as well.'

'We need to get you and the boys over for lunch one

weekend when neither of us is working,' said Mark. 'I promised you a barbecue, too.'

'Keep it simple, for God's sake. If those boys get near a barbecue, there won't be any sausages left for Hamish. Have you told Debbie about the investigation being dropped?'

'Last night. She's pleased, obviously – after all, they didn't charge her with anything and it was a flimsy case against me anyway.'

'And the girls?'

'Louise was sounding a lot happier when I spoke to her afterwards.' He snorted. 'Anna's in her own little world still – I think Debbie kept as much from her as she could last year. She was more interested in when she can come and stay again.'

'She misses you.'

'She misses Hamish.'

They laughed while Mark scrolled through the messages on his phone to find the address they needed.

'If you take this next right, the Tillcotts' place is about five minutes away.'

He was reading through copies of the couples' original statements when Jan slowed and turned between a pair of granite-hewn gateposts, the name of the property carved within the stonework on his left.

Wrought-iron gates had been staked open, the black paint glistening with raindrops from the previous night's storm and a paved driveway curved lazily towards a two-storey house that had once been a substantial farmhouse.

The Tillcotts' sports car was parked outside one of two garages housed within a converted stable block, a black four-by-four beside it with the name of their property company emblazoned across the doors.

Jan strode across to the solid oak-panelled front door and rang the bell while Mark straightened his tie.

When Simon Tillcott opened the door, Mark saw his colleague's grim expression and guessed the man looked even rougher than on Tuesday night when she'd spoken to him at the crime scene.

A day's growth covered his jaw, and he wore a creased light grey T-shirt stuffed into faded jeans, his feet bare. A tiredness clouded his eyes, a resignation that his life had changed forever after discovering the young woman's body, and Mark recognised the exhaustion in the man's posture.

'Simon, this is Detective Sergeant Mark Turpin,' said Jan, making the introductions. 'We wondered if we could have another word with you and Julie?'

'Sure. Why not?' The man led the way through to a large open-plan kitchen and dining area that looked out through cantilever windows across a wide lawn.

His wife stood next to a sink within a central worktop and peered over her shoulder as they entered, her hands holding a colander under running water.

She set it aside, turned off the tap and dried her

hands before introducing herself to Mark. 'I take it you've got more questions?'

'Just a few,' Mark said.

'Have a seat.' Julie pointed to a long six-seater dining table that had been carved from a single piece of chestnut tree. 'Do you know who she is yet?'

'Our enquiries are ongoing,' said Jan.

'That's a "no", then.' Simon pulled out a chair beside his wife and scratched his chin. 'Was she murdered, or hit by a car?'

'It's too early to say for sure,' Mark explained. 'We're waiting for more results from our forensics team following the post mortem earlier this week. In the meantime, we've got a few follow-up questions regarding the statements you gave on Tuesday.'

'When you were leaving the pub that night, did you notice any cars travelling in the opposite direction to you?' said Jan.

'Sorry, excuse me.'

Simon pushed back his chair and crossed to the sink, picked up a glass from the draining board and filled it. After taking a gulp, he wiped his mouth with the back of his hand and turned to face them once more. 'I can't stop seeing her.'

'He hasn't been sleeping properly,' said Julie. 'Our doctor's given him some sleeping pills but he refuses to take them—'

'They make me groggy in the mornings.'

'I'm sorry to hear that,' said Mark. 'Are you keeping in touch with your GP?'

'Yeah. I'm seeing someone next week. Counselling.'

'What about you, Julie – how are you doing?'

'I'm okay.' She grimaced. 'As soon as Simon saw her, he pushed me away. I saw enough, but not as much as he did.'

'Was… was she dead before she ended up like that?' Her husband returned to the table, his face grey. 'Or did she die there?'

'We're unable to say for sure at the moment, I'm sorry.' Mark watched while Julie slipped her hand across Simon's. 'I am interested in the moments before you found her though. Would you mind if I asked you some more questions?'

Julie frowned. 'I'm not sure that's a good idea. You heard what Simon said – he can't sleep at the moment. I don't think—'

'It's okay. I want to help.'

'We just have a couple of questions,' said Jan. 'Before you stopped the car, did you see any other vehicles?'

'No one passed us,' said Simon. 'It's pretty quiet along there at that time of night.'

'What about ahead of you?'

The man chewed his lip for a moment. 'Maybe… I'm not sure.'

'I didn't see anything,' Julie said.

'What do you think you saw?' Jan asked, keeping

her gaze glued to Simon, ignoring the comment from his wife.

'Perhaps – look, like I said, I can't be certain – it might've been a brake light.'

'Where?'

'Along the road, almost out of sight. There's a corner farther along there from where... where we found that woman. I thought I saw a brake light flash on then off.'

'Just the one?'

'Yeah.'

'Was it a motorbike, or a car?' said Mark.

'I-I don't know.' Simon exhaled, then frowned. 'Actually, I think it might've been a car. The light was too low down to be a bike. It could've been a small van, I suppose.'

'That's great, thank you.' Jan wrote down the new detail, then put her notebook away while Mark stood.

'Is that it?' said Julie, her eyes darting to her husband.

'For now.' Mark gave what he hoped was a reassuring smile. 'But it's good information to have, thank you.'

'I'll show you to the door.' Simon scraped back his chair, ushering them along the hallway.

When he reached the front door, Mark thrust out his hand.

'Thanks again, Mr Tillcott.'

'No problem.' He followed them outside, and pulled the door closed. 'Listen, before you go…'

'Something the matter?'

Simon glanced over his shoulder, then walked a few more paces towards their pool car before turning and shoving his hands in his jeans pockets. 'I couldn't say anything in front of Julie.'

'About what?' Mark saw the fleeting look of confusion crossing Jan's face, echoing his own.

'I recognised the dead woman.'

'Pardon?'

'The woman we found on the side of the road. I've seen her before.'

Mark took a step forward. 'Where?'

'You can't tell Julie, all right? She doesn't know. She can't know.'

'Where did you see her, Simon?'

'At an event, about three months ago.' The man's gaze dropped to the gravel driveway, and he kicked at a loose stone, his mouth downturned. 'Look, I'm not proud of myself. I broke it off soon after.'

Mark crossed his arms, waiting.

'I was having an affair with someone I met through the business. She works for a real estate developer, and she had tickets to this corporate event at one of the big hotels in Oxford. It ran over two days, so I told Julie I'd stay overnight because I wanted to network in the evening and at breakfast—'

'Except you were doing a different sort of networking,' said Jan.

Mark held up his hand to silence her, then glared at Simon. 'Go on.'

'That night, there was a black tie dinner. Lots of schmoozing, you know? Anyway, whoever the organisers were, they had a string quartet playing all night, tucked away in the background. You had to walk past them when you went to the toilets.'

'Where did you see the woman?'

'That's the thing. She was in the band. Playing violin.' He sighed. 'She was really good, too.'

# CHAPTER TWENTY-ONE

A different energy filled the incident room by Monday morning, the news quickly spreading that a potential breakthrough in identifying their victim was imminent.

Mark tucked his mobile phone in his pocket and flicked through a stack of files that Tracy had left on his desk, working through the official documentation and signing his name where pencil crosses dictated. Flipping the last one closed, his attention turned to the heightened conversations around him, the knowledge that they might finally be a step closer to some answers, and a motive.

Voices were louder, uniformed and civilian personnel walked past his desk at a hurried pace while more and more details came through by email, phone and social media posts.

Kennedy tempered the charged atmosphere within seconds of starting the briefing.

'Settle down,' he growled, putting on his reading glasses and glaring at the agenda in his hand as if it was to blame for his next news. 'After Simon Tillcott provided Mark and Jan with the hotel details, Alex gave them a call and spoke to the events manager. Unfortunately, her predecessor left six weeks ago – and he's the one who booked the string quartet.'

'We can go and speak to him this afternoon if she gave his details, guv,' Mark said.

'Good luck with that, Turpin – he's currently bobbing around in the Pacific on a cruise ship.' Kennedy flapped the agenda in the general direction of the windows. 'He left Southampton for Rio de Janeiro last week, and won't be back in the country until June at the earliest.'

'I left a message on his voicemail,' said Alex. 'Hopefully he hasn't changed his number – it didn't say it was out of service, so…'

'…we have to wait until he's got enough signal to get a notification.' Mark tapped his notebook against his knee with impatience. 'Why can't the events manager at the hotel give you the string quartet's details?'

Alex turned in his seat, resting his arm across the back. 'Because they hadn't played there before. The band that was booked had to cancel at the last minute, and the events manager at the time – the guy on the ship – phoned a mate of his who knew someone who could step in at the last minute.'

'Can't they trace them from the invoice?' said Jan.

'No, because the hotel didn't pay the band. Apparently the guy on cello owed the events manager a favour or something, so they did it for free.' Alex shrugged. 'Probably hoped they'd get a few more gigs there out of it.'

'Bugger,' Mark said. 'So we're stuck until we hear back from this bloke?'

'For now,' said Kennedy. 'In the meantime, Tracy – get in touch with media relations and ask if they can update the social posts to ask if anyone knows of a missing violinist. Who's processing the CCTV footage from Bereton's neighbourhood watch lot?'

'Me, guv.' Nathan shuffled past three colleagues before moving to the whiteboard. 'Only one of the residents' cameras was any good to us because the others were either turned towards driveway entrances from the direction of the road, or such poor quality that digital forensics couldn't clean them up enough for us to watch them. The doorbell ones again only showed enough to see driveways – none of those faced the road.'

'So what did you get on the one that was useful?' said Mark.

'We'd already seen that it picked up the Tillcotts' car going past, and we didn't spot anything going the other way but when we went back and watched the recording based on what Simon Tillcott told you today, we got a brief glimpse of the car he said he saw.'

'How brief?' Kennedy asked.

'The camera is positioned within a tree at the end of the driveway so if there's a breeze, the branches obscure the lens.' Nathan gave a small shrug. 'Sorry, guv. Forensics tried their best, but all they can confirm is that it's a four-door late model saloon. I was going to suggest that we start phoning around to request security camera footage and council-operated CCTV within the area to see if we can get a better angle.'

'Do it. The sooner the better, too.' The DI frowned at the agenda once more. 'Caroline – anything from the calls to the opticians you were making on Saturday?'

'No luck yet, guv, but we ran out of time before some of them closed at lunchtime. We'll continue this morning.'

'How far have you had to widen the search?'

'We've sent the prescription out to everyone within a wider radius now. I'll extend that to include Abingdon, Didcot and Oxford today,' said Caroline. 'I'm starting to think whoever our victim is, and given that she might have played in that string quartet, then she kept her private business in one area and the burglaries and fraud in a different one.'

'If she was playing gigs regularly around Oxford, then that makes sense,' said Mark. 'Although there are burglaries around Wallingford, Banbury and Witney, none of them match the descriptions of the cases further south.'

'Get a list of attendees to that event Simon Tillcott mentioned from the hotel, Alex,' Kennedy said. 'Divide them up between yourself, Mark and Jan and ask if anyone's got photographs of the musicians. Even if they're in the background, we might be able to get forensics to tidy them up for us enough to get a clear shot of the violinist to confirm she's our victim. Otherwise we could be chasing after the wrong lead here. We've only got Tillcott's opinion it's the same woman at the moment.'

'Do you think one of them might have a business card for the band, or perhaps know who she is?' said Nathan.

'We'll soon find out, constable.' The DI gave a grim smile. 'And when we do, we're one step closer to finding the bastard who did this to her.'

# CHAPTER TWENTY-TWO

Jan took a sip of soft drink, slammed the can back onto her desk and picked up the phone once more.

Resisting the urge to hold her head in her hand while she waited for the call to be answered, she ran her eyes down the list of names and numbers Alex had given to her, and then peered over her computer screen to where Turpin sat.

An equally exasperated expression creased his features, his dark hair ruffled where he'd been running his hand through it repeatedly.

His voice remained patient, but she could see the strain in his eyes as he ended the call.

'Hello?'

She blinked, her attention turning to the voice in her ear. 'Hello, is that Harvey Petersham?'

'Who's this?'

'Detective Constable Jan West, Thames Valley

Police. I believe you attended an event in Oxford a little while ago?' She explained about the string quartet. 'We're wondering if you might've caught the name of the quartet, or perhaps got a business card from one of them?'

'Why the hell would I ask them for a business card?'

'I don't know, I was just—'

'The whole thing was a waste of time, I tell you. It was advertised as a networking opportunity for pharmaceutical relations – a way to meet new clients and like-minded peers.' Petersham snorted. 'Honestly, if it weren't for the four-course dinner I don't think I'd have bothered. The hotel has a reputation for an excellent wine list, did you know that?'

'I didn't,' Jan murmured. 'Um, I don't suppose you took any photographs while you were there, did you?'

'Photos? Of course I didn't. Why would I?'

'It's just that—'

'I didn't have time to take bloody photos. I was trying to make the most of a situation that was otherwise a complete waste of time. Mind you, I did meet a chap who's working on a patent for a new surgical instrument to improve surgery times for colonoscopies...'

Jan closed her eyes while Petersham droned on, then exhaled when he paused long enough for her to get a word in. 'Thank you for your time.'

She crossed out his name on her list, then dialled the next number, hearing the same weariness in Turpin's voice as he ended another call.

The ringing in her ear changed to a monotone beep, and she hung up, resigning herself to trying again later in the day.

'Any luck yet?' Turpin said.

'No.' She looked over her shoulder to where Alex sat next to Sam Owens, both hunched over their desks with phones to their ears. 'I'm not hearing any eureka moments from over there, either.'

When she turned back, her colleague was running his hands down his face.

'Two hundred attendees,' he groaned. 'You'd have thought they would've had an official photographer or something.'

'Saving money, according to the hotel's events organiser. I suppose they figured everyone would have mobile phones with them – a bloke I spoke to earlier said they were all given a hashtag to quote on social media if they uploaded any photographs so I've asked Nathan to look through those while we do this.'

'Thanks. With any luck, he'll find her before we're done here.' Turpin checked his watch. 'Let's phone a couple more each, then go and get a coffee and some fresh air.'

'Sounds good. I could—'

Turpin's phone rang, interrupting her, and he frowned. 'That's the media team's extension. Hello?'

Jan held her breath while he listened.

'Give me his address and phone number – we'll go

over there now.' He hung up and pushed back his chair. 'That coffee's going to have to wait.'

'What is it?'

'They just got a call from someone who saw one of the social media posts. He thinks he knows our victim.'

'Was he at this event?'

'Yes – he plays cello in the same string quartet.'

# CHAPTER TWENTY-THREE

Mark stabbed the doorbell with his forefinger, then took a step back, mindful of the overflowing black wheelie bin beside him.

A sweaty tang of rotting vegetation and greasy pizza boxes accompanied a fouler smell emanating from a soil pipe beneath a frosted downstairs window, and he wrinkled his nose.

'Ah, shared houses. Takes me back to my younger days,' Jan said under her breath.

'Do you miss it?'

'Hell, no.' She bit back a smile as the door opened.

The man in front of them was well-dressed despite the exterior of his house resembling a mottled concoction of health hazards. Taller than Mark by a couple of inches, his rake-thin frame bowed a little by way of greeting, his floppy brown fringe falling into his eyes.

'I take it you're the police.'

'Mr Spencer Rossbay?' Turpin held up his warrant card and made the introductions. 'We understand you have some information regarding a missing woman we're trying to trace.'

'I think so, yes.' Rossbay stood to one side, waving them towards an open door into a living room. 'Take a seat.'

Mark traced his gaze over the cello and violin cases propped against a bookcase, a large gleaming instrument on a stand beside the television.

'Are these yours?'

'Yes. Well, the cello's mine.'

He hovered beside the front window until Mark had settled into a ragged armchair, Jan taking a seat on a sofa opposite, then scooped up a collection of vinyl records and books beside her and sank down with a sigh.

'I'd offer you a hot drink, but I'm out of milk.'

'No problem,' said Mark. 'You mentioned on the phone to our media team that you shared this house with a violin player from your quartet. Is she here?'

'Hilary's in Portugal at the moment,' he explained. 'Her sister's a travel writer so she gets all sorts of free holidays in five-star hotels. Life's a bitch, right?'

He brayed with laughter, a bitterness rising to the surface despite the forced humour.

'When is she back?'

'Not for another week.' Rossbay's face fell. 'We had

to turn down a couple of gigs because of her trip. Well-paying ones, too.'

'You said you think the woman in our social media post is your other violin player, is that correct?'

'She played viola, not violin. We had a bit of a falling out a while back.' The musician scowled. 'Her fault, but I still felt bad afterwards, when I'd cooled off a bit. I sent a couple of text messages that she didn't reply to, so I tried to call her last week to see if we could sort it out. I couldn't get hold of her.'

'When was that?'

'Monday night.' He chewed his lip. 'About seven, I suppose.'

'Did you report her missing?'

'God, no. Should I have? I mean, I don't know her parents' names or whether she had any friends. Wouldn't they have done that if they were worried?'

'That's okay. When was the last time you actually saw her?'

'Three months ago.'

'Was that when she left the quartet?'

'That was when we fired her, yes.'

'Why?'

Rossbay stood and wandered over to the window again, silent for a moment before his shoulders sagged.

'She'd changed. When she first joined us she was all enthusiastic, eager to turn up for practice sessions, good at helping with marketing the quartet. She's been playing since she was eleven, and a natural. She only had a year to go at uni studying music but dropped out during the first term. One of the big orchestras in London already had its eye on her, so it seemed strange to me. She loves music. Lives for it, in fact.' He turned back to them, his eyes downcast. 'She even has a tattoo of a clef and a heart on the inside of her left wrist so she can see it while she's playing.'

Mark saw Jan's head twitch up from her notebook, her pen frozen above the page. He pulled out the photograph, keeping it folded between his fingers.

'Spencer, I need to show you a photograph. A young woman was found by the side of the road just north of Wantage on Tuesday night—'

'It's Sonya, isn't it?'

'We don't know yet. We haven't been able to identify her, which is why I'm hoping you can help.'

The musician's Adam's apple bobbed in his throat. 'Is it… is she…'

'There's no blood. This was taken before the post mortem.' Mark grimaced. 'Look, I have to tell you it's only one side of her face. The other was too—'

'Let me see.'

Rossbay crossed to where Mark sat and took the photo. A sharp gasp escaped when he unfolded it, then he closed his eyes and handed it back.

'It's her.'

'Thank you. I know that wasn't easy.'

'Can I get you a glass of water, Spencer?' Jan said.

'No, that's okay. Thanks.' Rossbay slumped on the sofa next to her and wiped tears away. 'Poor Sonya.'

Mark gave him a few moments, then leaned forward. 'You say her name's Sonya – what's her surname?'

'Raynott. Sonya Raynott.'

'Do you know why she dropped out of uni?'

'Haven't got a clue. We all told her at the time she was crazy. Honestly, she was flying through it. Not a prodigy, but up there with the best.' Rossbay sniffed. 'I... God, I always thought this happened to other people, that it'd never happen to someone I know... knew...'

'Do you have anyone you can stay with tonight, or who you can talk to?' Mark said.

'I, er, my parents live in Woodstock.'

'Give them a call after we're gone, perhaps stay with them tonight.'

Rossbay's eyes widened. 'Do you think I'm in danger?'

'No, but receiving this sort of news about a friend is hard,' Jan said. 'And if you can be with someone, then you should.'

'Oh. Thanks. Perhaps I will.'

'Going back to Sonya – you said you had to fire her from the quartet. Why was that?'

Rossbay gave another sniff, then leaned his elbows on his knees. 'Her playing was still top notch, but she just kept missing practice sessions. She was distant, wouldn't join us for a drink after the practices she did turn up for – we sometimes go for dinner somewhere afterwards, you know – socialise a bit. We all get on really well usually so we used to look forward to it. But Sonya started leaving the hall where we practised as soon as we finished, almost as if she couldn't wait to leave, or had to be somewhere. She stopped doing the marketing without telling us until we wondered why the bookings were starting to dry up.' He paused. 'It was almost as if something else had taken over being the most important thing in her life.'

'You said Hilary's away at the moment, your violin player. Who replaced Sonya in the quartet when you fired her?'

'Graham Tiegler.' Rossbay managed a smile. 'He knew a friend of a friend and was always dropping hints that he wanted to join us if an opportunity came up. He's not as good as Sonya, but he can play all the pieces – and he turns up on time.'

'We'll need his contact details.'

'Of course.' Rossbay pulled a mobile phone from his pocket and turned the screen to face Jan while she jotted down the name and number. 'Do you think… I mean, I don't know any of her friends or her family. They never came to any of our gigs because we tend to play private bookings, but do you think you could let me know when they arrange her funeral? I'd… we'd like to pay our respects.'

Mark stood, and nodded. 'I'll be sure to pass on

your details to them when we speak to them in due course.'

'Thank you.' Rossbay showed them to the door, then paused with his hand on the latch, his shoulders stiffening. 'I hope you find whoever did this to Sonya, detectives. She didn't deserve to die like that, not alone and left like that.'

'Nobody does,' said Mark.

# CHAPTER TWENTY-FOUR

'Do you think this Graham bloke is our killer?' said Jan, her eyes flicking to the GPS map on her phone stuck to the dashboard before the traffic lights turned green.

Mark managed a chuckle. 'Well, I know Rossbay said he was keen to join them but I don't think he'd kill Sonya to get the part, do you?'

Jan wrinkled her nose. 'It's a bit desperate, isn't it?'

'We'll see. How far away is his place?'

'Five minutes, according to that map.'

'Okay.' Mark swiped his phone screen and hit speed dial. 'Alex, we've got a positive ID for our victim. She's a viola player by the name of Sonya Raynott. Spencer Rossbay confirmed she used to play in his string quartet, and we've got an address as well. Can you get uniform to go round there once you've got a search warrant? Jan and I are going to be interviewing another member of the string quartet. Right. Thanks.'

'Any news from that end?' Jan said.

'He says Kennedy's doing a briefing at five o'clock – and Caroline's waiting to hear back from an optician who might be able to help us too.'

'Finally.' Jan bumped the steering wheel with her fist. 'It's starting to feel like we're getting somewhere.'

'What number house am I looking out for?'

'Fifty-three. It should be up here on the left.'

Graham Tiegler's home was a stark contrast to Rossbay's, with a neat driveway striking a wide path up to a newly painted garage door and a lush lawn bordered with bright spring flowers.

'According to what I found on social media, he's married, with an eleven-year-old son,' said Mark as they parked behind a tidy blue hatchback, blocking the driveway. 'He works for an engineering firm in Radstock, and apart from the string quartet he plays badminton in his spare time. His wife is a teaching assistant at a local school.'

'All seems quite normal.' Jan locked the car and followed him towards the front door. 'Hello, is this him?'

The door opened when they were only halfway up the driveway and a man appeared, his freshly shaven head gleaming above a crisp blue shirt.

'Spencer said you were on your way,' he said.

'Bugger,' murmured Jan.

Mark provided the introductions, then tucked his

warrant card away. 'We just have a few questions we'd like to ask.'

'Ben's doing his homework at the moment, and I don't want him disturbed.' Tiegler shut the front door, then crossed to the hatchback and leaned against it, crossing his arms. 'Ellen thinks I'm mowing the lawn anyway, so we can talk out here.'

'No problem.' Mark waited until Jan was ready, then took out his own notebook as well.

Tiegler shuffled from foot to foot, his eyes bloodshot. 'Is it true, then? Is that dead woman I heard about on the news actually Sonya?'

'How well did you know her?'

'I saw her from time to time – in passing, mind. If I was in Oxford I might bump into her shopping. We used the same music shop to get strings from, you see, things like that.'

'What's the name of the shop?' Mark said.

Tiegler told him, then dropped his arms and shoved his hands in his trouser pockets. 'I saw her at a couple of concerts organised by the university last year. She was really good.'

'Jealous?'

'Pardon?'

Mark gave an easy smile. 'Were you jealous of Sonya? Was she better than you?'

The bloodshot eyes narrowed. 'She was better than everyone, detective. Not just me.'

'When was the last time you saw Sonya?'

'About four weeks ago. She walked right past me in the Westgate shopping centre. I said hello, but she ignored me and just kept walking.'

'Was that odd behaviour for her?'

'I just thought she was getting full of herself, that's all. It's like that business with dropping out of uni, and then getting fired from the quartet. She thinks… thought she was above all of that.'

'Do you think she might've had other things on her mind when you saw her?'

'I don't know. None of my business, right?'

'You look a little under the weather, Mr Tiegler,' said Jan. 'Everything all right?'

'Apart from finding out a fellow musician's been murdered, you mean?' He scowled. 'I'm fine. I was just out late last night. Playing at an event out near Witney – a fortieth wedding anniversary.'

'Where were you last Tuesday night, between half six and eleven?' said Mark.

Tiegler looked away, his gaze fixing on the fascia boards of the house.

'Mr Tiegler?'

The man turned back to face them. 'Look, I suppose I've nothing to hide, and let's face it – if I don't tell you now, it'll just look bad, won't it?'

'Tell us what?'

'I had a gig in Lockinge late on Tuesday afternoon. A private garden party raising money for charity. I play guitar as well as viola, you see. I finished at five o'clock and drove home.'

'Which way did you go?'

Tiegler lowered his gaze to his hands. 'I'd had a couple of drinks and didn't want to risk the main road, so I cut through the lane that goes past Denchworth.'

'You mean the one that leads to Charney Bassett?'

'Yeah.'

'What time?'

'About five thirty I suppose. I was trying to avoid the commuter traffic that was building up.'

'Is this your car?' said Jan.

A flush began at the base of Tiegler's neck, quickly spreading to his jowls. 'It's my wife's.'

'Where's your car?'

'In the garage, where I always park it. It's more secure if I have instruments in there. I don't like waking Ben up while I'm unloading it if I'm late home after a gig.'

'Show me,' Mark said, and took a step back as Tiegler pushed himself away from the hatchback.

'I'll need to open it from the inside.'

'We'll wait here.'

Pacing the concrete pavers while Tiegler disappeared back into the house, Mark hoped there wasn't an easy exit from the back garden and into the next road, or that the man wasn't desperate enough to run.

Then there was a clang and a scrape from behind the garage door before it lifted from the floor, flipping upwards to reveal Tiegler standing in front of a bright blue hatchback, a slightly older model than that on the driveway.

Jan emitted a surprised grunt when the man stood to one side.

There was a large dent in the front bumper.

Mark took a step forward. 'Mr Tiegler—'

'Hold it right there. Before you start accusing me of killing Sonya, I didn't and I certainly didn't run her over, either.' Tiegler jabbed a finger at the car. 'That was caused by a courier van pulling out in front of my wife while she was driving this three days ago. She's lucky she didn't get a whiplash.'

Mark dropped to a crouch and used his phone screen to illuminate the bumper and the corner of the front wing. Sure enough, white flecks of paint were embedded amongst the scratches, a sure sign of transference from the impact.

Straightening, he nodded to Tiegler. 'Fair enough. We'll need details of your insurance claim and the other driver to corroborate that. Going back to Sonya – did she have any other interests that were taking up her time, perhaps affecting her decision-making?'

The man leaned against the car and ran a hand over his smooth skull. 'Did Spencer tell you about Nolan Creasey?'

'No. He didn't mention him. Who is he?'

'Sonya's boyfriend. At least, I think he is. Was. Not a very nice bloke.'

'You met him?'

'Sort of. On a couple of occasions.'

'Got any idea where we might find him?'

'No. To be honest, I stayed clear of him. I think he was counselling her about something or other but they seemed closer than that to me.' Tiegler crossed his arms over his chest once more. 'I mean, I could be wrong about the whole boyfriend thing but he seemed very protective of her. Didn't like her mingling after the concert I saw her at. Kept pulling her away, introducing her to different people than the ones she seemed interested in chatting with, that sort of thing.'

'Thanks for your time, Mr Tiegler.' Mark pulled a business card from his pocket. 'If you think of anything else that might help us, my direct number's on there.'

The sound of a lawnmower starting up carried across to the pool car when he got in, Jan tossing her handbag next to his feet before settling behind the wheel.

'So,' he said, while she fastened her seatbelt, 'it seems Sonya Raynott was a viola prodigy before she turned to fraud.'

Jan stabbed her key into the ignition. 'I always thought it was drummers who died in mysterious circumstances.'

# CHAPTER TWENTY-FIVE

Caroline was waiting impatiently beside Mark's desk when he and Jan walked back into the incident room half an hour later.

She thrust a printed-out email at him before he could remove his jacket, and grinned.

'An optician in Wantage returned my call this afternoon confirming a patient of his matched the prescription we sent over,' she said before he'd finished reading. 'Her name's Marie Allenton.'

'It can't be,' said Jan. 'She's Sonya Raynott. We've just spoken to two blokes that knew her as a viola player. Spencer Rossbay was the one who recognised the tattoo from the social media post we put out.'

'Not according to this email,' Mark said, handing it to her. 'So, does our victim have an alias, or is this mistaken identity?'

'Spencer confirmed it was Sonya from the

photograph, Sarge. You heard him. He was adamant.'
Jan frowned. 'How long had she been going to this
optician?'

'On and off for three years. He said her last
appointment was in February for a routine check-up.
That's when he had to tweak her prescription because
there'd been a slight deterioration in her right eye.'
Caroline took back the email and looked over her
shoulder as Kennedy approached. 'They've got a
different name for her, guv.'

'Oh?' The DI listened while Mark updated him.
'Interesting. That goes a long way to explaining why
Alex just informed me that uniform found very little at
the address Rossbay gave for Sonya Raynott. Again, no
ID, and basic living arrangements. Not many clothes,
and certainly no musical instruments, let alone a viola.
We weren't able to trace a next of kin, either.'

'Did the optician give you an address for Marie?'
Mark said.

'Yes, I phoned him after his email came through.'
Caroline hurried back to her desk and returned holding
out a sticky note. 'She lives in a village just west of
Didcot, according to him.'

'Get another patrol over there now,' said Kennedy.
'And put those details into the system before you leave
tonight. If uniform can't find anyone to speak to at the
house then you'll need to apply for a search warrant for
us to use in the morning.'

Jan shook her head. 'What the hell was she up to?

It's a lot of subterfuge for someone conning people out of their valuables, isn't it?'

'Have you had a chance to find out anything about Nolan Creasey?' Kennedy asked.

'He's on a career networking site listed as running some sort of counselling service, which ties in with what Graham Tiegler told us,' said Mark. 'Neither Tiegler or Rossbay had any direct contact details for him, so in the circumstances we thought we'd drop in and speak to him in the morning. He's got an office here in Abingdon, just off East St Helen Street.'

'All right – tomorrow morning, Caroline, start phoning around local GP surgeries with both names. We need to track her parents before they find out about this by accident through the news or social media – the more witnesses we interview, the more the rumours are going to start circulating soon.'

'It'd be good to have a list of the dates she was at the optician's too,' said Mark. 'Just in case it ties in with any other burglaries in that area we haven't linked to her and her accomplice yet.'

'No problem,' said Caroline. 'I'll get some help with that from uniform so hopefully we'll have some answers by tomorrow afternoon.'

———

Mark cradled a mug of hot tea between his hands, a gentle breeze ruffling his hair while he sat cross-legged on the roof of the narrowboat and squinted at the night sky.

The light pollution out here wasn't too bad. The boat was moored far enough away from the bridge into town to avoid the harsh street lights, and the Abbey Meadows behind him were quiet at this time of night. The houses that bordered the gardens were far enough away that he could only hear remnant sounds from the streets beyond.

He wondered if the repairs to his old rental house had been completed, or whether new tenants had moved in.

He hadn't been back since the fire.

'I thought I'd better grab this to keep us warm.'

Turning, he saw Lucy throw a tartan blanket onto the roof before lifting up Hamish, and then she scrambled up to join him.

After arranging the blanket across their shoulders, she took the mug he held out to her with a smile.

'Thanks.'

'Cheers.' He clinked his drink against hers and blew across the surface before taking a tentative sip.

'I can see the International Space Station, look.' Lucy pointed to their eleven o'clock position and smiled. 'Rather them than me.'

'You don't fancy going into space?'

'Nope. I like terra firma, thank you. Why, would you?'

'I don't know. I like it from this angle, I have to admit.'

They sat in silence for a moment, and Mark watched while Hamish trotted to the far end of the boat and lay down, his ears pricked towards the bridge and the four other boats in the distance.

He emitted a growl under his breath at the sound of reeds slapping together on the opposite bank, and then a single sharp bark as a water vole plopped into the water.

'Shush, boy. Don't disturb the neighbours,' Mark said.

Lucy rested her head against his shoulder. 'Dare I ask how the case is going?'

'Frustrating. I can't tell you much, except that we found out this afternoon our victim has an alias.'

'Why would she do that?'

'I don't know yet.' He put his mug to one side, then wrapped his arm around her, drawing her closer and tucking in the blanket around them. 'I'm wondering if she did it to throw off anyone like us trying to catch her, or whether she was doing it to protect herself in another way. Most of the time she was going by one name – certainly publicly, anyway. The other name cropped up from an optician's appointment she had earlier this year. We were just lucky they were searching for a prescription rather than a name, otherwise we might not have ever made the connection.'

'Are you going to put out the new name to the news sites and social media in case someone can help?'

'Not yet. Not until we understand more about why she was using that name. After that, we'll have to dig around to see where else she was using it – and which one is her real identity.'

Lucy shifted under his arm, then peered up at him, her brow creased. 'I suppose there's always the chance she might have had more than two names as well, isn't there?'

Mark groaned, then drained his tea.

'Just what I needed to hear before I try to sleep.'

# CHAPTER TWENTY-SIX

The next morning, Mark turned away from the wrought-iron railings separating the street from the river to see Jan hurrying towards him, her heels clacking on the uneven stone pavers.

'Sorry I'm late. The twins decided they wanted to go to an outdoor activity centre this morning, and we couldn't find Luke's swim shorts.' She rolled her eyes. 'I found them in his drawer after he swore blind he'd left them in the tumble dryer last night.'

Mark grinned. 'No problem. Do you want to get your breath back?'

'No, I'm all right.' She huffed her hair from her eyes, her breathing returning to normal. 'Right, where's this counsellor's office?'

'Round the corner. Nolan Creasey has his office in one of those old houses backing onto the river that's been divided up into different businesses. Lucy's had some of her work in the little gallery next door a couple of times.'

They fell into step and passed St Helen's Church before turning right, the street narrowing as Georgian and older buildings cluttered the old Roman imprint.

A few more metres, and then Mark paused outside a courtyard entrance.

'This is the place.'

A wide wooden gate had been staked open leading into an asphalt driveway in need of patchwork repairs, a three-storey house in front of them and what appeared to be three converted stables off to the left.

'You'd never think they'd be able to squash this in between all the other houses,' said Jan. 'I'm always amazed by what I find hiding down here.'

'The stables are let out as temporary pop-up businesses, but Creasey's got his office in the main house according to his website.'

'Lead the way, Sarge.'

Mark walked through the front door then found the counsellor's details listed on a pin board with plastic letters setting out each business name at the base of a staircase that split the building in two.

Following the treads up to a second-floor landing, he saw a sign pointing to the left and followed the carpeted hallway to a frosted glass door at the back of the building.

'River view then,' he said under his breath.

'Very nice,' said Jan, then pushed open the door into an airy reception room.

Bright sunlight poked between vertical blinds at a wide window overlooking the river. A cheap-looking sofa had been placed underneath the sill with a metal and glass coffee table in front of it, a vase of flowers and a couple of health magazines arranged on its surface.

A solid oak door on their left stood ajar, and Mark could hear movement in the room beyond.

'Hello?' he called. 'Anyone here?'

A shuffling of paperwork and a grunt carried through from the other room, and then a man in his late thirties flung open the door, his shirt sleeves rolled up and surprise colouring his features.

'Sorry to disturb you,' said Mark, holding up his warrant card. 'We wanted to speak with Nolan Creasey.'

'That's me.' The man frowned. 'What's this about?'

'Sonya Raynott.'

Creasey took a step back. 'Sonya?'

'She's a client of yours, correct?'

'Yes, but what's that—'

'Shall we sit down?' Mark gestured to the sofa. 'We have a few questions.'

'Um... well, I'm expecting a client at nine-thirty.'

'This won't take long, I'm sure.'

The man's shoulders sagged. 'Best come through here, then.'

He shoved the door open wide, then stalked towards a desk in the centre of the inner office.

Mark followed Jan inside, admiring the floor-to-ceiling bookcases and the tasteful decor.

Two well-worn leather chairs had been placed in a corner beside a small wooden table and reading lamp, and the bay window had been fitted with a comfortable-looking window seat. Sunlight streamed through the open blinds, pooling onto a richly coloured carpet that deadened his footsteps.

'Quite a place you have here, Mr Creasey.'

'I try to make my clients feel at ease when they come to see me.'

'How long have you been here?' Mark pulled out one of the chairs facing Creasey's desk for Jan then took the one beside her, easing into the wooden frame.

'About three years. You said you wanted to talk to me about Sonya. Is something the matter?'

'I'm sorry to inform you that a woman matching Sonya's description was found dead at the side of a road north of Wantage last week. We've only just managed to identify her in the past twenty-four hours. Your name was passed to us by one of her acquaintances.'

'God, that's dreadful.' Creasey paled. 'What happened?'

'That's still part of our ongoing enquiry. When was the last time you saw her?'

'A couple of weeks ago.'

'Here?'

'Yes. She had an afternoon appointment on… hang on.' He swivelled his chair around to face his computer and moused across the screen. 'Thursday before last, three o'clock in the afternoon.'

'What exactly was your relationship with Sonya?' said Mark.

'There was no relationship. Sonya was a client, that's all.'

'What sort of services did she pay for?' Jan said. 'Counselling?'

'Not at all.' Creasey gave a benevolent smile, gesturing to the certificates lining the wall. 'Although I hold a degree in psychology, I offer clients a range of services to better equip them for their individual circumstances. Mindfulness, breathing techniques… I'm a qualified sports coach and nutritionist as well, so I hope to offer people a whole life package to benefit their day-to-day lives and wellbeing. It helps them both physically and mentally. I also offer assistance with different addictions – gambling, alcohol, that sort of thing.'

'Anyone else work with you?' said Mark, pausing to lift one of the heavy psychology tomes from the desk and weighing it in his hand.

'It's just me. If I'm very busy with referrals from local GP surgeries I use a telephone answering service and a virtual assistant for general email enquiries but both of those are remote working arrangements.' Creasey leaned back in his chair, the leather creaking under the movement. 'It's cheaper for a start, but allows me peace and quiet here in between seeing my clients. I don't like to be disturbed while I'm meditating on a particular problem or issue.'

'So what were you helping Sonya with?'

'That's confidential, and between me and my client, detective – you know that.'

'Your client is dead, Mr Creasey,' Mark snapped. 'Found dumped on the side of the road in the middle of nowhere with her head caved in. We're trying to find out who did that to her.'

'I know.' The other man held up his hands. 'I'm sorry. I tend to be very protective of my clients' privacy.'

Mark said nothing, and waited while Creasey tapped a few buttons on his keyboard before sighing under his breath.

'Here we are. I last spoke to Sonya almost two weeks ago, like I said. At the time she was suffering from anxiety-related issues, something for which I'd treated her before a year, or so ago. We did some breathing exercises, and I consulted her about lowering her alcohol intake and some other minor diet changes to help with her insomnia.'

'Did she seem scared about anything at the time?' Jan asked.

Creasey frowned. 'No, not that. Anxious, definitely. When I asked her what she thought the cause of that might be, she declined to say.'

'Doesn't that defeat the purpose of coming here?' said Mark.

'Getting someone to share their innermost fears takes time, detective,' Creasey scolded. 'And like some of the other creative types I've worked with over the years, it only takes a minor setback to knock their confidence. Sonya was no different.'

'Were you aware that she was involved in a series of burglaries around Wantage and Stanford in the Vale?'

'Sonya? Christ, no. Are you sure?'

'We've had her identity confirmed by more than one of the victims.'

'Jesus.' Creasey blinked. 'I had no idea.'

'Did she say why she stopped playing viola all of a sudden?'

'No. I never got to the bottom of that.'

'It's been inferred that she lost interest after meeting you.'

'By whom?' Creasey's jaw dropped. 'That's outrageous.'

'You're absolutely sure there was nothing more between you than professional interest?'

'Of course I'm sure. I have a business to run here. A reputation to protect—'

'And yet before Sonya cut short her music career, you were seen with her at a couple of her concerts.' Mark raised an eyebrow. 'Did that fall under your professional remit as well?'

Exasperated, Creasey pushed back his chair and

crossed to the bay window, his hands on his hips. When he finally spoke, his voice was low, dangerous.

'Detective, I take the wellbeing of my clients very seriously. I only went to two concerts at Sonya's invitation. I enjoy classical music, and she was quite insistent.' He turned to face them, his eyes boring into Mark's. 'I never took advantage of her sexually, and I resent you walking in here trying to undermine everything I've achieved.'

'Where were you between the hours of half six and half eleven last Tuesday?'

'I was here all day with appointments and then left at six. I met friends for dinner here in Abingdon. We went to a little Italian place off Ock Street to celebrate a birthday, and we stayed until eleven. After that, we went back to theirs for coffee because my first appointment on Wednesday wasn't until ten o'clock.' He pulled a mobile phone from his pocket. 'And you can have their phone numbers because I know you're going to ask anyway. Was there anything else?'

'That's all for now.' Mark dropped one of his business cards onto the desk as Jan snapped her notebook closed. 'Give me a call if you think of anything that might help us.'

Creasey remained standing beside the window. 'You can see yourselves out.'

# CHAPTER TWENTY-SEVEN

Mark dropped his notebook next to his computer keyboard, then walked across the incident room to Kennedy's office and rapped his knuckles against the open door.

'Got a minute, guv?'

The DI looked up from a collection of reports strewn across his desk, removed his reading glasses and rubbed his temples. 'Anything to get me away from these personnel forecasts. How'd you get on with Creasey?'

'He confirms he saw Sonya a couple of weeks ago for an appointment, and says he hadn't seen her since then. He did seem genuinely shocked that she was dead.' Mark pulled out one of the visitor chairs and sat, frowning at the paperwork Kennedy was scooping up. 'That's not our investigation, is it?'

'No – summer rosters. We can still expect a full contingent on this one for at least a few more days.'

'That doesn't make me feel better.'

Kennedy gave a grim smile and shoved the documentation into a manila folder before tossing it onto a pile in his in-tray. 'It is what it is. Was Creasey able to shed any light on Sonya's involvement in the burglaries?'

'No, and he seemed taken aback at that.' Mark wrinkled his nose. 'I don't think it came up in the counselling sessions he'd had with her. He came across as a bit too smooth for my liking though, and I'm sure he had feelings for her – he tried his best to deny it, but Jan picked up on the way he spoke about her too, and there's the business of him going along to her concerts. That's stretching the counsellor-patient relationship a bit far in my view.'

'Alibis?'

'They check out for the Tuesday evening.'

Kennedy drummed his fingers on the desk. 'Unless he dumped her on the roadside before going out to dinner.'

Mark exhaled. 'If he had, then surely Graham Tiegler would've spotted her on his way home from that garden party he finished playing late Tuesday evening.'

'Not if he was three sheets to the wind rather than the two drinks he says he had.'

The DI looked up at another knock against the glass panelling of the door, and Mark twisted in his seat to see Alex hovering at the threshold.

'Which one of us were you after?' Kennedy asked.

'Both of you, actually.' Alex remained where he was until the DI pointed to the seat next to Mark, then scurried over and cleared his throat. 'It might be nothing, but...'

'Spit it out,' Mark said, and smiled. 'Knowing you, it's not nothing.'

'I was reading through the email Caroline circulated with the details from the optician's place in Wantage, and – I don't know – I guess I just wanted to know more, so I phoned up and asked them if any of our burglary victims were customers of his as well.'

Kennedy leaned forward, resting his elbows on the desk. 'Why?'

'I was struggling to find a connection between Sonya – Maria, whatever her name is – and all the burglary victims. We still don't know how she selected them, so I thought I'd go back to one of our earlier theories that she must've overheard them giving their address out to someone somewhere.' Alex jerked his thumb towards Mark. 'We thought maybe GP surgeries, pharmacies, places like that where you're often asked to confirm your address.'

'Okay. Go on.'

'So I figured opticians would fall under that theory as well. I just got a call back from the one who gave us Sonya's alias to say he does recognise one of the names – Sally Fernsby.'

Kennedy straightened. 'Good work. How does it tie in with the burglary side of things?'

'I'm not sure yet. When Sonya coerced her way into Sally's house she was posing as a concerned social worker regarding her five-year-old daughter's health – her accomplice got upstairs and stole jewellery and some cash Sally kept for emergencies. She was distraught.'

'I know she's dead, but that's a disgusting thing to do,' said Kennedy.

'It's how they targeted a few of the single parents on our list.' Mark shook his head. 'Sally was one of too many.'

'Where does Sally live?'

'On the outskirts of Grove, down one of the older lanes,' said Mark. 'She was burgled back in January. Absolutely terrified by the experience – by the time the patrol reached her, she already had a locksmith there replacing all the front and back door locks and adding more to the downstairs windows.'

'Poor woman.' Kennedy's gaze moved to the clock on the wall above his filing cabinets. 'Get yourself over there in the morning, Mark, and have another word with her. Find out how long she'd been going to that optician's, and whether she'd seen Sonya anywhere else before that. Somewhere along the line, we're going to find her accomplice.'

'Will do, guv.' Mark pushed back his chair and rolled up his sleeves. 'And when I do, I'm going to make sure he pays.'

# CHAPTER TWENTY-EIGHT

The next morning, Jan walked up a stone path towards a neat end of terrace cottage.

She swerved past an overturned plastic play table then a box-shaped sandpit that had been dug into the corner of the lawn, a faint smell of cat piss wafting towards her.

Wrinkling her nose, she peered up at the pebble-dashed fascia, eyed the curtain twitch at the uppermost window, then turned to Turpin.

'When were you last here?'

'Back in February. A few weeks after the burglary when Alex and I started linking the cases together.' He reached out and pressed the bell to the right of the front door and lowered his voice. 'Sally lost her two-year-old daughter just before Christmas. Leukaemia. Her husband walked out three months before that – he couldn't take the impending loss by the sound of it, and left her to face it alone, which is why she's reverted to her maiden name. She was burgled – by Sonya – in January. She, or her accomplice anyway, stole a watch and two gold necklaces, as well as a diamond ring that belonged to Sally's grandmother.'

'Jesus, the poor woman.' Jan exhaled, her chest still tight as the door opened.

A woman in her late twenties with her hair scrunched up in a messy ponytail gave Turpin a wan stare.

'Caught them yet?' she said.

'There's been some progress,' Turpin replied.

The woman emitted a scornful snort in response.

'Could we come in, please, Ms Fernsby? My colleague, DC Jan West, and I have some questions we'd like to ask.'

Sally pushed open the door and turned away, not waiting to see if they followed. 'I've just dropped off Charlotte at school, so I'm about to go and catch up with friends at the market.'

'This won't take long.' Turpin waved Jan ahead of him, shutting the door behind her then following Sally into a tiny kitchen at the back of the cottage.

Jan could smell remnants of porridge and something sweeter in the stuffy room, the aroma mingling with coffee as the other woman picked up a mug with a child's wobbly drawing printed on the side and took it over to a battered pine fold-out table in the corner.

Pulling out her notebook, Jan wandered over and

pulled out a seat beside her while Turpin leaned against the worktop. 'Sally – can I call you Sally? – we haven't met before but I'm helping Detective Turpin with his investigation.'

'I hope you're having better luck,' the woman mumbled, then took a sip.

'Do you wear glasses?'

The mug was set down on the table with a sharp smack. 'What?'

'Tell me about the optician's in Wantage. How long have you been registered there?'

'Only recently. I was getting headaches occasionally so I thought I'd better have my eyes tested.'

'When was that?'

'Um, March I think.'

Jan frowned. 'Not earlier in the year?'

'No. Why?'

Turpin stepped forward. 'One of the theories we're following up is that the people who targeted you in January might've overheard you give out your address somewhere, such as a pharmacy, or a GP surgery perhaps. Yesterday, we got a positive identification for a woman found dead by the side of the road not too far from here. It's the same woman who was involved in a spate of burglaries similar to yours...'

'I heard about a woman's body being found.' Sally shivered. 'But I don't—'

'We received one of the positive identifications from her optician here in Wantage. The same optician you registered with.' Mark's voice softened. 'Except that doesn't fit in with our theory about how she got your address in the first place to target you in January, because you've just told us you registered with that optician in March. After you were burgled.'

Jan waited, watching while the woman's jaw worked, her eyes downcast as she tapped her fingernails against the side of the china mug.

'How did you know her?' she said gently.

'What's happened to her?' Sally looked from her to Turpin.

'That's what we're trying to find out,' said Jan.

'Jesus.' Sally paled. 'I… I don't know her. Didn't know her, I mean. I… I just followed her.'

'When?'

'In March. Like I said, I try to catch up with a couple of friends at the market – it gets me out of the house every week, otherwise I'm just sitting around here.' She gave a sad smile. 'Apparently, that's not good for me even though I work most of the time.'

'What do you do?'

'I'm an executive assistant for a real estate company, just online these days. You know, virtually.'

'So, going back to the day you followed her.'

'What's her name?'

Jan's gaze flicked to Turpin's before answering, and he gave a slight nod. 'We've got two names for her. Sonya Raynott and Marie Allenton.'

'Oh.' Sally raised the mug to her lips, her hand

shaking. After taking another sip, she slumped in her chair. 'I recognised her. I'd just said goodbye to Michelle, one of my friends, next to the King Alfred statue and was about to cross the road when I saw her walking along the pavement on the other side. A bus was pulling in at the stop, and she looked up at the number on the windscreen. That's when I saw her face. She must've been wearing a wig or something though, because her hair looked too dark for her features. She turned away, and I… I don't know, I just wanted to see what she did. She was in a hurry, as if she was late for something so like I said, I followed her.'

'Where did she go?'

'She left the marketplace, then went into the optician's place round the corner.' Sally pushed the empty coffee mug away, her eyes downcast. 'It was just so fucking normal. After everything she did, after she took…'

She broke off, tears cascading over her cheeks.

Jan waited while the woman composed herself.

Sally sniffed, wiping at her tears with the sleeve of her sweater, then reached across and tore a sheet from a roll of kitchen towel. After blowing her nose, she forced a bitter smile.

'God knows what I was thinking, but I gave it a couple of minutes then crept past and looked through the window. She was sitting in one of the chairs, waiting to see the optician I guess.'

'What did you do?'

'I kept going, then after another five minutes I circled back and went inside.' Sally pushed back her chair and lobbed the tissue in the kitchen bin. 'She wasn't there anymore but I wanted to see if she recognised me. I wanted... I don't know what I wanted. Of course, by then the two women working behind the reception counter were all over me, asking how they could help, and I ended up paying for an eye test I didn't really need. That's how you linked me to her, isn't it?'

Jan nodded. 'Sally, we have to ask this. Where were you between the hours of half past six and ten-thirty last Tuesday night?'

The woman's jaw dropped. 'Why? Do you think I killed her?'

'Can you tell us where you were?' Turpin said.

'I was here. With Charlotte. My mum came over and stayed the night – Dad was off on a fishing trip with a couple of his mates so we watched a film after Charlotte went to bed.'

'We'll need her number,' said Jan.

'For goodness sakes.' Sally crossed the kitchen to the table and snatched up a mobile phone. 'Don't you have any sympathy for me as a victim?'

'We do,' said Turpin calmly. 'And I do want to see someone brought to justice for what happened to you but until we find out what happened to her, and who killed her, we can't find her accomplice. The man who stole your jewellery and everything else while she kept you distracted.'

Sally's shoulders dropped. 'I know. It's just…'

'You've been through a horrible experience after everything that's already happened to you,' said Jan, 'and you've every right to be angry.'

She jotted down the phone number Sally recited.

'What happened after you finished your eye test?' said Turpin.

'I thought I'd lost my chance,' Sally replied, 'and I was angry with myself. I mean, it was a pretty dumb thing to do, right? Except she didn't recognise me at all. She was standing at the till, paying for a new pair of contact lenses, and walked out without a backward glance.'

'What did you do?'

'I followed her. I paid for my eye test as quickly as I could, rushed out the door and saw her walking back through the marketplace. When I got there, I saw her heading towards an alleyway at the far end. I stopped then.' She twisted her fingers together. 'I started thinking I was paranoid, that it couldn't be her. Then on the other hand, I was thinking that I never forget a face. I'm rubbish at names, but not faces. She might've changed her hair colour – she was blonde when she turned up here – but I guess I got worried. That alley's a dead end. What if she knew I'd been following her? What if she was waiting for me? I couldn't let anything happen to me. I couldn't let Charlotte grow up without… without…'

She gulped back fresh tears.

'Why didn't you tell us this before?' said Mark. 'Or for that matter, report it to the officer assigned to your burglary case?'

'Because I thought you'd be angry with me for taking a risk. Because I didn't want her, or whoever she was working with, to come back here.' Sally rubbed at her arms and glanced over her shoulder out the kitchen window. 'I don't sleep very well at night as it is these days. Not now. All I can think of is protecting Charlotte. I'm all she's got.'

Five minutes later, after thanking Sally Fernsby for her time, Jan walked to the far end of the path and along the road to where the pool car was parked, and turned to Turpin as he caught up.

He took one look at her face and frowned. 'What's up?'

'That alley that she mentioned. Just off the marketplace.'

'What about it?'

'It's where Marcus Targethen has his shop.'

# CHAPTER TWENTY-NINE

Mark strode across the cobblestones, his jacket flapping in the breeze while Jan tried to keep up.

She emitted a muffled curse under her breath as her heel caught in the corner of a drain, straightened and then grabbed his arm.

'Sarge, wait.'

He paused, glaring at her. 'What?'

'Maybe calm down before we go bursting in there. Just in case he's not on his own.'

Taking a deep breath, he allowed her to lead him over to one side of the alleyway beside a boarded-up shop, then cast his gaze farther along to where Marcus Targethen's junk shop stood.

The door had been propped open by a set of old fireplace tools with a wicked-looking brass poker dangling from a hook beside a brush and tongs. A motley collection of chairs and a small wooden coffee table were arranged below the window, dragged out from the shop and lined up alongside crates of bric-à-brac, their contents tumbling out over the cobbles.

'He lied to us,' Mark hissed.

'Of course he did,' said Jan cheerfully. 'Everybody does.'

He snorted a laugh. 'Thanks for the reminder.'

'You're welcome. Calmed down?'

'Let's do this.'

He led the way along the remainder of the alleyway, the sound of Targethen's radio carrying out through the door as they entered and dust motes tumbling in the late morning sunlight.

Blinking, his eyes adjusting to the gloom of the interior, Mark saw the pawnbroker behind the cluttered counter.

The man had his chin in his hand, his attention fixed on a velvet-lined tray of marbles he was sorting into different colours and sizes.

The place smelled even worse than it had on Saturday, and Mark wrinkled his nose at the stench of a blocked drain seeping through the building. Making his way past a precariously stacked collection of books, he kept his hands in his pockets and hoped his tetanus shot was up to date.

Targethen pushed the velvet-lined tray to one side, the contents wobbling within their individual holes, and then swept his hand across the dust on the glass counter before leaning his forearms on it.

'Detectives,' he said, leering in Jan's direction. 'What brings you back here?'

'Tell me about Sonya Raynott,' Mark said, relishing the shock that flittered across the man's eyes.

'I don't—'

Mark slammed his hand on the counter.

The tray of marbles exploded into the air and scattered across the tiled floor.

'I'm not in the mood for bullshit, Mr Targethen,' he said, 'so don't try my patience.'

'I've never heard of her. I told you that on Saturday.'

'I don't believe you.' Mark leaned closer and tried not to inhale the man's body odour. 'I saw your reaction to her photograph. You *do* know her.'

'All right.' Targethen's jaw worked, his lips trembling. 'But I ain't seen her for a while.'

'When was she last here?'

'I don't know. January, February maybe.'

'Try again,' Mark said. 'Because we've got a witness who can place her here in March.'

'Wait here.'

He watched while Targethen disappeared behind a faded brocade curtain into an inner room behind the counter, the sound of boxes being shuffled around and a grunt before the pawnbroker returned.

'She wanted me to sell this.'

He lifted a black violin case onto the counter and opened it, revealing a sleek spruce and maple viola, the ebony fingerboard worn but polished and gleaming under the poor light.

Mark frowned. 'Why?'

Targethen shrugged. 'Like most people who come in here – she said she needed the money.'

'Was this in March?'

'Yeah.'

'After she left the quartet,' Mark murmured. 'So she wasn't planning on going back.'

'She said she had a better one at home so she didn't need this – she told me she'd been using it as a back-up, that's all.' Targethen turned the instrument in his hands. 'I'm waiting for the right buyer to come along. It's worth a bit, this.'

'Did she sell you anything else at the same time?' Mark asked. 'Perhaps some jewellery, or a laptop computer, something like that?'

'Are you selling stolen property, Mr Targethen?' said Jan. She had wandered off to the side, feigning interest in a display of necklaces and bracelets beside the counter. 'Is all of this legit?'

'Look, I told you – I don't deal in stolen goods.' Targethen took a step back. 'I don't fence anything here.'

'Not here, but what about at your lock-up? The one you use for your house clearing business?' Mark said. 'What are you storing there?'

'You can't come in here, accusing me of things like that. You'll ruin my business.'

'We can get a search warrant,' Mark snapped.

'Fine.' Targethen straightened and crossed his arms. 'Then get me a solicitor before you ask me anything else.'

# CHAPTER THIRTY

Four hours later, the sun already lost behind a line of beech trees and a stiff wind buffeting him, Mark waited while a locksmith grappled with the aluminium door to Targethen's storage unit.

The unit was one of a dozen rented out behind a crumbling farmyard two miles west of Wantage, and one easily located via Targethen's house clearance website. From time to time, he held auctions at the lot, with the farmer receiving a commission on sales.

The headlights from the pool car illuminated the concrete hardstanding outside the row of twelve units while a pair of uniformed constables stood next to Targethen's, one aiming a torch beam at the lock.

'Is Kennedy all right about this?' said Jan, climbing out of the car and buttoning up her thick woollen coat.

'He's fine,' Mark said over his shoulder. 'The

warrant was signed off an hour ago, and we've used this chap before. He only lives down the road.'

He nodded towards the locksmith, who turned away from the garage and handed Alice Fields a broken lock.

'Looks like we're in, Sarge,' she called over.

Hurrying over, he paused at the gaping opening.

Jan nudged his arm. 'Here.'

'Thanks.' He pulled on the disposable gloves she held out and peered into the unit, eyeing the boxes and furniture piled four deep beyond Alice's torchlight. 'I kind of wish I had one of Jasper's full protective body suits and a mask.'

Jan moved off to the side and ran her hand down the exposed cinder blocks. 'Great. No light switch.'

'Have you any spare torches?'

'There's one more in the car.' Nathan Willis walked over, handing one to Mark as the locksmith's van pulled away. 'What are we looking for, Sarge?'

'Jewellery.' Mark reached into his jacket pocket and pulled out a photocopied list. 'This is what was taken from the most recent burglaries, so since Targethen would probably have wanted anything he'd fenced moved on as soon as possible, we'll work on the basis anything stolen prior to March will have been sold by now. If you do find something that isn't on this list, put it to one side just in case. We'll photograph it and compare it to the master list back at the station.'

Alice blew out her cheeks. 'Right, well I'm the

smallest so why don't I climb over to the back and start from there?'

'Sounds good. Nathan, you squeeze down that right-hand side, and Jan and I'll take the left half between us with this spare torch.'

They split up, the sound of Alice scrambling over chairs and boxes filling the single garage-sized space for a moment before Mark turned his attention to the first box Jan aimed the torch at.

Pulling out his keys, he sliced through the packing tape and reared back as a child's blue eyes peered out at him.

'Jesus.'

Jan managed a laugh. 'It's a doll, Sarge.'

'I hate anything like that.' He pulled it out and grimaced. 'Who the hell buys something like this for a kid?'

'It's china. I think it's antique.'

Placing the doll on top of another box beside him, he rummaged deeper into the contents. 'No, nothing here. These are all old toys, things like that. Okay, on to the next one.'

Ten minutes later, Alice's torch beam flashed against the back wall, and he heard an excited cry.

'I've got something,' she said, then dived headlong into an open cardboard box that was almost as tall as her and emerged with a pair of gold hoop earrings. 'Bugger. Not on the list.'

'Bring them anyway, just in case. As well as anything else you find in there.'

Mark selected another box, ripping open the packing tape with his keys.

Jan peered inside. 'This'd almost be like Christmas if it wasn't for…'

'Yeah, I know.'

'What if we don't find something on the list? What if he's telling the truth?'

'He's hiding something. He's got to be. Okay, Sonya traded in the viola but she already knew he'd give her a fair price. That suggests to me she knew him before that, and that he respected her enough not to try and short-change her.'

Lifting away crunched up old newspapers, Jan reached deeper and withdrew a set of pewter candlesticks, then a copper kettle. 'This isn't looking hopeful.'

'Try the next one.'

He flashed the torch along the wall, counting the boxes.

There were at least another twenty of varying sizes, and each time they opened one their chances diminished.

'There has to be something here,' he muttered.

Jan pushed past a table stacked upside down on an oak dresser, reaching out to steady an antique lamp as it wobbled precariously, then stabbed her keys through the tape sealing the next box.

'About time he had another clear-out or one of those auctions,' she grumbled. 'When was the last time he was here?'

'According to the bloke who owns the place, about three weeks ago.' Mark took the torch from her while she started rummaging through the contents. 'Maybe he's waiting for the weather to warm up so he gets more people here.'

'Sarge?'

Mark turned to see Nathan holding up a diamond choker against his neck, the stones sparkling in the constable's torchlight. 'It doesn't suit you.'

'Never mind that.' Nathan grinned. 'It's on your list.'

# CHAPTER THIRTY-ONE

When Mark and Jan walked into the interview room the next morning, Marcus Targethen was slumped in a grey plastic chair next to the duty solicitor appointed to represent him.

He ran a calloused hand over greasy hair that was now pulled back into a small ponytail at the base of his skull, accentuating the flares of white at his temples. Worry lines creased his brow and eyelids while Jan set up the recording equipment, then his gaze dropped to the transparent evidence bags that Mark placed on the table between them.

He lowered his eyes to his hands while Mark recited the formal caution.

'My card,' said the duty solicitor while introductions were made for the recording.

'Thank you, Mr Williams. Hopefully we can keep this brief if your client helps us.' Mark's attention swung back to the man beside the solicitor. 'Mr Targethen, when we spoke to you earlier today, you reiterated your original statement from Saturday that you don't deal in stolen goods. Would you care to amend what you told us now that you're under caution?'

Targethen remained silent.

'Okay, well let's see what we found in your storage unit a few hours ago. Perhaps that'll jog your memory.'

Mark pulled on disposable gloves and gently removed the diamond choker Nathan had discovered, and then a pair of matching earrings.

These were followed by a jade brooch, two watches estimated to be worth over four thousand pounds each, and more than a dozen sets of gold earrings, some inlaid with precious stones.

'There's more, of course.' Mark glared across the table. 'But you already know about that. What I find interesting is that every single one of the items here matches jewellery reported stolen during a spate of burglaries that took place between November and late March. Burglaries we suspect were carried out by Sonya Raynott.'

'How did they come to be in your possession, Marcus?' said Jan. 'And don't tell us you bought them – not unless you can provide receipts.'

Targethen swallowed, then turned to his solicitor and beckoned him closer.

The two men exchanged whispers, and Mark replaced the jewellery in the bags before opening a manila folder beside Jan and removing a formal document.

'This is a search warrant that was executed half an hour ago,' he said. 'It gives us power to search your shop premises as well.'

Targethen's head snapped round, his face grey. 'You can't do that.'

'We can, and we are.' Mark checked his watch. 'In fact, our team should be turning up there in the next ten minutes, I reckon.'

'No!' Targethen shoved back his chair. 'You don't understand.'

The duty solicitor put a restraining hand on the man's arm and pulled him back to his seat. 'My client would like to advise that although he's in possession of these goods, he categorically denies killing Sonya Raynott.'

'Finally. We're getting somewhere.' Mark shut the folder and clasped his hands. 'Right, the stolen goods – tell us about all this. When did Sonya first start bringing this stuff to you?'

'Early December,' Targethen mumbled.

'You'll have to speak up for the recording,' said Jan.

'Last December.'

'Why haven't you sold any of it on yet?' Mark asked. 'Surely even you knew it was a risk hanging on to it.'

'I couldn't sell it in the shop, could I?' said

Targethen. 'She'd nicked it all locally. I was waiting until I had a chance to make a trip down south somewhere. Sell it on to someone else or do a market or something.'

'How did she know you'd buy it off her?' Mark asked. 'Been fencing stolen goods for a while have you?'

Targethen glowered at him. 'I hadn't for a long time. Figured it was too risky.'

'Why do it for Sonya, then?'

'She was desperate. Wouldn't take no for an answer. Said she knew some people who'd be interested in my history if I didn't help her. I thought she was going to grass me up anonymously, so she didn't leave me any choice.'

'How did she know to ask you?'

'I don't know. Someone must've told her, I s'pose. Maybe she bumped into someone I used to deal with.' Targethen shrugged. 'Thought they were all inside. Perhaps someone got let out and she knew them. People tend to stick with who they know, I guess.'

'So, she started using you to fence goods in December. When did you next see her?'

'Early in the new year.' Targethen frowned. 'She was nervous – she couldn't wait to get out of the shop, and she was wearing a blonde wig too. Gave me a fright when she first walked in and started talking about needing a price for some special pieces. Thought she was you lot trying to set me up. She reckoned that was funny, but I saw her hands shaking when I handed over the cash.'

'Why was she nervous?'

Targethen shook his head, lowering his gaze to the table.

'When was her next visit?'

'The middle of February, and then the end of March. When she sold me the viola.'

'And was she bringing in the same sort of stolen items like this every time?'

'No. Most of the time it was just bits and pieces. It depended on how... how successful she'd been.'

'Was she always on her own?'

A silence followed his words.

Mark leaned forward. 'Targethen? Look at me. We know Sonya had an accomplice. A man. Was that you?'

'No, it wasn't.' The man's chin rose, and he gave a ragged sigh. 'I don't go in for robbery.'

'You'd rather leave other people to do your dirty work, is that it?'

'No – you have to believe me. Until she turned up on my doorstep, I hadn't touched anything dodgy for years.'

'Who was he, the man working with Sonya?' Mark cocked his head to one side. 'You know him, don't you?'

'He came into the shop with her once, that's all.'

'Who is he, Targethen?'

'He'll bloody kill me if I tell you lot.'

'I'm sure he won't be very happy when he finds out we're searching your shop for incriminating evidence into Sonya's death, either,' said Jan.

'Christ.' Targethen smeared a shaking hand across his mouth.

'Where were you between six-thirty and ten-thirty last Tuesday night?' Mark asked.

'I told you – watching footy in the pub. I told you that last time you asked.'

'So who killed Sonya? Give us his name, Targethen.'

'I can't.'

'Why do you think she was killed?'

The pawnbroker shrugged. 'If I had to guess, it was because she wasn't handing over everything I paid her for this lot.'

'His name, Targethen.'

'Shit, he'll kill me.'

'We'll find out anyway. It's only a matter of time.'

Targethen looked at his solicitor, who gave a slight nod, then sighed and turned back to Mark.

'Nolan. Nolan Creasey.'

# CHAPTER THIRTY-TWO

Mark gritted his teeth as Jan accelerated between parked cars along East St Helen Street before turning into the driveway of the converted Georgian house.

Two patrol cars followed, one parking diagonally across from the stables housing temporary craft workshops, the other blocking any escape through the open gates.

Doors slammed, shoes and heavy boots stomped across the asphalt driveway, and then Mark shoved open the front door into the shared reception area.

'Upstairs, second floor and round to the left, Grant.' Mark stepped aside to let the uniformed constable and his colleague lead the way, then turned to see Jan staring at the wall.

'Sarge?' she said, and pointed at the cork board displaying company names. 'He's not on here anymore.'

His stomach clenched, and then he gripped the

wooden banister and took off after the two constables, his heart racing with every step.

By the time he reached the second-floor landing, John Newton was waiting for him, his face stony.

'The place has been cleared out, Sarge,' he said, stepping aside to let Mark pass. 'There's only some furniture left.'

'Christ.'

He raced across the landing, through the open frosted glass door and into what had been Creasey's reception room.

All that remained were the two sofas.

A waste bin in the corner contained the flowers and magazines that had been on the coffee table and the blinds had been raised, exposing worn and chipped window sills that were covered with dead flies.

Grant emerged from Creasey's office, holding open the door for him. 'I've searched the filing cabinets in here, but they're all empty, Sarge. So are the desk drawers.'

Mark walked into the room, his throat dry.

All the bookshelves were empty, the chairs were gone, and all that remained of Creasey's business were dusty outlines of his computer and keyboard on the desk's surface.

'What the hell's going on?' he murmured.

'Bloody hell. He's done a midnight flit.' Jan stood on the threshold, her eyes wide. 'We only spoke to him two days ago.'

Mark spun on his heel. 'Grant, John – make a start interviewing the other business owners in the building, starting with the ground floor. Get the other patrol to interview the ones in the old stable block.'

He pulled out his phone and hit speed dial. 'Alex? We've lost Nolan Creasey – he's disappeared. Can you find out the landlord's name for this place and ask him for a copy of the lease?'

When he ended the call, Jan was already pulling out her notebook.

'There are two more businesses on the top floor,' she said. 'Shall we speak to them while we're waiting to hear back from him?'

'What are they?'

'One's an IT consultancy, the other's an investment firm.'

'Lead the way.'

The stairs narrowed between the second and third floors, echoing the original layout of the Georgian house and the fact that the top floor would have been inhabited by whatever servants the original homeowners employed.

Mark had to duck his head under the sloping ceiling when they reached the landing. He followed Jan across it to a smart aluminium plaque denoting the investment firm's office.

She rapped her knuckles against a glass panel in the door then pushed it open.

A man in his fifties using a landline phone turned

away from the window as they entered, the cord wrapped around his finger while he spoke.

He unravelled it, pointed to a cheap-looking sofa off to one side, and turned his attention back to the caller.

'James, I'm going to have to wrap it up. Unexpected visitors. Yes, yes. Will do. Give my regards to Trudy. Ciao.' He replaced the phone in its cradle with a delicate sweep of his arm, then looked at Mark. 'How may I help you?'

'Detective Sergeant Turpin, and my colleague DC Jan West. Are you the owner of this business?'

'Yes. Sebastian Mapleton. Is something the matter?'

'Nolan Creasey. Do you know where he is?'

'Nolan? No – haven't seen him for a while actually. I tend to use this place as a satellite office, for meeting potential clients and that sort of thing. Most of the time I work from home.'

'Were you here on Tuesday or yesterday?'

'No – Thursdays tend to be when I come in. I set up all my meetings from nine o'clock.' He looked pointedly at his watch. 'Speaking of which...'

'Who owns the building?'

'This place? It's a small investment company based out of Enstone – can't recall the address off the top of my head.'

'Phone number?'

'At home, I'm afraid. I rarely have to call them so I don't have it in my phone. They're very easy to deal with, given the circumstances.'

'Circumstances?'

'Yes – they're selling the place for redevelopment. Apparently they reckon they can squash six two-bedroom flats into here.' Mapleton snorted. 'Hate to think who'd end up here though. A bit boxy, isn't it?'

'Are you saying you're only on a short-term lease?'

'Oh yes, they don't offer anything over six months and it's got a clause to say either party can break it without penalty – it means they can kick us out the minute the sale goes through and the developers can make a start, you see.'

'When is your lease up?'

'In about eight weeks. I'll see what happens then.' He gave a slight shrug. 'Like I said, it's handy for formal meetings and doesn't cost too much so I might extend it. Saves having to find somewhere else.'

'Thanks for your time, Mr Mapleton.' Mark handed over a card, taking one of his in return. 'We'll be in touch if we have further questions.'

'Shit,' said Jan as they reached the landing once more. 'No wonder Creasey was able to get out quick.'

'What about that IT company?'

Jan shot him a grim smile as they approached the door opposite, then pushed it open with her forefinger.

It swung inwards, revealing a dusty empty space.

'Long gone, by the look of it.'

'Fuck.' Mark ran a hand over his head. 'Okay. Back to the incident room. We might as well give Kennedy the bad news.'

# CHAPTER THIRTY-THREE

'What the actual…?'

Mark held up his hand in response to Kennedy's spluttered outburst when he walked into the incident room, and steered the DI towards the whiteboard.

'How's Alex getting on with finding the address, guv?' he said. 'Anything?'

'Not yet.' Kennedy waited until Jan caught up with them before jabbing his thumb towards the photograph of Sonya. 'What's your thinking with these two then? Was Creasey her counsellor first, then tried to get in on the house burglaries, or…'

'Or maybe they already knew each other before she went to him for counselling, and that was just a front,' said Mark. 'I'm not sure yet.'

'Perhaps he found out something about her during those counselling sessions and used it against her,' Jan said. 'Blackmail, to keep her under his control.'

'Has anyone spoken to Marcus Targethen again?' Mark asked.

'I had a quiet word with him twenty minutes ago,' said Kennedy. 'He insists he didn't know where Creasey's office was, let alone where he lives.'

'Do you think he's telling the truth?'

'Either that or scared shitless, yes.'

'What about CCTV, guv?' said Jan. 'Any sign of him leaving the office on that? There are cameras all around the exit points from East St Helen Street.'

'We've requested it, but apparently there's a backlog – staff shortages,' Kennedy growled. 'I've escalated the request to Melrose. Hopefully he can find some extra bums on seats for us – and fast.'

'We ought to consider an all-ports flag as well,' said Mark. 'He's already run once – we have no idea where he is, or how far away he could go.'

'Leave that with me,' said Caroline, joining them. 'I'll also alert neighbouring forces.'

'Thanks.' Kennedy turned back to the whiteboard. 'Okay, so what does this look like? These two have a falling out about what? Who to burgle next? What to do with the takings? What?'

'Maybe she wanted to stop,' said Jan. 'And maybe that wasn't something Creasey was prepared to do.'

'Targethen said she blackmailed him into buying the stuff she took into his place to sell. Maybe she tried a similar stunt with Creasey and it backfired,' Caroline added.

'Good point,' said Mark. 'Yes, she's a victim but she wasn't necessarily a nice person. She may well have pushed her luck with Creasey.'

'I've got it!'

Mark glanced over his shoulder to see Alex dodging past two admin assistants to reach him.

'I've got the address,' he said, handing a sticky note over to Kennedy. 'It's a smallholding on the outskirts of Lockinge.'

'What did the landlord have to say about Creasey?' the DI asked.

'Always paid on time, on a two week basis – that was part of their arrangement due to the imminent redevelopment,' said Alex. 'Creasey phoned him Tuesday afternoon to say he was closing down his business immediately and would be leaving before the end of the week. There was another week to go on that particular payment, so the landlord didn't mind – he got to keep the money anyway.'

Mark looked at the map that was pinned to the cork board off to one side. 'Where is it on this?'

'Here.' Alex reached out and tapped a solitary narrow lane that snaked away from Lockinge. 'That's the address on the lease, which was signed a year ago.'

'Okay, I want search engine satellite images for that place on my desk in ten minutes,' said Kennedy, handing the note back to Alex. 'Before anyone goes racing over there, I want to know the layout of the area. Jan, Mark – once we understand what we're dealing with, you can head over there with a couple of patrols to back you up. Caroline, check out Creasey's social media accounts and see if there's anything to suggest he might turn violent.'

'What about road blocks in the meantime?' said Mark. 'Just in case he tries to make a run for it before we're ready to go over there and arrest him?'

Kennedy wagged his finger. 'Good point. I'll arrange with Control to send a patrol out at the end of that lane with a diversion. If anyone matching Creasey's description tries to drive through, they can delay him.'

'We'll need a search warrant as well, guv,' said Jan. 'I'll make a start drafting it if you don't mind...'

'I'll get it signed off, don't worry.' The DI glared at each of them. 'Well? Why are you all still standing here? Get a move on – we've got a killer to arrest.'

# CHAPTER THIRTY-FOUR

Jan gripped the signed search warrant in one hand and the strap above the passenger door in the other, her heart racing while Turpin powered the car through Wantage and out the other side.

Behind them, two patrol cars followed, their blue lights flashing but the sirens silent.

'No sense in telling him we're on our way,' Turpin had said at the briefing thirty minutes ago.

Urban sprawl turned to a countryside exploding with colour, blossom-laden trees blurring past Jan's window as he accelerated, his jaw tight.

He only slowed when the temporary diversion appeared at the fringes of Lockinge, then lowered his window before drawing to a standstill beside the two uniformed constables who manned it.

'Any sign of him?'

'Nothing, Sarge. We've only had a couple of

vehicles past here since we arrived – a tractor belonging to the farm up the road there, and a motorcyclist. She was on her way to work at the supermarket in Wantage, and her address checked out okay.'

'All right. Stay here for now, just in case he tries something when we get to the smallholding.'

'Will do.'

Jan swallowed, her throat tight with anticipation.

Like Turpin, she wanted to arrest Sonya's killer and she also wanted some answers for their victims – and perhaps the chance to return more of the stolen jewellery to its rightful owners.

There was still a pile of valuables that wasn't on Turpin's list being worked through by uniform at the station in the hope that it could be traced.

Turpin turned left into the narrow lane leading to Creasey's address, the silence in the car only broken by the sound of small stones spitting under the wheel arches and the occasional groan from the suspension when it met a deep pothole.

The hedgerows here were high, towering over the car and creating a tunnel-like effect while vegetation slapped against the windows and paintwork.

'It doesn't look like people come here much,' she murmured, then blinked as a bramble smacked the windscreen.

'Probably why he likes it here.' Turpin's grip tightened on the steering wheel as the lane ended and a metal five-bar gate came into view.

It had been left open, caught up amongst the long grass that bordered a stony track leading off into the distance. There was no name on the gatepost, and no indication that someone lived there.

But there were fresh tyre marks in the drying mud under the sycamore trees that bordered the gates.

Turpin inched the car forward.

In the door mirror, Jan saw the two patrol cars following as they bounced across the uneven surface, their emergency lights now subdued.

She turned her attention to the track as it widened to form a yard, framed on either side by a building.

The house on her left was a low-set brick home, slate shingles glistening from a late rain shower and faded net curtains across the three windows facing the yard. A single oak-panelled door remained resolutely shut between the first and second windows.

On the other side of the yard was a large wooden barn with a corrugated steel roof arching over it. Double doors prevented her from seeing inside, and a large padlock gleamed on the latch.

'Wait here a minute,' Turpin said, ratcheting the handbrake. 'We'll find out where he is first.'

Jan held her breath as he got out of the car and joined two of the uniformed constables beside it. They spoke in hushed tones, and then one of them and Turpin strode up to the front door. He tried the doorbell off to the right of the frame first, then hammered on the door with his fist when he got no response.

A moment later, Jan watched as he sent two constables racing around the back of the bungalow while he wandered along to the front windows and tried to peer in.

'Bugger this,' she said under her breath and climbed out, leaving the warrant on the passenger seat. 'What about the barn, Sarge?'

He nodded, falling into step beside her. 'I don't like the look of this.'

'We've got a search warrant, and if we're worried about his safety…'

'Yeah, I know. We'll break down the door after we check the barn though, otherwise we'll never hear the end of it from Kennedy.'

Jan slowed as she drew closer to the large outbuilding, and craned her neck to peer around the sides. 'I can't see any windows.'

'Those doors are falling off their hinges though.' Turpin walked up to the right-hand side of one and peered through the gap. 'I can't see a bloody thing. It's too dark in there.'

'And we're not getting past this.' Jan lifted the padlock in her fingers. 'This is quality, even if the hinges aren't.'

'Okay, enough. We're going in. Wait here and I'll see if one of this lot's got some bolt cutters in their car.'

She watched while he jogged back over to the vehicles as the two constables returned from the back of the house shaking their heads.

Turpin issued orders to them, and then walked over to one of the patrol cars and waited while the driver rummaged in the back.

Before he handed over a set of bolt cutters to Turpin there was a resounding *crack* as the front door was breached by a size twelve boot and three uniformed officers charged into the house.

Jan grinned as Turpin walked back to her. 'Well, if these don't work, we could always ask Grant to repeat that exercise with this door.'

'Hopefully these'll do the trick. Stand back.'

It took three attempts and a lot of swearing but eventually Turpin managed to snap the padlock hasp in half.

He kicked it to one side in the dirt, then rested his hand on the latch.

'Ready?'

She nodded, reaching out for the other door.

'Use it as a shield, just in case. On my three. One, two…'

Jan wrenched the door open, doing as Turpin suggested and standing well behind it for a couple of seconds.

When nothing happened, she peered around it into the gloomy interior.

'Christ,' said Turpin, echoing her own thoughts.

Scrape marks covered the dusty crumbling concrete floor, evidence of heavy objects being dragged across its surface intermingling with scuffed boot prints.

At the far end, just visible from the faint grey light poking its way into the barn, she could see piles of old farm machinery, chairs stacked beside upturned tables and an old moth-eaten armchair.

There were boxes strewn over the floor to her left and right, some still taped shut with felt tip pen scrawled across the sides denoting their contents.

'Shit.' Turpin stood in the middle of the barn with his hands on his hips as he surveyed the detritus. 'He's cleared out of here as well, hasn't he?'

'We'll have to let Kennedy know,' said Jan, leading the way back outside.

Opposite, the three constables were already standing next to their cars, waiting for further instructions.

'I take it there's no sign of him in there either?' said Turpin as they drew closer.

'Looks like he's gone,' Grant said. 'He was here – there are bills addressed to him on the kitchen counter but there're no clothes in the bedroom. It looks sort of a temporary living arrangement anyway – there's no TV or microwave, nothing like that. He wouldn't have had time to clear out his office and here, would he? It's only been forty-eight hours.'

Turpin opened his mouth to respond, but was interrupted by Grant's radio crackling to life.

'It's the team up at the road block,' he said, then turned up the volume.

'Sarge? We've got a neighbour here who says she saw a rental truck leaving the track late yesterday.'

Jan saw the excitement in Turpin's eyes as he took the radio from Grant.

'Did she get a licence plate number?'

'No, Sarge – but she does remember the name of the rental company that was printed down the side.'

# CHAPTER THIRTY-FIVE

Mark paced back and forth while the temporary diversion was dismantled, his phone to his ear and a sinking sense that the whole situation was slipping through his fingers.

'Caroline, can you confirm the rental company's got back to you with the licence plate?'

'Twenty minutes ago, Sarge. It's been passed on to a team to check cameras in the area. How's the search going?'

Mark had driven back to the main road, leaving Grant and his shift partner to sift through the contents of the house and barn in the vain hope they might find something to tell them where to find Nolan Creasey, but it was taking time.

Too much time.

'He isn't here, and we haven't found anything to

suggest where he's gone,' he said. 'What are uniform doing about the ANPR checks?'

'They're working on it, Sarge. We're also waiting for the rental company to let us have the GPS tracking details for the van – they fit them on all the vehicles in case someone does a runner without paying.'

'Well, get on to them, then chase up the cameras.' He lowered the phone, his eyes clouding with frustration. 'She put me on hold.'

'Well, she can't chase up the CCTV footage or the rental company if she's talking to you, Sarge.' Jan walked over and stood in front of him, keeping her voice level. 'Give her a chance.'

Mark exhaled, squinting at the bright phone screen as dusk settled around them.

Off to his right, Grant Wickes was finalising the neighbour's statement with her, the woman hugging a well-worn anorak around herself while he repeated her words in a low murmur.

A steady stream of vehicles were passing by now, a mixture of late commuters and nosy neighbours, evidenced by the way the drivers ignored the uniformed constables' attempts to wave them past and ogled through their windscreens at the police presence instead.

Caroline's voice dragged him from his reverie.

'Hello? Hang on, I'll put you on speaker.' Mark turned and held out the phone between them before toggling the volume. 'Jan's here too.'

'Sam Owens was on his way down here when I phoned him,' said Caroline. 'Got a pen handy? He's got another address you can try. The rental van was spotted on the A34 at seven twenty-two last night, but Sam lost it after it turned off just after Abingdon. I've spoken to the rental company's head office – they've got GPS coordinates for a lane just the other side of Boars Hill. There are only a couple of houses down there, and the rental firm told Sam the van hasn't been returned yet. It should be easy to spot.'

Jan smiled. 'That's great, Caroline. We'll head over there now and get one of these patrol cars to follow. They'll call it through to Control on the way.'

'No problem. I'll text you the address corresponding with the GPS coordinates now.'

'Caroline? I owe you one,' said Mark. 'Tell Sam that was good work, too.'

His phone pinged seconds after ending the call, and he jogged towards the car, only slowing to tell the constables packing up the road block to follow them.

Handing his phone to Jan, he started the engine. 'Pop that into the sat nav, will you? I'll make a start.'

'Are they sending anyone else?'

'I don't think there is anyone else.' Mark spun the car around, then floored the accelerator. 'At least there won't be much traffic.'

He saw Jan reach out for the strap above her window while she programmed in their destination.

'My driving's not that bad.'

'Just get me there in one piece, all right?'

It took twenty-five minutes and the patrol car's emergency lights and siren to cut through the traffic on the dual carriageway, but by the time he turned into the road matching the GPS coordinates, Mark's heart rate had returned to normal and his focus was on his current surroundings.

'God, the size of these houses,' said Jan. 'Even the smaller ones cost over seven figures.'

'Makes you wonder how he can afford to live here. Mind you, some of them have been converted into flats, I think.'

She said nothing in response, too busy gawping through the windscreen as the next five-bedroom property flashed past the window.

'This should be the place, up here on the right,' she said.

He slowed a little, then turned his attention to the radio fixed to the dashboard and called the patrol car behind them. 'Lights off, lads. No need to disturb the neighbours.'

Spinning the wheel, he turned into a wide gravel driveway and peered up at the two-storey house.

A white render had been applied to the brickwork, stark under the car's headlights, and only one light shone through a downstairs window, curtained off from the outside world.

To the left of the house was an older model hatchback, and a white van with a local rental company's name printed across its rear doors.

'Gotcha,' said Jan.

'Not yet. Come on.'

Mark crossed the driveway, waited until one of the uniformed constables sprang from the patrol car now blocking the exit, and then stepped into a slate-roofed porch and banged his fist against the door.

'I'll take the back,' said Jan.

'Go with her.'

Mark waited while the constable and his colleague disappeared from sight, then hit his fist against the solid oak surface again.

No answer.

He searched for a letterbox to shout through, then bit back an exasperated sigh at the sight of a mailbox fixed to the left hand side of the porch.

Before he could debate the paperwork if he were to follow Grant's example and try to kick down the door, he heard the sound of footsteps on gravel.

'Found him, Sarge.'

He turned to see Nolan Creasey being led towards the patrol car, the man's blue shirt untucked and covered with grass stains, and his hair dishevelled.

'Did he try to run?'

'The back garden leads out to woodland,' said Jan and grinned. 'He didn't bank on Carl running ultramarathons in his spare time. He hadn't got far by the time we got round there, but he gave it his best shot.'

The uniformed constable grinned before leading Creasey towards the cars.

Mark's shoulders dropped a little, some of the strain easing from his chest. 'Get on to Kennedy and let him know Creasey's in custody. Best tell him we're going to need another search warrant for this place, too.'

'No problem.' Jan pulled out her phone. 'Do you want to wait for that and take a look?'

'No,' said Mark, nodding towards the patrol car as it pulled away. 'I want to speak to Creasey and find out why he murdered Sonya Raynott.'

# CHAPTER THIRTY-SIX

Mark paused at the bottom of the staircase leading up to the incident room and watched through the security glass while Marcus Targethen was processed out of custody by Tom Wilcox.

The broad sergeant guided the pawn shop owner through a series of documents, his voice a low undertone as he explained what would happen next, and that Targethen should expect a letter regarding a court date. His face turned serious as he reiterated what would happen to Targethen if he failed to show up for that, then he shoved the man's belongings across the counter towards him.

Mark entered the front reception area as the reinforced glass door swung shut behind Targethen and waited for Jan to join him.

'Did he see Creasey being brought in?' he asked.

Tom shook his head. 'Figured we'd wait. No sense

in putting him in danger if he's telling the truth about Creasey.'

'Thanks. Which room are we in?'

'Four. His solicitor's been in there for the past ten minutes.'

'Long enough,' said Jan. She walked over and handed Mark a manila folder. 'That's everything. I'm ready when you are.'

When they entered the interview room, Nolan Creasey broke away from his murmured conversation with the woman beside him and gave them a defiant glare.

He remained silent while his solicitor passed across her card, only confirming his details when Jan prompted him for the recording, and then slouched in his chair.

'Ms French, I take it you've made your client fully aware of the offences we intend to charge him with,' Mark said.

'I have, and he denies all of them,' she replied, her voice even.

'I'll bet he does.' Mark flipped open the file and shoved across two photographs.

'This is what happened to Sonya Raynott,' he said, watching as Creasey blinked and looked away. 'This is how she was found last Tuesday night. God knows what she went through in the last moments of her life.'

Creasey said nothing, his gaze returning to the table as Mark swept away the images.

'We have a witness who states you were selling

stolen goods with Sonya,' Mark continued. 'You were selling stolen jewellery you'd taken during a series of burglaries throughout the Stanford in the Vale area. Sonya was the one you sent ahead to divert your victims' attention away from the fact that she made sure you could follow her inside and steal as much as possible before you both made your escape.'

Jan laid out photographs of some of the items that had been traced back through the list of thefts.

'We can link several incidents of burglary and fraud to you and Sonya,' she said. 'She often wore different disguises – did you? We don't think so. We think you were so confident in her abilities that you didn't bother.'

'Here's what's happening upstairs at the moment, Creasey,' said Mark, leaning forward. 'We have a team of officers ready to make a visit to each of those burglary victims with a photograph of you. How many people are going to be able to identify you, do you think?'

'I reckon at least a dozen,' said Jan. 'Easily.'

'What happened to her, Creasey?' Mark watched as the man's eyes flickered back and forth across the photographs. 'Why did you kill her? Did you have a falling out? Did she want a bigger share of the profits and you said no? Was that when you argued? What did you kill her with?'

'Stop.' Creasey threw up his hands, sweat beading at his temples. 'I didn't kill her. I don't know what's going on.'

He wiped his hand across his mouth, then leaned towards his solicitor, whose mouth formed a perfect moue as she listened.

Finally, she gave a curt nod and turned to Mark.

'My client wishes to make a statement, however he will deny any involvement in Sonya Raynott's death.'

'All right, let's hear it.'

Creasey cleared his throat before shuffling in his seat, his gaze fixed on the photographs. 'I'll admit to helping Sonya steal some stuff.'

'Back up.' Mark saw Jan open her notebook in anticipation. 'How did you and Sonya meet?'

'Legitimately. She came to me about a year or so ago, seeking help for an addiction.'

'Stealing, you mean?'

'Yes.' Creasey raised his chin. 'She wanted to stop, I really believe she did.'

'I'm not interested in what you believe, Mr Creasey. I want to know why Sonya was murdered.'

'After about three or four sessions – she was seeing me every two weeks – I asked her what she stole, and how she stole it.' The man glanced down and clasped his hands, taking a breath before continuing. 'I don't know, I suppose I was fascinated with her. Here she was, a talented musician with her whole life ahead of her, and she was going around conning people and stealing from them. When she first came to me, I thought she had a drug addiction to finance. It turned out her addiction was the process of stealing. She didn't even have any interest in keeping the stuff afterwards.'

'How did you get involved?'

Creasey exhaled. 'I had some debts. Quite large ones. Gambling, mostly.'

'Ironic,' said Jan. 'And yet you sell your services as an addiction counsellor.'

'I'm careful which clients I take on. I don't mix with other gamblers.'

Mark heard the defensive tone in the man's voice and held up a finger to silence his colleague. 'Tell us how you ended up helping Sonya.'

'It must've been three or four months after she first came to see me, and she was showing no sign of quitting. I was intrigued. I mean, I could understand my own addiction, but not one where there were so many… risks. So many chances of something going wrong, and getting caught. Sorry, could I have a glass of water please?'

Jan crossed to the door, leaned out and spoke to a young probationary constable. Moments later, she returned with a plastic cup filled to the brim.

Creasey took a large gulp, then wiped his mouth with his sleeve. 'Thanks. She agreed, anyway. I think she was a bit nervous at first because on the way there she kept reiterating what I had to do, what I shouldn't do, that sort of thing. I was too… too excited to notice at the time, but it was almost as if she was reluctant to let someone get that close to her.'

'Where did you go?'

'A farmhouse between Stanford in the Vale and the road that heads towards Swindon. An older couple, probably in their seventies.' Creasey frowned. 'I had to nip around the side of the house while she did her thing on the doorstep trying to get them to let her inside. I think she was pretending to be from the Highways Agency that day, saying the dual carriageway was going to be widened and some of their land might be purchased for the project.'

Mark's jaw clenched, but he said nothing, reminding himself that one false step by him would have Professional Standards breathing down his neck again.

Creasey took another sip of water. 'As soon as she was in, I gave her a few seconds then went inside. She told me to look for small things, nothing big or difficult to carry.'

'What did you take?'

'I was worried the stair treads would creak – it was an old place, probably last decorated in the eighties – so I did a quick recce of the living room. I didn't find much, to be honest. Some silver rings in an old bureau and an antique clock. She was livid when she saw them later on. Said they weren't worth anything. So before we did it again, she taught me what I needed to look for next time.'

'And you became as addicted to stealing as she was.'

'I-I can't explain it. It's – was – such an adrenalin

rush. I mean, we could've been caught at any time.' Creasey turned the plastic cup between his hands. 'I just didn't expect her to be murdered for it. I cared about Sonya, I really did.'

'Such as encouraging her addiction, instead of curing it,' said Jan.

Creasey glared at her. 'I didn't know it was going to end like this.'

'How incredibly naïve of you,' she snarled.

'What happened, the last time you conned your way into someone's house?' Mark said. 'Did something go wrong?'

'I wouldn't know. I didn't always go with her.'

'Are you suggesting that Sonya was conning people over and above the victims you targeted together?'

'That's it exactly.' Nolan's eyes darkened. 'And she was breaking into people's homes if they weren't in. I had my suspicions for a while, and then I confronted her about it a month ago. She didn't even bother to deny it, just said that there were some jobs she was better at doing alone. I told her she was taking too many risks, and that she'd get caught.'

'Did you kill her because you were afraid she'd expose your involvement?'

'What? No – no, that's not what happened.' Nolan twisted around to face his solicitor. 'I didn't kill Sonya, I swear.'

'And yet you didn't seem surprised when we first told you.'

'Because I'd seen the news. Because I'm not stupid and put two and two together. I'd been trying to phone her since Wednesday morning. I didn't know she was already dead by then.'

Mark snatched up the plastic evidence bag containing Nolan's mobile phone. 'So we'll find her number on here?'

'No... I...' He sighed. 'I used a burner phone to call her. When I realised what had probably happened, I got rid of it. I was scared.'

'Scared of what?'

'This, of course! Being accused of killing her, when I didn't.'

Jan looked up from her notes. 'She was too useful to you.'

'That's what I'm saying,' Nolan insisted. 'Why would I kill her? We were doing all right until she went a step too far.'

'Was she working with somebody else?' Mark said.

'I don't know. She never told me. We argued about it, and she told me to mind my own business.' Nolan jutted out his chin. 'I told her it *was* my business. She was putting both of us at risk doing what she was doing. I told you – there was something wrong with her. It was more than an addiction, almost a challenge for her to see how far she could push her luck every time.'

'When did you last speak to her?'

'The last time I saw Sonya was the week before she was found dead. We met in one of the pubs in

Headington, near the hospital.' Nolan frowned. 'She was quieter than usual.'

'Did she say if something was troubling her?' said Jan.

'No, but she seemed distracted, like there was something on her mind. Worried, I thought. She wouldn't tell me why though.'

'I'll ask you again,' said Mark. 'Where were you between six-thirty and ten-thirty on Tuesday night last week?'

'I told you. I was in Oxford all day Tuesday at the clinic with appointments, and then I met an acquaintance and his wife for dinner at that new restaurant on the High Street at seven. We didn't leave until eleven, we had coffee at theirs and then I got a taxi straight home.'

'Do you know who killed Sonya Raynott?'

'No, I don't.'

Mark gathered up the photographs, slipped them back into the folder and eyed Nolan Creasey.

'You'll be formally charged for the thefts and profiting from selling stolen goods,' he said. 'I've a good mind to charge you with wasting police time as well. You should've told us all this when we first spoke to you.'

'She'd still be dead,' Creasey said quietly, his lips trembling. 'There's nothing I can tell you to change that.'

# CHAPTER THIRTY-SEVEN

A loud duck quack accompanied the sound of the cabin stove flickering to life the next morning as Mark refilled Hamish's water supply and scooped food into a stainless steel bowl on the deck.

The sun had crested the horizon thirty minutes ago, and he had reluctantly rolled out of bed, slipped on a sweatshirt and jogging shorts and pulled on a pair of well-worn running shoes.

His breath had fogged in his face while he'd set a fast pace towards the lock, crossing the weir and into the meadow while the small dog at his heels easily kept up with him.

Now, he stood for a moment, enjoying the sunlight warming his neck while Hamish buried his nose in the food.

He left the cabin door open for the dog to wander inside when he'd finished, and picked up his phone from the galley worktop while automatically finding the switch for the kettle.

There was nothing on the national news, but a quick scroll through the local news websites soon brought results.

Despite no media release being made about Nolan Creasey's arrest, a reporter from the *Abingdon Times* had somehow found out that the counsellor had been at the centre of attention yesterday, positing that the man was helping with enquiries.

Mark's frustration rose as he read the scant lines of text, the kettle rattling on the hob.

He made a mental note to speak to Kennedy about reminding everyone on the investigation about the penalties for speaking to the press, and to ask Sarah in media relations to issue a statement to calm the rumours before lunchtime.

In the meantime, the fact remained that Creasey's alibis were solid, and they still had no idea who had killed Sonya Raynott – or why.

'Might as well start all over again,' he groaned.

Mark sighed as Hamish scampered down the steps, scurried across the cabin and leapt up onto a blanket covering the sofa and faced the Abbey Gardens, paws on the cushions lining the seat.

The dog growled under his breath as two walkers strolled through the grassy expanse behind a spaniel, and then gave an excited yip when a canoeist passed the window.

'Settle down,' Mark murmured, stirring milk into one of the coffees and adding sugar to both. 'It's not your river, you know.'

Hamish whined in response, then jumped to the floor and crossed to his bed.

Yawning widely, Mark padded along to the main bedroom, toed off his running shoes and edged around to Lucy's side of the bed.

'You awake? I made coffee.' He set down her mug on her nightstand beside a thriller she'd been reading into the early hours.

She groaned in response, rolled over and blinked. 'What time is it?'

'Almost seven. Hamish has been out and fed, so don't let him tell you otherwise.'

Lucy rubbed her eyes, then smiled up at him. 'Those shorts are falling apart.'

'They're comfy.' He blew across the surface of his coffee, took a tentative sip and then wrinkled his nose as the hot liquid scorched his mouth. 'I'm going to take a shower.'

Rolling back the duvet, Lucy smiled. 'I can think of a better way to spend your time waiting for that to cool.'

Mark grinned, set down the mug and crawled in next to her, wrapping his arms around her shoulders before burying his nose in her hair. 'You smell nice.'

'That's what they all say.'

She giggled as he tickled her, then drew back, frowning. 'Is that your phone?'

He raised his head.

Sure enough, the familiar ringtone carried through from the galley. 'Bugger.'

Throwing back the duvet, ignoring Lucy's indignant cry at the sudden draft that swept over her body, he raced past Hamish and slid to a standstill beside the countertop.

Kennedy's name was splashed across the screen.

He swept up the phone before it went to voicemail, and answered.

'Been running?' the DI said by way of greeting.

'What's up, guv?'

'Just wanted to ask you to come in earlier this morning.'

'Has something happened?'

'Sonya Raynott's father has been in touch. He wants to meet us at nine o'clock.' Kennedy paused, a slurping sound reaching Mark's ears. 'I'd like to have a short briefing before that to see what we're left with after Creasey's interview.'

'Isn't he being kept up to date by the Family Liaison Officer that's been assigned to him?'

'He is, but apparently he still wants a word.'

'Have you seen the news this morning?'

'I have indeed. No doubt Mr Raynott has too, so I suggest you get here by eight sharp.'

Mark glanced at the clock on the wall before peering back towards the bedroom, then bit back a groan.

'I'll be there.'

# CHAPTER THIRTY-EIGHT

'Kennedy's waiting for an update.'

Mark glanced over his shoulder at Jan's words to see the DI standing beside the whiteboard, his shirt sleeves rolled up and the remains of a takeout bacon and egg sandwich in his hand.

The greasy aroma of hurried breakfasts and sweet energy drinks filled the incident room while a pale grey light penetrated the window blinds, adding to an already exhausted atmosphere that reeked of despair.

He looked away, then eyed the red flashing light on his desk phone and swore under his breath.

'See you over there. I need to check these voicemail messages, just in case.'

Mark watched her go, then made a start, his earlier good mood dissipating further with every voice he heard.

No, the rental company had never leased a vehicle to Sonya Raynott or someone called Marie Allenton.

No, none of Nolan Creasey's neighbours at Lockinge or Boars Hill recognised the woman.

And could he provide a quote for the *Abingdon Times* in time for their noon update? Off the record, of course.

Slamming the phone back into its cradle, he rubbed at already tired eyes, then snatched up his notebook and crossed to where Kennedy waited.

Caroline handed him a tepid breakfast burger and gave a small smile. 'Figured you might need something to eat.'

'Thanks. Sorry for yesterday. I know you're doing everything you can in the circumstances.'

She winked, then joined Alex sitting on one of the desks facing the DI and picked at the remains of an egg roll.

'Okay, thanks for the early appearances everyone,' Kennedy began. 'I spoke with DCI Melrose last night and he's agreed we can go ahead and charge Nolan Creasey with the offences relating to fraud and burglary. Creasey will be released later today, with a court date to be arranged within the week by the CPS. In the meantime, he'll be required to hand in his passport and check in with his local station on a daily basis.'

His jaw tightened as he eyed each of the team in turn. 'I know it's disappointing that we haven't got Sonya's killer in custody, but we have at least removed one problem from the original equation. Uniform are going to continue to work through the seized items so, where possible, they can be returned to their owners. Now our attention turns to who else Sonya came into contact with in the weeks leading up to her murder.'

'We could have another word with Spencer Rossbay,' said Mark, dusting crumbs from his trousers and swallowing the last of the burger. 'He was the cello player who was trying to get in touch with her before she disappeared. He gave us Graham Tiegler's details but he might know who else she'd contact if she was worried about something, like Creasey suggested.'

'Did Creasey have any suggestions?'

'No – apart from the two times Tiegler saw him at Sonya's concerts, he confirms the only time he spent with her was either at her counselling sessions or when they burgled people.'

'Right,' Kennedy said. 'Jan – can you do that this morning? Caroline, I need you to chase up Jasper about the lab testing for the fibres Gillian found in that head wound of Sonya's. It's been ten days, and considering Melrose approved it being escalated, they should have something for us by now.'

'I'll take a look at any offenders who might've been released on licence with a history of violence, just in case,' said Alex. 'I mean, it could be a random attack and not related to anything she'd been up to, but it's worth checking I suppose.'

Mark smiled at the detective team's youngest

member while Kennedy wrote down the DC's suggestion on the whiteboard.

Not so long ago, Alex had been a nervous probationary detective, unsure of his own capabilities and too afraid to speak out.

'Good thinking,' said Kennedy, then paused when Tracy walked towards him.

'Mr Raynott is downstairs,' she said. 'I've put him in the meeting room off the atrium.'

'Thanks, we'll be down in a minute.' He turned back to the group. 'Any more suggestions?'

'I'd like to speak to Marcus Targethen again,' Mark said. 'He gave up Creasey's name unwillingly and yet he must have known Sonya was skimming the profits from their operation. I wouldn't be surprised if he's more active than he says in dealing stolen property, and he might divulge some more names if we drag him back in here.'

'Do that.' The DI shot him a wolfish smile. 'Get uniform to pick him up. And when you talk to him, do it in interview room one. It's the least comfortable, and fucking freezing this time of year. It might make him more conducive to clearing his conscience once and for all.'

# CHAPTER THIRTY-NINE

When Kennedy opened the door into the meeting room downstairs, Sam Raynott turned away from the window with red-rimmed eyes, his face haggard.

'Is it true?' he said. 'Have you arrested the bastard who murdered my daughter?'

'We're very sorry for your loss, Mr Raynott. Shall we sit down?' Kennedy said, rolling one of the chairs away from the conference table and setting out his notebook and phone beside him.

Mark waited until Sam sat opposite the DI, taking in the broken features of a grieving man and father and wondering how much he had aged since receiving the news last week.

Joining the two men, he eased into his chair while Kennedy cleared his throat.

'The man we arrested last night will be charged with several offences relating to burglary and fraud,' he said.

'At this time, we won't be charging him with Sonya's murder.'

Sam blinked, his mouth opening and closing for a moment as if gasping for breath. 'But... but that's not what they said on the news. It says on social media that Nolan Creasey was arrested for her murder too.'

'Unfortunately, the media and some members of the public have a way of misinterpreting the facts to suit their own ends, Mr Raynott,' said Kennedy. 'We hadn't even released a statement before journalists and others were making their own minds up about his involvement. Although he has been helping us with our enquiries in relation to the circumstances leading up to her murder, we have no evidence yet to suggest that he was responsible for her death.'

'Oh.'

'I can assure you that my team are doing all they can to find out what happened to Sonya,' Kennedy continued. 'Both DS Turpin and I have daughters, and we're—'

'Yes, but your daughters are still alive, aren't they?' Sam wiped angrily at the tears spilling over his cheeks. 'You're not waiting for someone to say when you can have yours back to bury... you're not grieving, asking yourself why you, why her, why... oh, Christ.'

Mark got up and crossed over to a cabinet beneath a whiteboard, pulling out a box of tissues before returning and plucking a handful out.

'Here,' he said softly. 'I'm sorry. Of course we can't

relate to what you're going through. But DI Kennedy is right. I promise I'm doing everything I can to find and arrest whoever did this. I won't stop until I do.'

Sam nodded, then buried his face in his hands. 'I know you won't. I just…'

Returning to his seat, Mark waited while Sonya's father composed himself, burying his own emotions at the man's grief.

He clenched his fists under the table, knowing full well what he would do if anyone ever hurt Anna or Louise.

'I'm sorry,' Sam said eventually.

'No need to apologise.' Kennedy clasped his hands together on the desk. 'I wonder whether you would be able to help us with regard to some of the information that's come to light about Sonya over the past week, Mr Raynott? If now isn't the right time for you, then of course we can make other—'

'No, please. Go ahead and ask me.'

'This isn't easy, but you need to be aware that we suspect Sonya was involved in a number of burglaries in the area west of here, and that she profited from selling the proceeds from those. Did you know about this?'

'I didn't, no.' Sam exhaled. 'Look, she went through a phase when she was about fourteen or so. There were a couple of instances of shoplifting. The school got involved, so did your lot. It was a couple of bits of make-up but we knew we'd have to nip it in the bud or risk it escalating. We worked with the school and the police officer who came round to the house to give her the fright of her life in the hope she wouldn't do it again. We thought it'd worked.'

'When did you suspect it hadn't?'

Sam shifted uncomfortably in his seat. 'Within a few months. I think she just got better at hiding it, at making sure she didn't get caught. Neither me or my wife could prove anything though, and Sonya always categorically denied it.'

'Any ideas why she might've kept stealing?' said Mark.

'I think she enjoyed it,' Sam replied. 'It sounds crazy, I know, but we couldn't think of another explanation.'

'Mr Raynott, we understand from Mr Creasey that he first met Sonya when she went to him for counselling for her addiction – if we can call it that – to stealing,' said Kennedy. 'Except that instead of him curing her, she persuaded him to join her in conning vulnerable people out of valuables and cash they left lying around. That was last year. Was Sonya living with you at the time?'

'No, she was living at her flat. She hadn't lived at home since she started university,' said Sam, his voice cracking. 'I don't think she could wait to leave home. Sonya was our only child so I suppose we did spoil her – that's what makes me so frustrated about the stealing and all that. She didn't *need* to steal anything. She could've just asked me if she wanted something.'

Mark checked his notes. 'We're trying to work out why she registered with an optician in Wantage under the name of Marie Allenton.'

He heard a harsh intake of breath from the other side of the table and looked up.

Sam shook his head. 'That's her mother's maiden name.'

'Is your wife aware that your daughter was using her name?'

'Of course not.' Sam wiped his eyes. 'She died four years ago.'

# CHAPTER FORTY

Jan checked over her shoulder to make sure the door through to the atrium closed behind her, then hurried towards the row of plastic chairs bolted to the floor in the station's reception room.

Spencer Rossbay looked up at the sound of footsteps, flicked his overgrown fringe from his eyes with a practised twitch of his neck and stood.

'Thanks for coming in, Mr Rossbay,' Jan said. 'And at such short notice.'

'No problem. Have you caught him?'

She gave him a tight smile, waved him through the security gate and showed him into the larger of the interview rooms. 'Not yet.'

'Oh.'

Hearing the disappointment in his voice, she looked closer and took in the dark circles under his eyes.

'Did you have a concert last night?' she said, slipping a new tape into the recording machine.

'No. I, um... I haven't been sleeping that well since you told me about Sonya being found like that.' Rossbay removed his camel-coloured wool coat and looked around for a hook. 'Hot in here, isn't it?'

'It's one extreme to the other down here, I'm afraid,' said Jan. 'And you'll have to put that on the table or the spare chair there. We can't have anything like hooks in the rooms, just in case.'

His eyes widened. 'Oh. Oh yes, I see.'

Colouring a little, he shuffled from side to side, then wrinkled his top lip at the chipped and scarred table surface before folding the coat over his arm and sitting opposite Jan.

'Did you speak to your parents after we came to see you on Monday?' she asked.

'Yes. Thank you, by the way. I did go and stay with them.' His blush deepened. 'I didn't want to be on my own in the house. Hilary's back on Monday but it just seems too empty at the moment.'

'I understand. I'm glad you've got someone to talk to.'

'Me too.' He straightened. 'Is this what they call "helping police with their enquiries", then?'

She smiled. 'No. This is what we call a voluntary interview. I'll still recite a formal caution, just in case I learn something that could help our investigation, but you're not under arrest and you're under no obligation to answer my questions. We can stop at any time, too – just say so. Sound good?'

He nodded vigorously, his hair falling in his eyes once more and she wondered how on earth he made it through a whole concert without blinding himself.

'Ah, yes. All good.'

'Great. Here we go, then.' She went through the formalities, then shifted in the hard chair until she found a modicum of comfort in the meagre plastic padding. 'Right, thanks for your help on Monday, Spencer. When we spoke to you, you said you'd last seen Sonya three months ago. Can you recall where, and perhaps exactly when?'

Rossbay frowned, then reached into his trouser pocket and dragged out a phone. 'I can't, but I'm sure I'll have something in my calendar. I can't live without lists,' he said, already scrolling. 'If I don't write something down, I forget.'

'You and me both,' Jan said, matching the bright smile he gave her.

'I know it was the day after our quartet had played at a wedding in Banbury. Expensive do, too. I think Hilary found that gig. It paid good money but... I wasn't the only one who noticed Sonya was off colour that day. She looked tired, and cocked up a couple of times. Nothing that the reception party noticed, but it was clear to the rest of us that her playing was suffering more and more.'

'What did you do?'

'Ah, here it is. It was eleven weeks ago, so not quite three months. The gig was on the Saturday evening, and I phoned her on the Monday asking her to meet me for coffee that morning.'

'How did that go?'

'Ugh. About as bad as you'd expect. No one else had the balls to mention it, so they left it to me to swing the hatchet.' Rossbay sighed. 'Honestly, you'd think she'd realise what was going to happen, the way she'd been carrying on but I think it knocked her for six.'

'Is that when you argued?'

He nodded, putting the phone away. 'Yes. She stormed out of the café. I was going to go after her, but then I thought, bollocks. It's not me who's in the wrong, and if she can't accept responsibility then it's her problem. God, I wish now I had run after her. I wish I'd pestered her until she'd told me what was really going on. Do you think I could have stopped someone killing her if I had?'

Jan reached out and patted the young man's hand. 'No, I don't think so, Spencer. I think you probably did everything you could to accommodate her by the sound of it.'

'Hmm. Maybe.'

Jan skimmed through her notes. 'When we last spoke, you mentioned that you don't know any of Sonya's friends or family. What about acquaintances, people who perhaps you both had common interests with?'

She watched while Rossbay sucked in his bottom lip, his eyes finding the ceiling tiles.

'What about other people you saw around her at any time, then?' she prompted. 'Did she ever have people approaching her at your concerts, things like that?'

'Every now and again, yes.' He pulled back his fringe between his fingers before dropping his hand to his pocket once more. 'I might have some email addresses or something like that on my phone – if someone did speak to her at those, it was usually because we left her in charge of the marketing like I said. So she'd be handing out business cards with the group's email address on. We'd all get copied in for information but left it to her to respond.'

'That would be useful, thanks,' said Jan, updating her notes.

'You should probably speak to the university about the two concerts she played at before she quit too – they were ticketed events so they might still have contact details for everyone who came.'

She flashed him a smile. 'I will, that's a good idea.'

'Apart from that, I really don't know who she hung around with,' said Rossbay. 'I'm sorry, but we moved in different social circles outside the group's bookings and practices.'

'No problem.' Jan formally ended the interview and popped the tape from the machine. 'Thanks again for coming in.'

After showing Rossbay through to reception, she made her way back up the stairs, lost in thought.

How on earth had Sonya managed to keep her extracurricular activities from her quartet companions for so long?

And what was it about the burglaries she was committing on her own that she didn't want to share with Nolan Creasey?

When she walked into the incident room, Mark's chair was empty and Kennedy's office door was closed.

The tiny fine hairs on the back of her neck stood on end at the muted atmosphere amongst her colleagues, and she caught Caroline's eye as she sat and woke up her computer screen.

'All right, what did I miss?'

Caroline opened her mouth to reply, but Kennedy's door ripped open and the DI leaned out.

'Jan? Got a minute?'

She hurried over, Kennedy shutting the door behind her before moving to his desk and sinking into his seat.

Turpin looked up from one of the visitor chairs, his face furious.

'What on earth happened?' she said. 'You two look apoplectic.'

In response, Kennedy turned his computer screen.

An enlarged photograph of Nolan Creasey leaving the police station the previous night was emblazoned across it, his face clearly visible while he watched the passing traffic and held a phone to his ear. Beside it, a headline screamed for attention, staying just the right side of defamation while managing to suggest he was linked to the death of Sonya Raynott.

'Shit,' Jan managed.

'They somehow got his name as well,' said Turpin.

'I'll string up the fucking journalist when I find out who he is,' Kennedy rasped, jabbing his finger at the offending text. 'Staff reporter, my arse.'

'I've just spoken to Creasey's solicitor,' Turpin said. 'She'll warn her client not to speak to anyone. Hopefully no one figures out where his place in Boars Hill is and he can keep his head down until his court appearance.'

Kennedy groaned. 'I'd better give the CPS a call too. Melrose is already speaking to the editor of the newspaper.'

'How the hell did the reporter find out who he was?' said Jan. 'It can't be anyone here, surely? Everyone wants to find out who murdered Sonya – they wouldn't jeopardise the investigation like this, would they?'

'We think it was luck,' said Turpin. 'Word got around via Creasey's old workplace and his neighbour at Lockinge no doubt so the reporter and photographer knew whoever we arrested would be brought here. While the photographer waits on the other side of the road, the reporter could've been lurking anywhere near that front door and overheard the phone conversation.'

Jan leaned against the filing cabinet. 'What do we do, guv?'

'We're stuck until Jasper gets those lab test results to us, and he reckons that won't be until Monday,' Kennedy said resignedly. 'You may as well both take tomorrow off – there's no point us all trying to work while we're exhausted. Come in on Sunday and I'll speak to the editor of the newspaper again. With any luck I can persuade him not to sell the story to the national press, otherwise whoever killed Sonya is going to go to ground.'

'We can count out Targethen as a suspect while we're at it,' Turpin added, turning to Jan. 'I finished speaking to him five minutes before you got up here, and apart from a couple of blokes uniform had already arrested for other thefts last month, he didn't have any other names.'

'Christ,' she said. 'We're back to square one, aren't we?'

# CHAPTER FORTY-ONE

The following morning, Mark stood on the towpath upstream from the narrowboat with Jan's twin boys and a pair of bright orange fishing nets.

'Right, you two – there are only a couple of rules. One, don't fall in, and two – if you do, don't let your mum see.'

Luke giggled, holding out his hand. 'Okay. What can we catch?'

'That's half the fun – you'll have to find out.' Mark handed the other net to Harry, then peered into the shallow water nearest to them. 'Although by the look of it, minnows are your best bet. Where's your jam jar?'

'Here.' Harry turned and held up a large empty marmalade pot.

Taking it from him, Mark scooped up some water before setting it to one side. When he straightened, he saw Jan appear from the narrowboat's cabin with a mug of tea in her hand before she climbed over the gunwale and settled into one of the deck chairs Lucy had put on the towpath.

Sunlight dappled the watercourse, sparkling off the bow wave from a pair of swans that gracefully paddled past. A light breeze ruffled the boys' waterproof coats, carrying with it the sound of Saturday morning traffic from the bridge.

'Have you ever caught anything in here?' said Luke, already dipping his net into the water with a practised flourish.

'No – although I'll admit I haven't tried.' Mark pointed to the lock farther upstream. 'You can only do proper fishing past that, and I've never bothered getting a licence.'

Harry looked troubled. 'Are we allowed to do this, then?'

'Sure, you'll be all right. Besides, we'll pop everything back in the water when we're done.'

Happier, the boys crouched closer to the water's edge and soon their gentle banter fell quiet as each became entranced with the small creatures they could see darting above the clay silt.

Mark glanced down as Hamish scampered from the narrowboat, closely followed by Lucy who ambled after him, a coffee mug in her hand.

'You're a gem,' he said, kissing her. 'Thanks.'

'All the food's prepped. You'll just need to fire up the barbecue when the boys are done here. Jan says

Scott should be here in an hour, just as soon as he's finished doing a quote for a customer.' She smiled when Harry peered up at them. 'Caught anything yet?'

'They're too fast,' he grumbled, turning back to the water.

Lucy chuckled, squeezed Mark's hand, and wandered back to where Jan sat, Hamish at her heels.

Mark had suggested the brunch date with Jan and her family when they'd left the incident room last night, reluctant to take Kennedy's advice about taking a day off.

He knew the impact exhaustion could have on a large investigation team, and despite waking up with a lingering guilt that they were no closer to identifying Sonya's killer, he was looking forward to the day ahead.

Having two ten-year-olds to keep entertained would stop him worrying for a couple of hours, at least.

'Got one,' Luke sang out. He held up his net, a small minnow writhing inside.

'Quick, pop him in the jar then. Otherwise he'll die. We don't want that.'

Mark gently untangled the net and slipped the fish into the water. Handing back the net, his attention was caught by Jan suddenly leaning forward in her chair, phone to her ear.

A few seconds later, she was hurrying along the towpath towards him, her features bleak.

He exhaled, steadying his heart rate as he took in the look of shock on her face.

'Er, boys. Might have to stop what we're doing here for now. Sorry, but I think your mum and I are going back to work.'

Harry rose to his feet and handed back the net. 'I haven't caught anything anyway.'

'I think we scared the others away,' Luke added.

'Mark?' Jan gave her boys a sunny smile, then pulled him to one side. 'Caroline just called. It's not good news.'

'Where…?'

Jan shook her head and turned to the twins. 'Do you two fancy waiting with Lucy until your dad gets here, and then you can still have your barbecue?'

'Yes!' Luke grinned. 'I thought you were going to make us go home.'

'As if I'd make you miss out on food.'

Mark took the nets from the boys as he watched Harry gently pour the contents of the jam jar back into the river and then hurried back to the narrowboat in their wake. He gave Lucy an apologetic smile when she placed the nets on the narrowboat's roof to dry off.

'I'll take you out to lunch when all this is over, promise,' he said.

'You heard that, Jan.' She grinned. 'I've got a witness.'

Jan looked longingly at the barbecue set up on the deck and sighed. 'Shame we hadn't made a start. We could've had a takeaway.'

They said their goodbyes, and fell into step across the meadow, the long grass flapping at their heels.

'Okay, what did Caroline say?' Mark asked. 'What's this all about?'

'She and Alex were sent over to Boars Hill twenty minutes ago.'

'Boars…' Mark's heart rate spiked. 'Nolan Creasey?'

'It doesn't sound good, Sarge. Someone attacked him and left him for dead.'

# CHAPTER FORTY-TWO

Jan swung her car through the open gates of the Boars Hill address then braked hard, a gasp escaping her lips.

'Shit, Caroline wasn't kidding.'

Three patrol cars cluttered the driveway with Jasper's van alongside one of them while a mixture of uniformed officers and CSI specialists traipsed back and forth from the open front door of the property.

She parked off to one side, away from the commotion, and pointed through the windscreen. 'There's Alex.'

'Let's find out what's been going on.'

Mark strode towards the young DC, rolling down his shirt sleeves and buttoning the cuffs to offset the cool air under the enormous conifers that bordered the driveway.

'Sarge, you made it.' The relief in Alex's eyes matched his voice. 'Caroline said she'd spoken to Jan, but I didn't know if you—'

'Where's Creasey?' Jan asked. 'What the hell's been going on here?'

'Okay, so the ambulance took him about ten minutes ago – he was still breathing but he was unconscious when his father found him, and there's blood everywhere.' Alex led the way over to the front door, which was now being taped off by Jasper. 'Can we go inside?'

'There are spare suits in the back of the van,' said the CSI lead. 'Get them on, and I'll take you in.'

Mark took one of the sealed packs Alex handed to him, pulled on the protective booties and steadied Jan while she did the same.

'Did Creasey's father see anyone leaving the house when he arrived?' he said when they walked back to where Jasper waited.

'I don't think so,' said Alex. 'Caroline's interviewing him now, and then she's going to take him to the hospital.'

Handing the roll of barrier tape to one of his colleagues, Jasper pointed to the door frame as they passed.

'Neither this nor the back door was forced open,' he said. 'So whoever attacked him was invited in.'

'Or Creasey opened the door, and was then pushed back inside,' Mark suggested, gesturing to the scuff marks down one side of the hallway wall. 'Where did they go from here?'

'This way.' Jasper turned, his booties sliding on the

chequered tiled floor. 'After he answered the door, it looks like he was pursued through here.'

'Pursued?' Mark frowned, then followed him into a reception room and stopped, stunned. 'Jesus.'

Blood streaked the tiles and splattered the plasterwork beside a plush three-seat sofa, a large stain smudging its way down the wall before pooling across the floor next to a small wooden table.

'I'm thinking Creasey tried to use the sofa as a barrier between him and his attacker,' said Jasper. 'But it looks like he was cornered here, and that's where the majority of the attack took place. The blood between the front door and here would suggest whoever did this managed to stab him as soon as the door was forced open.'

'The paramedics said he had several stab wounds,' Alex added. 'There were defensive wounds to his wrists and hands, but most of the damage was caused by one to his stomach, and another to his neck.'

Mark pursed his lips while he surveyed the scene, taking in an upturned table lamp and small wooden coffee table. 'Will you try to lift prints off of these?'

'Absolutely.' Jasper pointed to several plastic markers placed around the room. 'We've found blood spots over here, and a partial footprint. As for the results, tell Kennedy we'll do our best.'

'Thanks. All right, we'll get out of your way.'

Once outside, Mark stripped off the protective suit and stuffed it into a biohazard bin in the back of Jasper's van, turning as Caroline emerged from the rear of the property, her face wan.

'Creasey's father, Garen, didn't see anyone leaving when he got home,' she said. 'There were no other vehicles in the lane, but he said he knew something was wrong when he saw the front door open. Apparently there was a reporter here earlier as well.'

'Does he know who?'

'Yes, I've got a name and number. I was planning to head back to the station and interview her, if that's all right with you, Sarge?'

'Who's arranging to take Garen to the hospital if you're doing that?'

'I can,' said Alex.

'Okay then, Caroline – you head off, myself and Jan will finish up here and we'll all meet back at the station in a few hours. Sound good?'

They nodded, then shot off to their respective cars, gravel spitting out from under the wheel arches as they sped away.

Mark exhaled, and cast a sideways look at Jan, who was staring up at the house, her face troubled.

'What are you thinking?'

'I was just wondering whether we've been looking at all this the wrong way.' She gave an apologetic shrug.

'Do you think this attack wasn't related to Sonya's death?'

'No, I think they're connected. Too much of a coincidence otherwise. What I meant was, what if

Sonya and Nolan went too far with their burglary enterprise? What if they stepped on someone's toes?'

'Like a territorial dispute?'

'Exactly. What if someone took exception to what they were doing and decided to eliminate the competition?'

# CHAPTER FORTY-THREE

Kennedy stormed out of his office at high speed as Mark headed towards the whiteboard, his face livid.

'According to the newspaper, only their social media mentioned Creasey by name,' he said through gritted teeth. 'The post was taken down after I called the editor yesterday, but—'

'It was already too late to stop someone from finding out where he lived.' Mark eyed Creasey's photograph on the board, and jerked his chin towards his colleague, who was standing next to her desk with her phone to her ear. 'Jan thinks the two murders might be linked to a turf war.'

'Right now, I don't know what to think, so it's as good an idea as any.'

The DI scrawled a new bullet point on the board and took a step back. 'This is a mess, Mark. I've already had Melrose on the phone demanding an explanation as to how this happened, and the Chief Super's going to want to have an update within the hour.'

'What about the journalist and photographer who published yesterday's story?'

'Contractors.' Kennedy snorted. 'Everyone's a bloody contractor these days. And insured up to the hilt in case something like this happens. They won't be working for a while though, I'll bet.'

'Oh, I don't know – plenty of nefarious news sites would snap up that kind of reporter in an instant.'

'Has anyone had a chance yet to look into how his attacker found Creasey's address?'

'He's still using the rental van. According to Caroline, his father told her that he used it to go back to his old office in East St Helen Street yesterday to pick up the rest of his stuff. It wouldn't take much for someone to locate the office and follow him from there, especially given that social media post. The van's easy to spot given it's from a local firm rather than a national company – it stands out more. They don't have that many hire vehicles in their fleet yet.'

'Do you think Marcus Targethen is involved?'

Mark shook his head. 'I think Targethen is a small-time dealer. Remember, he was worried when we made him give up Creasey's name. I don't think he's up to doing something like this. Then there's the fact that his alibi for Sonya's murder checks out.'

'Where was Sonya Raynott's father at the time of the attack on Creasey?'

'Caroline spoke to him on her way back here. He was at his sister's house – he's been staying there to avoid the media.'

'What about that vigilante group leader – what was his name?'

'William Bereton.'

'Get him in here. In fact, get the whole bloody lot of them in here and find out whether they're behind this. I'll speak to Kidlington and ask them to send someone over to that other pawnbroker's place in the morning – Brenda Stephens. Perhaps she can shed some light.'

'It's a long shot, guv.' He saw Kennedy's mouth harden. 'But I'll get Jan and Caroline to give me a hand. We'll aim to speak to everyone by the end of the weekend. I'll ask Alex to work with uniform to get hold of CCTV footage from any petrol stations, shops, anything around the Boars Hill area that might show Creasey's attacker. With that much blood at the scene, his clothes must have been spattered with it. I'll have them speak with neighbours along that lane too – maybe someone noticed a strange vehicle or someone on foot leaving the house.'

'Do that. What about Jan's hypothesis? Do you think there's any merit in that?'

'It's a fair analysis, guv.'

'But?'

'The attack on Creasey...' Mark rubbed his chin while his gaze meandered over the sweeping notes and photographs pinned to the board. 'It just looked too personal. Too angry. I mean, we won't rule it out – but it feels like there's something else going on here. Something that hasn't come to light despite all the people we've spoken to, and all the questions we've been asking. We've missed something.'

Kennedy looked down as his mobile phone started ringing, and grimaced when he looked at the screen.

'That's Melrose. Hang on.'

Jan walked over while Kennedy paced the carpet, his voice low while his features remained grim.

'He wants us to speak to Bereton's vigilante group before the end of the weekend,' Mark murmured. 'Are you going to be able to do that?'

'I've already called Scott to let him know I'll be working tomorrow.' She gave a small smile when he opened his mouth to respond. 'Don't worry. We sort of expected it with this one. Who's Kennedy speaking to?'

'The DCI.'

They both turned as the call ended, and Kennedy lowered the phone.

'Melrose spoke to someone at the John Radcliffe just now,' he said. 'Creasey was pronounced dead twenty minutes ago.'

Mark exhaled and eyed the man's photograph pinned to the whiteboard.

'So now we've got a double murder enquiry on our hands.'

# CHAPTER FORTY-FOUR

The next morning, Mark swallowed the dregs of his second coffee, gathered up his notebook and a folder full of paperwork and made his way downstairs.

Passing through the atrium of the station, he glanced at the muted television screen fixed to one wall and eyed the news ticker along the bottom.

So far, Creasey's death had received a flurry of interest from the larger local newspapers and a suitably subdued reaction from the one that had published his photograph.

Mark had no doubt that the editor of that particular enterprise was still contemplating his options with his legal team.

'Are you ready?' Jan emerged from the toilet, straightening her blouse and looking none the worse for starting her shift at seven o'clock that morning. She squinted at him. 'How many coffees have you had, Sarge?'

'Only two.'

'Jesus, we're going to have to find you something stronger.'

'I'm not a morning person,' he protested, holding open the door into reception.

'I've noticed.'

Tom Wilcox was behind the front desk when they walked in.

'William Bereton's in interview room two,' he said. 'Alex and Caroline have made a start on two of the other members of his group who arrived about an hour ago.'

'How long's Bereton been here?' Mark asked.

'Only fifteen minutes.' Tom winked. 'He had the sense to turn down the offer of a coffee from the vending machine.'

Mark grinned, then followed Jan through the security gate and along a tiled corridor, the door to their interview room ajar.

William Bereton rose to his feet when they entered, his bulky stance matching the glare he shot at them.

'I don't appreciate being told what to do,' he growled. 'Especially at eight o'clock on a Saturday evening. What the hell's the meaning of this?'

'Sit down, Mr Bereton,' said Jan, patting the table. 'We're speaking to everyone from the White Horse

Home Protection Group over the course of today. You're not being singled out, believe me.'

Mark closed the door as the man lowered himself into his seat, then gave Jan a nod.

If Bereton was already fired up about the interview, then having a female officer lead it might calm him down.

As it was, the man's eyebrows shot upwards when Jan read out the formal caution, his face turning scarlet.

'We took a look at your group's social media account last night,' Jan began. 'How did you find out about Nolan Creasey?'

'It was all over the news,' Bereton said, his gaze sliding to Mark, then back. 'All we did was reshare the post that newspaper put up.'

'That post was taken down an hour later, after our chief inspector requested it. Creasey's name hadn't been released to the press, and they'd obtained that information by covert means,' said Jan. 'And now, probably because of that original post naming him, Mr Creasey is dead.'

'Dead?'

She opened the folder Mark slid across to her and removed a screenshot of a familiar social media site. 'As of fifteen minutes ago, your group still has that post displayed. We've sourced every other person who shared the post and they removed it as soon as they heard about Creasey's death yesterday. You haven't. Care to explain why?'

'I… I don't run the social site. You'll have to ask Charles.'

'We are. But you all have access to that site, Mr Bereton. Moreover, according to the site you're also one of the administrators for the group. You share responsibility for what goes on it.'

Bereton swallowed audibly, and Mark wondered if the man was contemplating his civic responsibilities or thinking about his rumoured political future.

Eventually, the man cleared his throat, leaned forward and lowered his voice conspiratorially.

'To be honest, I don't even like the site or what they stand for,' he said without a trace of embarrassment. 'I can't even recall being asked to administer the group's online presence. I'm more of a practical man myself, hands on with matters. Solutions, rather than creating problems, you know.'

'You told us that there were six members of your so-called protection group,' said Jan. 'Yet there are twenty-three members of the online version. Can you vouch for each of those? Do you run this as a closed group, or by invite only?'

'Again, you'll have to check with Charles,' Bereton said, straightening. 'I'm a busy man, detective. I don't have time to sit in front of a computer all day.'

'Where were you between nine-thirty and eleven-thirty yesterday morning?'

'I— what?'

Jan clasped her hands together and waited.

'I… I took the missus into town. She wanted to do some food shopping.'

'Which town?'

'Abingdon, of course.'

'What did you do while she was shopping?'

'Went for a walk, like I usually do. I can't stand supermarkets. Horrible places.'

'Where did you walk?'

'I don't know – through the market square I suppose, round by the church…'

'Which one?'

'God, woman, I don't know the name of the bloody place.'

'A bit more respect for my colleague, Mr Bereton, if you don't mind,' Mark snapped. 'It's Detective Constable West to you.'

Bereton pursed his lips. 'Of course. My apologies.'

'Where else did you walk?' Jan asked. 'Did you perhaps go down East St Helen Street towards the wharf?'

'No, no I didn't.'

'Did you walk past the buildings marked for redevelopment? Did you see Nolan Creasey with his rented van and decide to follow him home?'

'No!' Bereton's eyes widened. 'Jesus Christ, you think I murdered him, don't you?'

'Did you?'

'No. For God's sake, no. I went for a ten-minute walk around the market square, doubled back on myself and met the missus outside the supermarket as arranged so I could help her carry the bags back to the car. Then we went home. Where we stayed. I haven't left the house until this morning to come here.'

An air of desperation filled the room as he took a deep breath and stared beseechingly at Jan.

'I'm telling the truth, I swear.'

She flipped shut the folder, popped her pen and rose to her feet.

'I hope you are, Mr Bereton. But you won't mind giving us your wife's mobile number so we can check with her before we release you, will you?'

# CHAPTER FORTY-FIVE

Monday morning brought with it new levels of frustration within the tight-knit investigation team.

An exhaustive session of interviews with William Bereton's vigilante group the day before had produced no new leads, let alone a suspect for two cold-blooded murders.

By the time Mark stowed his mountain bike beside the back door to the police station, showered and jogged up the stairs to the interview room, a lethargy was setting in amongst the officers brought in to assist the team.

Kennedy's face was grim when he peered out from his office and beckoned to him.

Mark took the takeout coffee Jan thrust his way with a murmured thanks, then hurried over.

'We're going to lose at least eight of the officers out there so they can help investigate a fatal stabbing in

Cowley later today,' the DI said as he closed the door. 'Melrose has tried arguing our case with those above us, but...'

'We've haven't had a breakthrough in two weeks,' Mark finished. 'But what about the fact Creasey was attacked and died over the weekend? We'll need that extra help to finish with the CCTV and follow-up calls to neighbours.'

'It's political,' said Kennedy, glowering at his computer screen. 'And I got an email through five minutes ago confirming the change in personnel. It's out of my hands now.'

Mark sipped his coffee and peered through the blinds at the bowed heads, murmured phone conversations and administrative staff who were starting to arrive to deal with the copious amounts of documentation generated by such an investigation.

'Shit,' he said eventually.

'Indeed.' Kennedy crossed to his chair and sank into it. 'Clive Moore phoned ten minutes ago – Gillian's going to do Creasey's post mortem at nine-thirty, so take Jan with you to that. Perhaps that will give us another angle to look into.'

'Okay.' Mark reached out for the door handle.

'And, Turpin?'

'Yes, guv?'

'Given his performance so far on this case, I think Alex deserves a more active role. Let's not waste that talent, otherwise Melrose will snap him up.'

'Understood.' Mark opened the door and looked across to where the young detective constable was staring at the whiteboard, his jaw clenched. 'He's definitely come on leaps and bounds this past year.'

'That he has. I've got a meeting in Kidlington in an hour so I'll be off in a moment—' Kennedy's phone chirped, and he raised an eyebrow. 'I have to take this. We'll talk later.'

Mark left him to it, walked over to where Alex stood, and nodded at the board. 'Any new theories?'

'No,' came the glum reply. 'Jasper will be here in a moment though, so hopefully he's got something for us.'

'He's coming here?'

'Apparently he was working at the lab yesterday, trying to get on top of the backlog. He's got some results for us and wanted to go through them with us on his way back there this morning.'

Hope threatened, and Mark battened it down immediately. 'What about Bereton's wife? Did she confirm his alibi?'

'Yes, and all the other members of his group checked out as well. They've removed the shared post off their social media page too.' Alex sighed. 'Talk about stable doors and horses, though.'

Pinching the bridge of his nose, Mark then swept his gaze across all the looping notes. 'What the hell have we missed?'

'I was sort of hoping it'd jump out at me if I kept

looking. I can't see the connections though. I mean, yes, Sonya and Nolan knew each other, but his alibi checked out for her murder, and Caroline spoke to her ex-quartet friends late yesterday and they've got alibis for when Creasey was killed.'

'Jan mentioned that perhaps this is all about a territorial dispute. I'm starting to think she's right…'

'I'm right about what?' His colleague wandered over with Caroline in her wake.

'A turf war, rather than revenge,' Mark said. 'Oh, and Kennedy says we're losing half the support staff today, so whatever we come up with, we're on our own from now on.'

Jan's eyes widened. 'Shit.'

'That's what I said.'

'Jasper's here,' said Alex, jerking his chin towards the door and beckoning to the CSI lead. 'Morning.'

'Morning, all.'

Mark watched while the technician set down his battered leather briefcase on a nearby desk and rolled his shoulders, dark circles under his eyes. 'Kennedy said you were working yesterday too.'

'You owe me,' said Jasper without rancour. His eyes were sparkling despite the evident tiredness that remained. 'I might have something for you.'

'The stage is yours,' said Caroline, standing to one side and executing a mock bow. 'Don't keep us in suspense any longer.'

Extracting copies of a printed report from his

briefcase and distributing one to each of the detectives, Jasper then pointed to the photographs of Sonya.

'First of all, the rash that was on her arms and legs,' he said. 'Gillian didn't want to assume anything during the post mortem simply because she was in two minds how to interpret what she was seeing. We got in an expert of ours to analyse the swabs. That's what delayed us,' he added apologetically. 'However, he confirmed late on Friday that Gillian was correct about the carpet burns, and that the rash is an allergic reaction to a plant – possibly something such as euphorbia that has an irritant sap and causes a rash or blistering to the skin.'

'How would she have come into contact with that?' Jan asked. 'It's a garden plant – it wouldn't have been in the verge where she was found, would it?'

'No, we definitely didn't see anything like it at the crime scene. I spoke to Gillian yesterday about the positioning of the rash marks.' Jasper unpinned one of the photographs from the board. 'The rash is here, you see – on Sonya's left thigh, the palms of her hands and her left forearm.'

'Perhaps she accidentally brushed against it,' said Mark. 'Maybe a day or so before being killed.'

Jasper nodded. 'That's what Gillian and I are thinking. Wherever she was, I'd posit someone had pruned the plants the same day so the sap was still exposed.'

'Both Creasey and Targethen confirmed Sonya was carrying out her own burglaries more often,' Caroline said. 'If she was interrupted and had to escape, she might have gone through a garden to get away in a hurry.'

Mark nodded, already writing the new information on the board while Jasper replaced the photograph. 'What else do you have for us?'

'We've managed to narrow down the composition of the weapon used to hit the back of her head.' The CSI lead took one of the reports from Jan and flicked through the pages before handing it back. 'Here. The samples Gillian removed from the wound contained traces of acrylonitrile and fibreglass. I'm still waiting on the results from a final test – there's some powder mixed in with the acrylonitrile that I want confirmation on first.'

'What's acrylonitrile?' Alex frowned. 'Acrylic based, obviously, but—'

'It's a specialised glue, used in binding fibreglass and carbon fibre compounds together,' explained Jasper.

Mark looked up from the page. 'So, the same sort of composition as a bicycle fork, that sort of thing?'

'Exactly.' Jasper picked up his briefcase. 'I'll get more information to you as the results come in, but I thought you'd want what we have so far. I've emailed all of it to Tracy too.'

'Thanks.' Mark watched as Alex walked the CSI lead out, then wandered back to his desk, head bowed as he skimmed over the contents of the report once more.

Sinking into his chair, he looked over his computer screen to see Jan staring into space.

'Penny for your thoughts?' he said.

She blinked, turning to him with a frown. 'Nothing at the moment. Just something I've seen but can't remember where. It'll come to me.'

'Well until then, grab your keys – we're due at the mortuary within the hour.'

---

# CHAPTER FORTY-SIX

Jan tapped her fingers on the steering wheel while she waited for the traffic to surge across the Headington roundabout the moment the lights turned green, Turpin's voice mere white noise until she heard her name.

'What?'

Then the van behind them honked its horn and she pressed the accelerator, colour rising to her cheeks.

'Sorry, Sarge – I was miles away there.'

'I noticed.' He grinned. 'What's up? Still thinking about Jasper's report?'

'Mm-hmm.' She slowed to turn into the hospital complex and found a parking space close to the mortuary.

Turpin got out, folding up his jacket and leaving it on the back seat. 'If you want another word with him, we could set up a conference call this afternoon. He might have more information for us by then.'

'True.'

She squinted up at the sky as the clouds parted, revealing splotches of blue and a tantalising end to the rain that had plagued the country for the past two weeks. 'Fingers crossed it stays like this for Easter.'

'What have you got planned?' Turpin opened the door to the morgue and followed her inside. 'The boys are off this week, aren't they?'

'It depends.' She gave him a resigned smile. 'If we're not working, then Scott and I were planning on taking them camping for a week down in Dorset. Are the girls staying with you?'

He nodded. 'For a few days. Debbie wants to spend some time with her mum, so I'll go and pick them up from Swindon on Thursday...'

They fell silent as they walked towards Clive's desk, both realising that if they didn't find Sonya and Nolan's killer or killers by then, neither of them would be seeing much of their families.

'Morning, both,' said the pathology assistant, sliding across the visitor log for them to sign. 'Gillian's just prepping, so if you could go and get changed and meet us in there, we'll make a start.'

'I'll see you in there.' Jan walked into the changing room off the corridor and put her bag and jacket into a locker before removing one of the complimentary protective suits from its plastic wrapping. After tying the plastic booties over her shoes, she closed the locker and rested her forehead against it, emitting a deep sigh.

She glanced up at a sharp rap against the door.

'You ready, Jan?'

'Yes.' Scuffing over the worn tiles, she opened the door to see Turpin pacing the corridor. 'Sarge, before we go in – do we know if any of Creasey's other clients were burgled by Sonya?'

He paused, his jaw dropping.

'It's just that, I was thinking,' Jan continued, 'if he found out during the course of one of his counselling sessions that someone was particularly vulnerable, he might've passed on that information to Sonya, mightn't he?'

'Bloody hell,' said Turpin, already pulling out his mobile phone. 'Alex? What are you doing right now? Okay, stop that for a moment. Get Caroline and a couple of uniforms to help you go through all the original burglary files and see if you can find anyone who corresponds with Nolan Creasey's client lists. If his solicitor refuses to hand those over, get a warrant for them. Yes, this is urgent. Thanks.'

Jan moved to the window, staring at the cars outside while Turpin then spoke to Kennedy, who had evidently overheard the conversation and wanted to know what was going on. She glanced over her shoulder at an impatient cough from the end of the corridor to see Gillian peering out, and held up her hand.

'Two seconds,' she said. 'Something urgent came up.'

Gillian gave a slight shake of her head and let the double doors swing shut.

Jan took a step forward as Turpin started to end the call, and took a deep breath. 'Sarge? There's something else—'

'Hang on, guv,' Turpin said to Kennedy, then stared at her. 'What?'

'The carbon and fibreglass splinters Jasper mentioned. When we went to interview one of the burglary victims last week, he had a set of golf clubs in the hallway. His game was cancelled because of the rain.'

'Can you remem—'

'Michael Phillips. The bloke that works for that company in Didcot. His wife has—'

'Guv? We need uniform to go and pick up Michael Phillips. Alex has all the details... No, not an arrest. Not yet. We need to talk to him about his golf clubs though, and— Yes, okay. Thanks, guv.'

Jan exhaled when he ended the call and cocked an eyebrow at her.

'You don't do things by halves, do you, West?' he said, smiling.

'I could be wrong.'

'We'll soon find out.' He wagged a finger at her as they walked towards the examination room. 'You could also be onto something.'

'Well, it's nice of you both to join us at last,' said Gillian, looking up from her work as they entered.

'It's a murder investigation,' said Turpin. 'You know how it is.'

Jan moved closer, taking in the pale form of Nolan Creasey, and grimaced at the puckered wounds that littered his skin. 'How many?'

'He was stabbed a total of nine times,' Gillian said while she ran swabs under the man's fingernails, passing each to Clive to record and seal. 'I ran X-rays on the deepest one here, above his pelvis. The blade scored his hip bone.'

'Jesus.' Turpin hissed through his teeth. 'Is that the one that eventually killed him?'

'No, that's this one here.' Gillian handed the last swab to Clive, then gently rolled Creasey's body onto its side. 'This one pierced a major artery in his neck. Hence the enormous blood loss at the crime scene.'

Settling the victim onto his back once more, she rested her gloved hands on her hips. 'He didn't stand a chance after that, especially given all his other wounds.'

'Any thoughts about the knife used?' said Jan.

The pathologist nodded, beckoning her closer. 'If you look at the wound to his hip, you'll see minute bruising around the rise of the bone. That's where the hilt punched against the skin as it sank in. There's a similar pattern here, just below his ribs.'

'A shorter knife then, not something like a carving knife,' Turpin suggested.

'Exactly, and with a serrated end to it, more like a hunting knife.'

'Caroline managed to get a full inventory of knives in the house from Creasey's father yesterday, and there were none missing from there,' said Jan.

'So your killer took it with him.' Gillian plucked a scalpel from Clive's fingertips.

'Was that neck wound a lucky strike for the killer?' asked Turpin.

'Maybe.' The pathologist's mouth twisted. 'Not for Mr Creasey though. But you have a point – this looks like a frenzied attack to me, fuelled by anger. Look at the way the wounds have been inflicted – there's one to his waist, to his stomach, several to his arms while he was trying to defend himself, and then the final thrust to the neck as he was turning away, I suspect. Whoever did this was determined to make him suffer, and die.'

'He wasn't going to survive,' Jan murmured.

'No, because I don't think your killer was going to stop until he did what he went there to do.'

Turpin stepped away from the table and reached under his gown for his phone.

'Mark, you know my rule about mobile phones in my examination room,' Gillian scolded.

'I know,' he said, already pressing buttons. 'But I need to get a patrol out to Wantage. I'm worried whoever did this to Sonya and Nolan isn't finished yet. We need to make sure Marcus Targethen stays alive until we have a chance to arrest a suspect.'

# CHAPTER FORTY-SEVEN

Mark sniffed the collar of his shirt, then wrinkled his nose.

Despite the protective overalls, despite taking ten minutes to visit the men's locker room and have a shower the moment he and Jan returned to the station, and despite the spray of deodorant he'd squirted over his chest and arms, he was sure the stench from the post mortem lingered.

He had tried the age-old remedy of dabbing vapour rub under his nose before Gillian had revved up her preferred electric saw, but it never failed to amaze him how easily the smell lingered in his nostrils for at least a day.

Sometimes longer.

Sighing, he lifted his chin, adjusted his tie, then turned his back to the mirror and hurried upstairs to the incident room.

Jan was fluffing up her hair, her jacket over the back of her chair, and gave a resigned smile as she dropped a small bottle of perfume into her bag and kicked it under her desk.

'Some things don't change, do they?' she murmured.

'At least we won't repel Michael Phillips before we've even had a chance to ask him a question,' Mark replied. He looked past her to where Caroline was walking towards him. 'Is he downstairs?'

The other detective constable nodded. 'Uniform brought him in twenty minutes ago. Wilcox has him in interview room three, and his solicitor's just arrived.'

'What about Targethen?'

'He was in the pub in the square.' She scowled. 'Already three sheets to the wind, and it was only half eleven. He told the patrol that went in there that he didn't want their help, and that they could sod off.'

'Just as well we got Phillips into custody when we did, then.' Mark extracted his notebook from his backpack, then beckoned to Alex.

'Did you get anything useful from the CCTV footage we obtained for last Tuesday night after speaking to the Tillcotts again?'

'Nothing, Sarge, sorry,' Alex said. 'Mr Tillcott might've seen another vehicle on that lane ahead of them, but we found nothing on camera along that stretch of road. By the time it joins the main Swindon to Oxford road at that time of night…'

'It would've been lost in traffic.' Mark nodded as

Jan tapped her watch. 'Well, let's go and see what Michael Phillips has to say for himself.'

————

'This is outrageous,' fumed Leonard Sparkford, thrusting his business card towards Mark the moment he entered the room. 'My client denies all the charges, and—'

'We need to make this formal,' Mark snapped, handing the card to Jan. 'So hold your horses until we're ready. And take a seat, please.'

Michael Phillips sat with his hands clasped on the rough and worn surface of the table, his Adam's apple bobbing while he watched his solicitor pull out a seat beside him, then turned to face the two detectives.

After starting the recording machine and reading out the caution required for the interview, Mark paused for a moment to gather his thoughts while Sparkford made a show of extracting a fresh legal pad from his briefcase and uncapping an extravagant fountain pen.

'Michael, when Detective West and I spoke to you and Patricia last week about the burglary that took place earlier this year, did you tell the truth about your whereabouts last Tuesday night?'

'I did. Why would I lie?'

'Can you state exactly what your movements were last Tuesday for the record please?'

'I told you. I was at work.' Michael's shoe heel

tapped against the tiled floor as he spoke. 'I left the office just after four. I'd been there since seven forty-five that morning and I had a couple of quotes to do when customers got home from work.'

'Where were those appointments?' Mark said, keeping his eyes on Michael while both the solicitor's fountain pen and Jan's cheaper ballpoint scratched across respective notebooks.

'Um, the first one… yes, that was in Wallingford, completely in the opposite direction to home. From there I stopped at an off-licence on the outskirts of Didcot to pick up a bottle of red for dinner that night, and then I went to my last appointment in Appleford. I left there at seven-thirty, like I told you.' Michael jutted out his chin, a pout on his lips. 'I told you all this last week.'

'Which route did you take home after the Appleford appointment?'

'I went via Steventon, and then picked up the Reading road back to Wantage, then home from there.'

'What time did you get home?'

'A little after eight, I suppose. Patricia will back me up.'

Mark raised his eyebrow at the man's words. 'Did you at any point between four o'clock and eight take a diversion along the lane that goes past Charney Bassett?'

'No, why would I?' Michael twisted in his seat to

face Sparkford. 'I didn't kill that woman. What's her name? Sonya?'

'What evidence do you have to make such a spurious accusation?' the solicitor demanded.

'Tell us about Saturday morning,' Mark said, ignoring the solicitor. 'Where were you?'

'At home, of course.'

'All morning?'

'Well, no. It wasn't too cold and Patricia needed some fresh air so we drove over to Uffington at about ten-thirty, and then had lunch in the pub in Woolstone.'

'Did you take any diversions on the way?'

'No.'

'Was Patricia with you at all times?'

'Yes, of course,' Michael said. 'Why wouldn't she be?'

'Michael, when we visited your house last week, you had a set of golf clubs in your hallway,' said Jan. 'Can you tell us what they're made from?'

The man frowned. 'They're graphite. Why?'

'Any carbon fibre in there?'

'Well, yes – that's how they're made. It's carbon fibre and epoxy resin, I think. When you heat it up, you get the hollow graphite tube. That's what the bloke at the pro shop said anyway.'

'Where do you keep them when they're not in your hallway?' Mark asked.

'Either in the boot of the car or in the garage just inside the door through to the kitchen. Why?'

In reply, Jan slipped a folder out from under her notebook, flipped it open and slid some stapled pages across the table to Sparkford. 'This is a copy of a search warrant currently being served on Mrs Phillips.'

While Sparkford spluttered, Mark turned his attention to Michael. 'We need to take your golf clubs for testing. When Sonya Raynott was murdered last week, it was with a long blunt instrument. She was struck so hard on the back of the head that minute particles of fibreglass, carbon fibre and an epoxy-like substance were embedded in the wound.'

'This is atrocious,' Sparkford exploded, shoving the warrant back across the desk. 'You can't—'

'Leonard, stop.' Michael reached out and placed his hand on the man's arm before looking at Mark. 'Take whatever you need from the house. Just promise me you won't upset Patricia, all right? Something like this could have a catastrophic effect on her health. I don't want police stomping through our house and stressing her out.'

'We already made sure the officers were fully briefed about your wife's circumstances,' said Mark. He watched as the other man relaxed a little in his seat, a sense of foreboding encroaching as the solicitor leaned forward and murmured in his ear.

Michael gave a slight nod, then raised his gaze. 'Leonard advises me I should explain why I'm so sure of my movements last Tuesday.'

'Please do.'

'I didn't go to Appleford to meet with a client.' The man's cheeks coloured. 'I went to see a therapist.'

'A therapist?'

'Yes. I-I get scared sometimes. Frustrated, about Patricia's illness.' Michael swiped sudden tears away with his hand, then sniffed. 'I don't have any close family down this way. My parents are dead, and my sister lives in Chester. We're not close, and sometimes... it all gets too much, to be honest.'

Mark sighed. 'We're going to need your therapist's name and phone number.'

'Sure.' He recited it, and then blinked as Jan shoved back her chair and hurried from the room.

The silence in the room spun out for another two minutes, and then Jan reappeared, her face giving nothing away.

She waited until she'd retaken her seat and shot an apologetic look towards Mark before continuing.

'Thank you, Mr Phillips. Your therapist has confirmed your alibi for last Tuesday night and stated that you didn't leave her consulting rooms until half past seven. Your wife has also corroborated your movements on Saturday morning.'

'I never killed Sonya or whatever her name is,' Michael said, his voice a little stronger. 'I hate her for what she did to Patricia, to us, but murdering her never crossed my mind. I just wanted you to find her and make her pay.'

'I know.' Mark turned to the solicitor. 'Mr

Sparkford, rest assured that no charges will be laid against your client.'

'I've also spoken to the officers at your house,' Jan added. 'None of your property will be removed from the premises, and they've updated your wife to let her know you'll be on your way home soon.'

Michael slumped in his chair. 'Thank you. You won't tell her about the therapist though, will you? I couldn't bear it if she thought I felt she was causing me any... any...'

'It's all right, we won't,' Mark assured him. 'I hope you'll let us move on to another angle of our enquiry that you might be able to help us with, if that's all right?'

The other man nodded. 'What do you need?'

'How long have you been seeing your therapist in Appleford?'

'About four weeks.'

'Were you seeing anyone before that?'

Michael snorted. 'Yeah – and what are the chances? It was that bloke, Nolan Creasey.'

Jan emitted a small squeak before turning it into a bad case of throat clearing while Mark tried to keep his face passive.

'Creasey? Why did you stop going to see him?'

'I had a bad feeling about him, that's all. It started off fine, the sessions, I mean. I found him online in the new year – by then, I knew I had to sort myself out otherwise I'd be of no use to Patricia at all. I had my first appointment with him the second week of January.'

'Why did you get a bad feeling about him?'

'He got too personal.' Michael shook his head as Mark opened his mouth. 'I know, I mean he's supposed to ask me questions, but after the second or third session – I was going once a week on a Tuesday – he started asking how much I made in sales, what I liked to spend my money on. He obviously already knew about family and stuff through our sessions. It's just that... something didn't gel, and I started dreading going there I suppose.'

'Okay, one last thing.' Mark held out his hand for a second folder that Jan had brought back into the room with her. 'These photographs show items of jewellery and other valuables that were seized during a raid on a storage unit last week. We'll need to check the provenance of course, but do you recognise anything here? I don't want to get your hopes up – you were burgled some time ago, and the chances of—'

'Let me see.'

Michael bowed his head while he sifted through the images, turning each one this way and that before pursing his lips or shaking his head and placing it to one side before repeating the exercise.

Jan was starting to collate the discarded photographs when the man emitted a shocked gasp.

'Oh my God.' He choked out a laugh, and then looked up at Mark, tears welling. 'I thought I'd lost these forever.'

Michael turned the photograph around to show a pair of gold cufflinks with a tiny diamond sparkling in one corner of each. He ran a hand over his mouth before speaking again, his fingers shaking.

'My father gave me these the morning of my wedding. He died four years ago, completely out of the blue. He wasn't an easy man, Detective Turpin, but he said the day I married Patricia was the proudest moment of his life. I miss him so much.'

# CHAPTER FORTY-EIGHT

Caroline closed the door to the meeting room on the ground floor with her heel before hefting a pile of manila folders onto the conference table.

'That's a copy of all the statements we've taken since the beginning of the two investigations,' she said to Mark as he and the others eyed the documentation. 'Tracy's sorted them into date order for us, so your burglary ones are first, then the statements relating to the murder enquiries. How do you want to do this, Sarge?'

Mark swallowed, the sheer amount of information overwhelming. 'Jasper's findings about the acrylonitrile is our reference point. If Sonya was killed by something made from a carbon fibre and fibreglass composite, then we need to background check each of the burglary victims we've interviewed to date. Separate out the ones we know correspond to the items recovered from

Targethen's storage unit and start with those. We can use social media to see if they have any interests that involve some sort of carbon fibre-based implement. And knives, obviously.'

He sifted through his notes, checked the number of folders again, then lifted his gaze. 'Jan also suggested that Creasey might've been identifying potential victims for the burglaries via his counselling services.' He cast a glance her way. 'I think you're on the right track, even if Michael Phillips wasn't our suspect.'

He saw some of the tension leave his colleague's face as she swept up two of the folders before taking a seat at the far end of the table and opening her laptop, then rested his hand on the remainder of the pile and turned to Alex.

'How many uniforms are left since this morning's cull?'

'Six, Sarge. Three of them are still working through the items we found in the storage unit that weren't on the recent burglaries list.'

'How much more have they got to get through?'

'About twenty evidence bags – a mixture of women's jewellery, watches and odds and sods.'

'Okay, take half of these and divvy them out amongst the other three. We'll take the rest. If the people we speak to from this other pile are able to provide solid alibis for Saturday as well as last Tuesday, then the next step is to ask if they recognise any valuables from the photographs that we couldn't match to their original statements. At least then we can pass them on to the officers out there to get that backlog cleared.'

Mark risked a glance towards the clock above the door as the other detectives spread around the room and settled in to the task.

In another few hours, it would be two weeks since someone murdered Sonya Raynott.

With every passing moment, the investigation lost momentum, memories became faded, and details were lost.

He shook himself from his reverie, dropped into a chair at the far end and started reading.

The next hour passed with occasional bursts of hope followed by frustrated swearing and a growing pile of folders in the middle of the table.

These were the cases where no connection could be made, where alibis had already been double-checked, and where social media showed the person had no interest in any activities involving a carbon fibre-based implement.

Only two possibilities had been slid across the table to him so far, a man in his eighties who had some old snooker trophies stolen and still kept his cues in his garage for his grandsons to play with, and an insurance broker south of Wantage whose social media showed a healthy passion for tennis.

'Snooker cues are wooden,' Mark said, flicking through the paperwork during the next break.

Caroline looked up from her laptop screen. 'I know. I figured it's worth asking him if we don't—'

There was a sharp rap on the door, and then Alice Fields peered inside. 'Sorry. Can I have a word, Sarge?'

'Come on in.'

The young constable held one of the evidence bags, her face flushed. 'I found this at the bottom of the box I was working through.'

Mark took the bag from her, angling it to see the contents.

Inside was a delicate silver hoop, intricately engraved with tiny animals and ivy.

'What is it, one of a pair of large earrings or something?'

'Looks too big for that,' Alex remarked.

'It's a christening bracelet. Check out the inscription on the inside of it,' said Alice, handing Mark a spare pair of protective gloves. 'It was in the storage unit, but it wasn't on the original list of valuables we collated from the statements.'

He bit back a sigh of frustration, wondering whether if uniform had had more manpower to investigate the original burglaries properly, the outcome might have been different.

Slipping on the gloves, he pulled out the bracelet and squinted at the tiny writing. '"Emma, with love from grandpa and grandma."' A chill wrinkled its way up his spine and across his shoulders.

'What is it, Sarge?' said Jan. 'You've gone pale.'

He held up the bracelet. 'Sally Fernsby's daughter was called Emma. The one I told you about who died when she was two years old.'

'Well, we can return it to her now – that's good, isn't it?'

Mark closed his eyes for a moment, then eyed his team. 'When we first spoke to Sally last week, we asked her what her movements were on Tuesday. She said her mum stayed over and they were watching a film together because her dad had gone on a fishing trip.'

'Shit.' Jan was already pushing back her chair. 'He'll have fishing rods. Carbon fibre.'

'Exactly,' said Mark. 'And he'll have knives.'

# CHAPTER FORTY-NINE

'Anything?'

Mark gripped the steering wheel as the car slewed through a bend before stomping his foot on the accelerator, his jaw clenched.

'Nothing here.' Jan scrolled through her phone in one hand while she gripped the strap above the car window with the other. 'Her mum's got her social media profile set to private so I can't see anything. The photos that show up don't help.'

'What about her dad?'

'Again, all set to private.'

'We're five minutes out from Sally's place.' Mark checked his mirrors. 'Where's the fucking back-up we requested?'

'Meeting us there. Two patrols from Didcot.'

'What about the locals?'

Jan gave a bitter chuckle. 'Four on shift today,

including a community officer. They're not available –
one's doing a school talk, two are currently interviewing
someone about a shoplifting incident in the Wantage
supermarket, and the other's checking out a complaint
about a man acting strangely down by the river. Possibly
suicidal.'

'Shit.' Mark smacked his palm against the steering
wheel as a tractor bumbled towards them and he had to
pull over to let it pass.

The moment it did, he took off again, haring across
the junction with the main road before tearing through
the narrow lanes.

When he brought the car to a standstill outside Sally
Fernsby's end-of-terrace house, Jan paused with her
hand on the car roof.

'Sarge, no disrespect meant, but perhaps take a
breath before storming in there. She might not know
anything.'

'She knows something,' he said, slamming shut the
car door and leading the way towards the cottage.

The sound of a child bawling carried through the
downstairs window, and he exhaled.

Whatever happened next could tear apart an entire
family, and right at that moment he hated himself
for it.

Sally opened the door a few moments after he'd
knocked, her face flushed. 'Oh. What's going on?'

'Can we come in for a moment, Mrs Fernsby?' Mark
said, already putting his shoe between the step and the

open door, his hand against the uPVC surface. 'We have a few more questions.'

The twenty-something glanced over her shoulder at another cry. 'Do we have to do this now? Charlotte's off school today – she's got an ear infection, and I'm—'

'Please.' Mark cocked an eyebrow.

Jan moved closer. 'Mrs Fernsby, I can sit with Charlotte while you speak with Detective Turpin, if that helps?'

Sally's eyes shifted from Mark to Jan, then back. She sighed, and thrust the door open wide. 'All right.'

After Jan disappeared through to the living room, her voice cooing to the sick girl, Mark jerked his head towards the kitchen. 'Shall we?'

'I don't know what else I can tell you,' said Sally, her shoulders slumped with exhaustion. She tied back straggly hair with a pink-coloured elastic and sank into one of the chairs beside the kitchen table. 'You know everything.'

Mark pulled out a chair beside her, and watched her automatically reach out and tidy away scattered colouring pens, bills and letters, pushing everything to the far side of the table.

When she turned back to him, he extracted the evidence bag with the bracelet and placed it on the table between them.

'Do you recognise this?' he said.

She paled, then reached out for the bag and slid it closer, her eyes reddening. 'It's Emma's.'

'Are you sure?'

'Yes. There's an inscription on the inside. My dad bought it for her christening.'

Mark nodded, satisfied.

'Where did you find it?' Sally asked, tearing her eyes away for a moment.

He noticed how she kept her hand on top of the bag, as if she were afraid that he'd take it away again.

'It was found in a storage unit belonging to a man we arrested last week in connection to the burglaries.'

'I thought I'd lost it forever.' She sniffed, smiling through her tears. 'Dad was even more upset, especially because it was one of the few memories we shared of Emma. He doted on her, you know. I knew he'd have spoiled her rotten if she'd... if she'd lived...'

'It was a lucky find,' Mark admitted. 'It wasn't on the original list of stolen items our colleagues took from you after you were burgled.'

Sally wiped at her eyes with her sleeve. 'I was in such a state when they turned up. I thought I'd told him – the policeman who turned up – about everything that was taken. Mind you, I started doubting myself for days afterwards, wondering if I should've realised I was being conned, wondering what would've happened if Mum or Dad were round here when she – that woman – knocked on the door. I only managed to pull myself together because of Charlotte.'

'When did you find out that this bracelet had been taken as well?'

'About a week after the burglary. I kept it in the bottom drawer of my bedside table. It was in a small red box and always got pushed to the back under other things. I was looking for something else – an old diary from a few years ago because I wanted the address for a friend who moved to Ireland. I didn't have her phone number anymore, you see, and that's when I realised they'd taken this as well. I phoned the number the policeman gave me to tell them.'

Mark bit back a curse, realising the message had been lost in the system, and why the bracelet had never appeared on the list.

If it hadn't been for Alice's attention to detail…

'I hated them for taking it. Dad was livid when I told him.' Sally's fingers tweaked at the plastic bag. 'Can I open this?'

'Yes, by all means. We've swabbed it for fingerprints, so there's no problem.'

She gave him a watery smile, then unzipped it.

Mark watched while she held up the bracelet to the light in shaking fingers, Jan's voice carrying through to them from the living room as a giggle burst from Charlotte.

Then he took a deep breath.

'Sally, did you tell your dad that you followed Sonya Raynott?'

# CHAPTER FIFTY

Greg and Maureen Fernsby's house lay at the far end of a tidy cul-de-sac on the fringes of Wantage, accessed through a convoluted set of mini roundabouts and short twisting narrow roads.

Squashed between a matching set of two identical homes, it boasted one of the smallest front gardens Mark had ever seen – and an empty driveway in front of a tiny garage.

'Shit. Did she warn him?'

Jan held up her phone. 'Carl Antsy says not – he's been with her since we left.'

Mark found an empty space behind a neighbour's car, saw one of the patrol cars approach the corner into the dead-end street, and turned his attention back to the house. 'Let's not hang around, just in case.'

After fetching a stab vest from the back seat and

handing another to his colleague, he strode up the short path and beat his fist against the front door.

He ran his hand down the velcro fastenings for the vest, trying to ignore the sickness that threatened to overwhelm him.

He'd been stabbed before, and was lucky to have survived that attack.

The front door edged open, and a woman in her sixties glared at him.

'Mrs Fernsby? Mrs Maureen Fernsby?'

'What do you want?'

Mark held up his warrant card. 'Where's your husband Greg?'

'He's… he's out at the moment. What's going on?'

He didn't respond, and instead glanced over his shoulder to the four uniformed officers who hovered at the end of the path and signalled to them. 'Check the back garden. I saw a gate around the side.'

Three of them peeled away, the remaining officer standing on the pavement in case Sally's father reappeared.

Turning back to Maureen, Mark kept his face passive. 'Can we come in, Mrs Fernsby? We've got some questions we'd like to ask you regarding two murders we're currently investigating.'

'What's that got to do with us?'

'Please, could we do this inside?' He placed his hand on the door, and it gave way under his touch as she took a step back, bewilderment in her eyes.

The hallway walls were strewn with family photographs amongst watercolour paintings of bucolic scenes depicting rivers and streams, and as he followed her towards a door to his left, he paused.

'Is this Emma?' He pointed to an amateurish photograph taken in a back garden, a backdrop comprising a fence and tomato plants behind Sally and the small baby she cradled.

Maureen gave a small nod. 'Three months before she was first diagnosed,' she said, her voice quivering. 'Nothing was quite the same after that.'

Her words punched him in the gut, and he traipsed silently into a living room with a high ceiling that offset its box-like size.

Two armchairs and a small sofa were placed around a glass-topped coffee table, and as Maureen eased into the far end of the sofa, she seemed to shrink under his gaze.

He heard footsteps behind him, a deep baritone voice murmuring to Jan, and then she was at his side.

'He's not here.'

Mark's eyes narrowed as he turned his attention to Sally's mother. 'Where's Greg?'

'He said he was going fishing. It's what he usually does on a Tuesday.'

'Do you know where?'

'If he's not at the fishery, then he'll be somewhere along the Thames up near Shifford – he likes it there. He was hoping to catch some bream.' She frowned.

'Why do you want to speak to Greg? What's this about?'

Mark waited until Jan sped from the room, her phone to her ear. 'Mrs Fernsby, I need to ask you some questions, and due to the nature of them I have to make this formal.'

Maureen paled when he cautioned her, and sat back with her mouth open.

'I want to take you back to two weeks ago. Did you visit Sally?'

She blinked, then nodded. 'I did, yes.'

'Why was that?'

'Greg said he wanted to go on a night fish – he hadn't done that for a while – and suggested I stay with Sally. It'd been a few weeks since I'd spent any proper time with her because I've been so busy with work.'

'Where do you work?'

'I'm part-time at one of the solicitor's offices here in Wantage.' She gave a tired shrug. 'Greg retired a few years ago but with the state of my pension I couldn't afford to, so I'm going to keep going as long as I can.'

'Did you go on your own to Sally's two weeks ago?'

'Yes – there's a bus route twice a day that gets me to the end of her road. It's only a half-mile walk after that.'

'What time did you leave?'

'After work, so I went straight from there. It must've been about five-thirty because I finish at five and had to wait around for the bus.'

'What time did Greg say he was going fishing?'

'He usually leaves here at half-three if he's going to Shifford. Sometimes he'll catch enough to come home early, other times he might be out until one, two o'clock in the morning.'

'What did you do the next morning?'

'I went straight from Sally's into work.' Maureen clasped her hands over her knee. 'Look, are you going to tell me what's going on?'

'I will, bear with me. When you came home that Wednesday afternoon, was Greg acting strangely in any way?'

'What do you mean?'

'Did he seem troubled, or unhappy about anything?'

'No, not at all. In fact, he was in a really good mood – he even bought me flowers.' She smiled, and then it quickly faded away again. 'He hasn't done that since Emma died. He even forgot our anniversary last year. Thirty years…'

'About Emma's passing – did either of you seek counselling to help you through your grief?'

Maureen's gaze slipped to the carpet, and he noticed how she dug her nails into her palms. 'I made him go. I was worried. Scared, in fact.'

'Greg didn't cope well?'

'None of us did, but he took it especially hard. He loved her so much.' She sighed. 'He obviously loves Charlotte too, but she's such a different character to

Emma – boisterous, whereas Emma was gentle, happy to play quietly. She'd crawl across the carpet here making a beeline for him whenever Sally brought her round.'

'Who was his counsellor?'

'Some chap over in Abingdon. I found him on social media. I didn't want us to use someone too local because people gossip, you know? I mean, I know the counsellor wouldn't but I didn't want people to see us walking in or out of his office.'

'Did Sally know about it?'

'God, no – of course not. She was getting a lot of help from her GP surgery, and us. It helped us, talking to a stranger who didn't make assumptions.'

'Going back to the Wednesday after you'd stayed at Sally's – Greg had been fishing you say, so what happened to the clothes he was wearing that night?'

She looked perplexed. 'Like I said, he was in a good mood when I got home, and he'd bought me a lovely bouquet of chrysanthemums. I asked him what he'd managed to catch, and he said just the one trout…'

'A bit strange, given he was out all night. Weren't the fish jumping?'

'That's what I said,' Maureen replied. 'But his clothes… they were folded up on the counter in the kitchen. They were the same as I'd seen him in on Tuesday morning – an old jumper and a pair of jeans he keeps for fishing, and I said to him he'd better not stink out the house. That's when he said he'd already washed them.'

'Was that out of character for him?'

'I suppose so, yes. I mean he'll pop in a load every now and again but I usually do a wash on Wednesdays. I normally stick a load in before I leave for work.'

'Where are his jeans and shirt right now? The ones you saw him wearing that Tuesday before he went fishing?'

'In the bedroom drawers, I expect. He was wearing his other old clothes when he left earlier – he has two lots for fishing. Unless he's put the shirt he wears underneath in the ironing cupboard. I don't usually do the ironing until the second wash is done on Saturdays, you see, because he likes to go fishing on Tuesday afternoons and Saturday mornings. It means I can get all the blood and fish guts out of the material straight away. I mean, sometimes I have to use hydrogen peroxide but then I...'

Mark was already out the door and halfway up the stairs before she finished speaking.

Pulling protective gloves from his trouser pocket, he quickly found the master bedroom with a fitted wardrobe against the outer wall, then saw the chest of drawers behind the door.

He found Greg Fernsby's old sweatshirt and jeans folded up in the bottom drawer, and tentatively held each to his nose.

There was a faint smell, underneath the distinct

aroma of the same washing pods he and Lucy used, and when he looked closer he could see several thumb-sized stains on the hem of the sweatshirt.

It seemed that Greg Fernsby wasn't as efficient at removing stains as his wife was.

Feet thundered up the stairs behind him, and Jan appeared holding an evidence bag.

'Figured you'd need this,' she said, shaking it open while he slipped the clothing inside. 'And I've spoken to Kennedy. He authorised the paperwork for the search here ten minutes ago and for the arrest of Greg Fernsby – if we can find him. There was a patrol about a mile away from the reservoir when he got on to Force Control, and they're on their way now.'

'Okay, let's go. We'll get one of the uniform patrols to stay with Mrs Fernsby and take a formal statement from her while they're waiting for Jasper's lot to arrive. We need the house and garage searched.'

When Mark reached the doorstep, PC John Newton lowered his radio.

'There's been no one reported matching Mr Fernsby's description or his car at the reservoir, Sarge. He must be at Shifford.'

'Same as he said he was two weeks ago when he killed Sonya,' Mark replied.

Jan tossed the car keys from hand to hand. 'Are you sure?'

'Well, Fernsby was definitely lying about night fishing there.' Newton tucked his radio back in his vest.

'It's not allowed along that stretch of the Thames – I've just checked.'

'Nice one, constable.' Mark held up his phone so Jan could see the maps app while he found the location. 'That explains how he knew about the lane going past Charney Bassett. It's a direct route to his favourite fishing spot.'

# CHAPTER FIFTY-ONE

Mark slammed on the brakes, his seatbelt etching a tide mark across his shoulders and chest before he eyed the small wooden hut at the end of the private road.

A red-tiled cottage stood behind it, a pretty rambling rose covering the roofs of both, with an information board and a life buoy outside the hut's open door.

A Thames Valley-liveried patrol car was already parked in front of the barrier, and he saw a uniformed sergeant speaking to a group of walkers farther along the tow path.

He climbed out, eyeing the compact two-berth cabin cruiser and its pilot waiting patiently in the lock while water gushed between the paddles, lowering the level.

Wandering over, he beckoned to the man and kept his voice as low as possible over the roar of water.

'Don't open the gates until I tell you, all right? We might have a situation here.'

The man swallowed. 'Okay.'

'Stay inside the cabin for your own safety, and don't move.'

Satisfied, Mark spun back to the car and followed Jan towards the lock-keeper, who was staring at PC Ian Knowles with a mixture of confusion and fear.

'Sarge, Mr Dunham here says Greg Fernsby's upstream, about quarter of a mile from the lock,' said the constable.

'It's his favourite spot. Swears by it for a good catch,' said Dunham. 'He'll be on or near the weir walkway.'

'You haven't seen him walk past here?'

'Not in the past twenty minutes, no. His car's parked on the other side of the cottage.'

'Are there any other exits for him?'

'Only the footpath from the weir along to the next hamlet.'

'Right, well as I've told that bloke in the boat, stay here until we tell you otherwise,' said Mark. 'Don't whatever you do poke your head out the door to see what's going on.'

Dunham nodded, edging back behind the low wooden counter. 'I'll be right here.'

'Jan, Ian, with me.'

Mark took off, pausing briefly to make sure Sergeant Peter Crosley kept the walkers corralled within the grassy expanse behind the cottage, and then turned his attention to the weir farther upstream.

Overgrown grass smacked against his trouser legs leaving wet stripes across the hems while a moorhen dashed from between bullrushes and paddled its way across to the other bank, startled by their sudden presence.

Mark didn't slow his pace, despite wondering for a fleeting moment whether he should have waited, should have got more back-up, should have…

He shook the thoughts away.

It was too late now.

As he got nearer, Jan and Ian's footsteps close behind him, he could see the water gushing through the metal gates, churning the river. A bridge crossed the water here, and beyond that a hunched figure was huddled on a fold-out camping chair, his face shadowed by the baseball cap pulled low over his eyes.

A fishing rod was clasped in his grip, the line cast out to the middle of the river and tugging slightly from the weir's flow.

Slowing, Mark held up his hand. 'Jan, stay here and make sure no one tries to cross the bridge. Ian, follow me but wait on the other side of the bridge when we get there. I don't want to crowd him in case he panics.'

He heard muted responses, then set off once more.

When he reached the other side of the river, the fisherman didn't look up to acknowledge his presence, but leaned forward and fastened the rod to a wooden stake driven into the ground.

'Greg? Greg Fernsby?' Mark slowed his pace and edged forward. 'My name's Detective Mark Turpin.'

He got within ten paces of the man before Fernsby reared from his chair holding a gleaming fishing knife in his hand.

The blade flashed against his dark clothing as he brought it up to his face and then placed it against his exposed neck.

'Don't come any closer, or I'll cut myself.'

Mark froze.

If Fernsby sliced his carotid artery, he wouldn't be able to save him.

He'd have seconds to reach him, seconds to stem the bleeding, and there probably wasn't an ambulance within a five-mile radius – if that.

'Greg, please. Put the knife down.'

'I was helping, you know. No one else was doing anything to find them. Sally did…'

'She's a smart woman, your daughter.'

Fernsby closed his eyes, and Mark watched as the knife shifted.

'Greg, I need you to put down the knife.'

'No.' The man's eyes flashed open, the blade straightening. 'I can't.'

'You can. I'm not going to hurt you. I'd like to talk. Would that be okay?'

'They took my Emma's bracelet. She was so lovely.' Fernsby's face crumpled. 'I miss her so much.'

'Greg, listen to me.' Mark risked another step

closer. He could almost touch the man. 'You have a loving wife, a smart daughter and a gorgeous granddaughter. Charlotte. They're worried about you, Greg. They need to know you're safe, that you're all right.'

'I didn't mean to do it.'

Mark heard it then, the slight shift in the man's voice, the hesitation as he repositioned the blade. 'Drop the knife, and we'll have a chat. How does that sound?'

His heartbeat rushed in his ears while he watched the man's eyes, fully aware that if Fernsby went for him, the stab vest would be of no use at all if he slashed out at his arm or his face.

'Greg, please. Think of Charlotte. Don't let her grow up without a grandfather.'

Fernsby's lip trembled, his eyes watering.

Then the knife slipped from his grasp, falling into the long grass at their feet, and Mark lunged at him.

'Sarge!'

Ian sprinted from the bridge, tearing across the embankment before helping him handcuff Fernsby and dragging him to his feet.

'Greg Fernsby, I'm arresting you on suspicion for the murders of Sonya Raynott and Nolan Creasey. You do not…'

Ian's words faded as he led the man back towards the bridge and away to the waiting patrol car.

Mark stood on shaking legs, brushed off the damp grass clinging to his trousers and straightened to see Jan on the footpath, arms crossed while she glared at him. 'What?'

'You could've been stabbed. Again.' She marched across the grass to join him. 'Honestly, Sarge – we should've waited for more back-up.'

'I don't think so.' He squinted against the fading sun as Ian reached the cars farther downstream. 'I think he would've hurt himself eventually if we hadn't been here to stop him.'

Jan sighed in response, and turned her attention to the fishing tackle. 'Mark, look. In the bag.'

She pulled gloves over her fingers, reached into the olive-coloured canvas bag beside the camping chair and held up the broken end of a fishing rod.

Hissing through his teeth, Mark saw the jagged edge and the tiny woven fibres protruding from it.

'Here,' he said, extracting a glove from his pocket and putting it over the rod. 'I'll give Jasper a call and get him to send over some of his team to process this lot. They'll need to check his car for any traces of Sonya's DNA as well.'

'I'll bag the knife while you're doing that.'

The CSI lead answered within a single ring. 'I was about to call you. Everything all right?'

Mark glanced over his shoulder as Greg Fernsby was guided into the back of Ian's patrol car, his hands cuffed behind his back. 'It is now. We've got something for you here though. What did you want me for?'

'While she was giving her statement to Carl Antsy,

Maureen said she smelled a chemical sort of burning a couple of weeks ago when she got home on the Wednesday. Apparently, Greg told her that one of the neighbours had been doing something over the road…'

'I sense a "but".'

'You'd be right. It's obviously rained since then but after we searched the back garden, we found the remains of a small fire close to the rear border and melted pieces of a driving licence. We've got some bits of debit card as well.'

Mark gripped the phone tighter. 'And?'

'It's hers,' said Jasper. 'Sonya's. We found remains of a credit card in Marie Allenton's name too, the alias she was using.'

Mark thanked him, ended the call and then watched to see the patrol car driving out through the lock-keeper's gate, blue lights flaring before it disappeared from view.

'Got you,' he murmured.

# CHAPTER FIFTY-TWO

By the time Mark and Jan walked into the interview room, a cool evening had enveloped the town and the rush hour commute had ended hours ago.

Greg Fernsby was sitting at the table, his sweatshirt, jeans and underwear bagged and being processed by Jasper's team while he huddled in a set of protective overalls, his eyes downcast.

His chipped fingernails were scrubbed and clean now, having been swabbed upon arrival at the station and before he'd been allowed to confer with the duty solicitor appointed to him.

That solicitor now slid a card across the table to Mark, and tried to find a comfortable angle for his spine against the hard plastic chair. 'William Hawsey – Hawsey and Wainwright Solicitors. I'll be representing Mr Fernsby for the purposes of this interview.'

Mark nodded in response, waiting until Jan pressed the "record" button on the equipment.

'I need to speak to my wife,' said Fernsby, lifting his gaze for the first time.

'Not yet.' Mark opened a file, spacing out a series of photographs on the table in front of him. 'Tell us about Sonya Raynott, or Marie Allenton as she was also known.'

'What about her?'

'Why kill her, Greg? If you suspected her, why didn't you tell us?'

'I tried!' Fernsby slammed his fist on the table.

Jan jumped in her seat, then cleared her throat and picked up her pen once more.

'When?' Mark said, unflustered by the man's response. 'Certainly not since I've been speaking to Sally about the burglary, and there's nothing on file.'

'Of course there isn't. Bloody typical.' Fernsby threw up his hands in disgust. 'I phoned up. I left a message with a woman back in February. She told me she wasn't sure who was dealing with Sally's case but that she'd find out and pass it on.'

Mark bit back his frustration, wondering how many more tip-offs and updates had been lost to junior or temporary staff passing through the station in the past year.

'Did you follow it up?'

'No. I figured you weren't going to do anything about it, and yet I was hearing about all these other burglaries in the area. I was worried that it'd happen again, and with Sally on her own in that house with a little 'un...' He shivered. 'You hear all the time that if people are burgled once, they're more likely to get burgled again. I had to do something.'

'You murdered Sonya, and left her body on the side of the road.'

Fernsby picked at a loose thread on the sleeve of the overalls. 'I didn't mean to.'

'I find that hard to believe,' Mark said, slipping across images from the crime scene. 'If anything, you planned this from the start. Including telling your wife and daughter that you were going night fishing that Tuesday, to give yourself time to clean up afterwards.'

'It wasn't meant to happen like that. It was an accident.'

'An accident?' Mark saw the same incredulous look on Jan's face that he was sure he wore. 'How did this "accident" occur?'

'I just wanted the christening bracelet back, that's all. Emma meant everything to us, to me. She was such a sweetheart. I... I knew Sally kept that bracelet hidden away. She couldn't bear to look at it after Emma died, but she knew how much it meant to me. When she told me it'd been stolen, I suppose I saw red. I mean, they took a laptop from her too but who cares about that? You can pick them up second-hand these days, can't you? They're replaceable.'

Mark remained silent, watching the man chew his lip before continuing.

'Me and Maureen were round at Sally's in March, and when her mum was busy with Charlotte and out of earshot, she told me she thought she'd seen the woman who'd conned her way into her house. I asked her where, and she said in an optician's in Wantage. Got her name and everything.'

'Sally didn't tell us she overheard her name when we interviewed her,' Mark said.

'Maybe she thought it wouldn't do any good.' A sad smile reached Greg's eyes. 'She told me about the alleyway too, so the next time we were in Wantage I had a wander along there while Maureen was having her hair done. I found the second-hand shop at the end. It wasn't hard to put two and two together after that. The bitch was stealing stuff with whoever she was working with, and then flogging it to that toe-rag.'

'Did you go in the shop?'

'No. I saw him step outside with another bloke. I pretended to be looking at something in that haberdasher's that's nearer the square, but they looked like they were mates.' Fernsby's gaze dropped to his hands. 'I'm not a big bloke, and I didn't fancy my chances with those two.'

'It's now April, Greg. You had plenty of time to come in and see us, even if you didn't get a response to your original message,' said Jan. 'Why didn't you?'

'I dunno. 'Spose by then, it was too late. I knew

what I had to do. I had to find her, and find out what she'd done with that bracelet.' He looked up, eyes hardening. 'And I wanted her to get it back. I mean, even if that shop owner had sold it, she could steal it again, couldn't she?'

'So, what did you do after that?'

'I started following her. It was hard at first – I didn't know where she lived, and even though Sally overheard her name in the opticians, I couldn't find her online, only a dead woman in her late fifties with the same name. So I started keeping an eye on the shop. I figured it wouldn't be long before she turned up again. I picked a different place to watch the alleyway from every day – I told Maureen I was going out for a walk, that I wanted to get a bit of exercise because I was putting on too much weight. She's been nagging me since Christmas about it, so that kept her happy…'

He drifted off, stretching out his legs before continuing. 'It took a couple of weeks, but sure enough she turned up at the end of March, bold as you like with a bag over her shoulder. It looked heavy the way she was carrying it, but by the time she left, she didn't have it anymore. I followed her to that car park near the square and got a look at her car as she drove out – she didn't even look at me. Next time, I made sure I parked in the same place as her.'

'When was that?'

'Two weeks ago. I kept an eye on the local news sites for reports about burglaries in the area that weekend, and the shop doesn't open on Mondays. That way, I had a pretty good chance of knowing when she'd go back there to flog what she'd nicked.'

'You're a patient man, Mr Fernsby,' said Mark.

'You need to be patient when you're fishing.'

'What did you do?'

'I was right, there was another burglary like Sally's that weekend. A woman conned a bloke over near Challow to let her in, and while he wasn't looking she stole some medals and a pocket watch. As soon as I saw that on the Monday, I told Maureen I fancied a bit of night fishing the following day.'

Mark cast his eyes down the timeline in his notes. 'For the purposes of the recording, can you confirm that that was on the Tuesday, two weeks ago?'

'It was.'

'What happened?'

'I waited until I knew Maureen would be at work, then drove to the same car park she – Marie, Sonya, whatever her name was – used the last time I saw her.'

'What time was that?'

'About half ten.' Fernsby shuffled forward in his seat. 'She was already there, her car was, I mean. I'd driven in thinking I'd better have a look around in case she was already there, and I saw her getting out of her car as I came around the corner. I braked and waited while she walked off. When I got out, I noticed there weren't any cameras pointing in my direction.'

He paused, shaking his head in wonder. 'Clever,

see? Means you lot couldn't prove she was ever there or see what she was carrying. It was further from the ticket machine and from the exit to the shops, so no one else was parking there. That's how I got a spot right next to her car.'

Trying to ignore his heart rate increasing, Mark took a deep breath. 'What did you do to her, Greg?'

'I followed her to the alleyway. Sure enough, she went into the shop.' Fernsby blinked. 'I hurried back to the car park and slashed her tyres. The ones nearest my car so she wouldn't see they were flat when she came back. Then I waited near the fire exit until she came back.'

He choked out a bitter laugh. 'The bitch had a smile like the Cheshire Cat when she appeared, striding towards her car like she'd won the fucking lottery, swinging the bag because it was lighter than before. You should've seen her face when she unlocked it and then saw the flat tyres. It was a picture, I tell you. I gave her a few minutes to stew – I could see her looking around, debating whether to call someone or wander off and ask for help, so that's when I walked over. I asked if there was a problem, and said I could help after she showed me the tyres. I told her I had a tool kit in the boot of my car…'

Mark held his breath, knowing what would come next.

'Look at me,' Fernsby said, spreading his hands. 'I look harmless, don't I?'

'What did you do, Greg?'

'I'd already managed to break one of my rods in two – I always keep a pair, and my fishing gear's always in the car anyway. I told her the jack was under the carpet and pretended to be looking at the rear tyre on her car while she opened the boot and started rummaging around. Then I hit her. I only meant to knock her out. I only wanted to take her somewhere and ask her what she'd done with Emma's bracelet. I wanted to know who had it now. I don't know... I panicked, I suppose. Especially when I saw her eye hanging out like that.' Fernsby swallowed. 'I managed to get the back seats lowered and bundle her inside. There was blood... over my sweatshirt. I locked her car, tossed the keys away, and drove out. I just... I just kept driving. I ended up near the Ridgeway for a bit, a quiet spot away from everything, and thought I'd be better off ending it all right then. But I still didn't have the bracelet, did I?'

He ran a hand over tired eyes. 'I waited until it was getting dark, and then I thought I'd better go fishing... after all, that's where Maureen expected me to be, and I didn't want her panicking. I-I tipped out her... her body on the way. I found some ID stuff in her jacket pocket but I never got a chance to go through her bag. It fell off her shoulder when I was trying to get her out of the car, and then I heard someone coming and I panicked so I drove off. I got to Shifford and managed to park the car around the back of the cottage away from the lock so Dunham didn't see me arrive, and went and fished until about eleven, I suppose. He saw me on the way back and waved, I remember that. I waved back, then got in my car and went home. It took me ages to get the blood out of my clothes. I didn't get to bed until two in the morning…'

'Why didn't you destroy your fishing rod, same as you tried to do with the debit cards and her driving licence?'

'I tried,' Fernsby mumbled. 'Fucking thing wouldn't burn so I put it in my bag. I didn't want Maureen to find it, and I knew I couldn't just put it in the rubbish bin outside. I was meaning to dump it but when I saw it in there today, I… all I could see was her face, her eye…'

'You deliberately killed Sonya Raynott.'

'No. I didn't want that. I wanted answers, and I wanted Emma's christening bracelet back.'

'But you didn't ask her, did you?' Mark insisted. 'You didn't give her a chance to explain. Instead, you killed her, and then dumped her body before you went fishing to give yourself an alibi, and then you drove home and tried to hide the evidence. We found the burned credit cards and driving licences, Greg. All of it. Those swabs that were taken prior to your interview are now being matched against the broken fishing rod found in your tackle bag, which in turn is being analysed to see if it matches the traces of carbon and glass fibre found in the wound to Sonya's head along with the blood samples taken from the rod. We're also processing your car for any traces of DNA. You didn't want answers from her,' he snarled. 'You wanted to kill her.'

Fernsby looked away, his jaw clenched.

'I think it prudent that my client be allowed a short break,' said Hawsey. 'And I'd like a word with him in private.'

Mark waited until Jan had paused the tape, then glared at both men. 'You've got ten minutes.'

# CHAPTER FIFTY-THREE

Ewan Kennedy was pacing the corridor when Mark and Jan stepped outside the interview room, his face grim.

'Well?' he said.

'He's admitted to killing Sonya Raynott, saying he didn't mean to,' Mark replied. 'He's trying to claim he only meant to knock her out so he could ask her where the damn bracelet was.'

'What do you think?'

'I think he saw red when he realised she enjoyed what she was doing. The fact that he went there having already broken that fishing rod with the intent to use it to hit her with says a lot.'

'Then there's the fact he didn't panic or try to revive her, or call an ambulance.' Jan shivered. 'To just calmly put her in the back of his car and drive around until it was dark enough to dump her body... that's cold.'

Kennedy held out his hand, and she passed across

her notebook. Skimming her handwriting, he pursed his lips. 'I'll listen to the tape later before we speak to the CPS. This business about the car park – I'll ask Caroline to get on to the council in the morning and get hold of the CCTV recordings, just in case they have picked up something. Even if it's Fernsby leaving there on the Tuesday morning, it supports what we've got already.'

'We'll need someone to go over and take another statement from the lock-keeper at Shifford as well, guv,' said Mark. 'Just to corroborate the timings.'

'No problem. Alex can head over there now.' Kennedy handed back the notebook. 'Have you got enough time in hand to continue the interview?'

'Plenty. He's talking, so that helps. Although I'm not sure whether he's feeling any remorse for his actions.'

'Mark's right, guv.' Jan glanced over her shoulder towards the closed door. 'I don't think he feels anything, to be honest.'

Kennedy grunted, then turned and started to walk away. 'Best get back in there, then. There's still another murder to solve.'

———

'Let's talk about Nolan Creasey.'

There was a palpable tension to the interview room when they entered, Mark waiting until Jan restarted the recording before speaking.

William Hawsey seemed to have created a few more

inches of distance between himself and his client, and Greg Fernsby appeared to have shrunk within the protective overalls in the past ten minutes.

He nervously nibbled at his thumbnail before spitting the filings to the floor, ignoring the glare that Mark shot at him and looking away.

'Is Creasey the counsellor you and your wife went to see after Emma died?'

'Bastard.'

'You'll need to answer yes or no for the purposes of the recording.'

'Yes.'

'When was that?'

'October, November last year perhaps. Can't remember. Maureen organised it. Said she thought it would help.' Fernsby gave a bitter snort. 'Fat lot of help he turned out to be.'

'Did you tell Creasey about Sally?'

'Yes.' He lifted his chin. 'Not at first though. Maybe after we'd been there three or four times.'

'Is that how he found out where she lived?'

''Spose so.'

'What made you suspect him?'

'Just a feeling I had. I wasn't sure, not until Maureen showed me that post on social media last week. When I found the original news story online, I realised his so-called "accomplice" was that bitch. Sonya, Marie – whatever she was calling herself. Had to be – that's how they were targeting some of their burglaries, wasn't it? He was passing on information to her, and then helping her to con people. And you lot let him go.'

'So you decided to go to his house and kill him, is that it? How did you find out where he lived?'

'Because I knew where his office was. I spoke to one of the people who owns a business in the courtyard there late Friday, and they said he'd cleared out but left some of his stuff behind. I figured he'd come back for it, and I was right. There was a rental van parked outside it on Saturday morning. Besides, there was a journalist hanging around too with a cameraman. They were taking pictures while he was trying to load stuff into the van. He shouted at them. I waited until he drove off, and followed. Once I knew where his house was, I parked down the road from it and walked back. Of course, he recognised me when he opened the door, but I was ready for that.'

'He was released on licence, Greg. We'd charged him with a series of burglaries he'd carried out with Sonya Raynott, and he was due to appear in court this week,' Mark said, angrily. 'He was facing a lengthy sentence too. Justice, not murder.'

'That doesn't get back all the memories he stole,' Fernsby spat. 'We – none of us – can get those back, can we?'

Mark tore open the folder beside him and slapped over a final photograph, stabbing at the image with his finger.

'We recovered Emma's christening bracelet from a storage unit owned by Nolan Creasey last Thursday,' he said. 'It was returned to Sally this morning after one of our officers identified it from the inscription.'

Fernsby reached out a shaking hand, pulling the photograph closer. 'She has it now?'

'Yes.' Mark bit back a sigh. 'You gained nothing by killing Nolan Creasey.'

'But it was me who led you to him. Me killing that Sonya he worked with that got you interested.' The man sat back in his chair, folding his arms over his chest. 'You wouldn't have found the bracelet otherwise, would you?'

## CHAPTER FIFTY-FOUR

Bright sunlight sparkled on the water when Mark emerged from the narrowboat the next morning, a dog lead in one hand and a hessian tote bag in the other.

He hadn't left the incident room until well past eleven the previous night after sending Jan home to her family, and now relished the thought of a late start and the chance to spend some time with Lucy and Hamish.

There was a warmth in the air, a promise of spring and perhaps an Easter weekend without rain showers, and he wondered whether to request some extra time off from Kennedy given the DI's current good mood.

'Have you got the list?'

'On my phone.'

Hamish shot out from the cabin door, leaping across the gunwale and onto the grassy embankment before standing and waiting with his tongue out.

'Anyone would think you haven't been walked this morning,' Mark said, clambering over to join him.

Lucy appeared next, her keys jangling while she locked the door, and he grinned.

'There used to be a time when you didn't bother doing that.'

She cocked an eyebrow at him and held out her hand for the bag. 'There used to be a time when I didn't live with a detective.'

Mark clipped the metal catch to Hamish's collar, checked that there were no new messages on his phone, and set off across the meadow towards the car park, his arm around Lucy's waist.

The dog pulled on the lead, unaccustomed to being restrained, but Mark wasn't taking any chances.

He pushed open the metal five-bar gate and scuffed his shoes to lose the worst of the mud. Satisfied, he set out along the pavement that bordered the main road, keeping Hamish to his right to avoid the small dog being buffeted by the traffic that shot past.

'Where first?' he asked, raising his voice to be heard.

'Supermarket. We'll do the bookshop on the way back otherwise we'll have extra weight to cart around.' Lucy grinned. 'I know what you're like once you're let loose in there.'

'Who, me?'

He nodded to another couple who waited at the far

end of the bridge to let them pass, then exhaled as some of the stress from the past two weeks began to subside.

Some of it.

There were still answers that needed resolving from the forensic evidence, a mountain of paperwork to prepare for the CPS, and that was before he turned his attention back to the cases he'd been neglecting since the Tillcotts had discovered Sonya Raynott's body.

'Hey.'

He blinked, then looked at Lucy. 'Sorry. Miles away. What did you say?'

She pointed through the supermarket windows. 'We only need a few things, and you're itching to phone Jan for an update so why don't you wait out here with Hamish?'

'Do you mind?'

'We only need a few bits and pieces. See you in a minute.'

Mark waited until the glass doors swished shut, made sure Hamish sat at his feet, and then pulled out his phone.

Jan answered within three rings. 'I thought you wouldn't be able to wait until you came in.'

'Everything all right?'

'Yes. Kennedy's on the phone to Melrose at the moment and the media relations team have just released a statement that'll probably be all over the news sites within the hour. Caroline's over at the council offices getting a copy of the CCTV footage, and—'

'Anything from forensics?' Mark bit his lip. 'Sorry.'

His colleague laughed. 'I was getting to that, Sarge. Yes, Jasper phoned this morning. He managed to fast-track some of the evidence, but we're going to have to wait for the formal report.'

'What about informal? What did he say?'

'It's Greg Fernsby, Sarge. We got him. The fishing rod he used to hit Sonya over the head with is made of a composite of carbon fibre and fibreglass, which is why fragments were found in that wound – it was the glass fibre particles that broke away from the rod on impact. And they found hair in the boot of his car that they expect will be a DNA match with hers.'

'So much for just knocking her out.'

'I've just been speaking to Gillian about that, and she said if an ambulance had been called and managed to save Sonya, there was every chance a blow like that would've left her with some sort of brain damage.'

He heard the sound of Jan flicking through pages, and resisted the urge to pepper her with more questions.

'Ah, here we go,' she said eventually. 'The blood on Fernsby's sweatshirt, the stains that he couldn't get out. Definitely Sonya's. The knife that we retrieved from his arrest also has traces of Creasey's blood embedded in the hilt.'

Mark thanked her, exhaling as he ended the call, and then smiled as Lucy appeared, the tote bag now laden and a pair of leeks sticking out the top.

'Was that Jan?' she said, winding her fingers between his before they walked towards the square.

'It was.'

'And?'

'It's him.' He lowered his voice as they passed a cluster of people outside a charity clothing shop. 'Jasper's confirmed the forensic evidence is a match for both murders.'

'Well done.' She pulled him to a standstill, and kissed him.

Then her stomach rumbled.

Mark laughed. 'Fancy something to eat before we go to the bookshop?'

'Have you got time?'

'I have.' He smiled. 'Jan's got it all under control. Besides, I know just the place.'

He led the way across the square towards a familiar café, several tables cluttering the cobblestones and bright tablecloths covering the surfaces.

Spotting a waitress emerge with a platter of scrambled eggs that she put in front of a man in a hi-vis vest before turning to clear away another table, he approached her with a shy smile.

Clare Baxter turned around and wiped her hands on her apron before pulling out a chair, and grinned.

'I'll go and get some menus.'

## THE END

# ABOUT THE AUTHOR

Rachel Amphlett is a USA Today bestselling author of crime fiction and spy thrillers, many of which have been translated worldwide.

Her novels are available in eBook, print, and audiobook formats from libraries and retailers as well as her website shop.

A keen traveller, Rachel has both Australian and British citizenship.

Find out more about Rachel's books at: www.rachelamphlett.com.

Lightning Source UK Ltd.
Milton Keynes UK
UKHW041024060922
408391UK00002B/407

9 781913 498856